CRIMINAL SPIRITS

EVA CHASE

GANG OF GHOULS

BOOK

2

Criminal Spirits

Book 2 in the Gang of Ghouls series

First Digital Edition, 2021

Cover design: Yocla Book Cover Design

Ebook ISBN: 978-1-990338-30-4

Paperback ISBN: 978-1-990338-41-0

one

Lily

As shocking developments go, seeing a childhood-friend-turned-sort-of-lover shoved up against a wall with a gun to his head was one I could have skipped. 0/10, would not recommend.

The man with the gun—a burly, lumberjack-looking guy—had Ruin pinned against the building in the lane over my basement apartment. He jabbed his pistol more firmly against Ruin's forehead and whipped his head around at the thump of the apartment door. Ruin's three friends and former gang colleagues were already hurtling up the stairs with murder emanating from their every movement.

A yelp caught in my throat as I scrambled after them. I had the urge to shout at them to be careful, which struck me as totally ridiculous at the same time. Both because these guys were never exactly careful, and because how the hell could anyone be *careful* when the life of one of our own was on the line?

That might have been the first time I'd really thought of myself as part of their group. An honorary Skullbreaker of sorts. But I was a little too frantic to contemplate the significance of my shift in mindset.

"Don't get any—" the lumberjack with the gun started to growl, but he didn't have the chance to finish his threat, because Nox barreled right into him.

The massive leader of the Skullbreakers slammed the gunman away from Ruin, his fists already flying to smack the pistol from the dickhead's hand and send the guy's jaw soaring upward with a pained grunt. Jett was there an instant later, bringing a knee to the asshat's gut and an elbow to his nose, setting loose an impressive flow of blood.

Freed from his attacker's grasp, Ruin spun around and added his own limbs to the mix. Despite the deadly situation he'd been in just seconds ago, he laughed as he slammed his heel into the guy's ribs, sending the douche-nozzle reeling into the opposite wall. The rhythm of fleshy thuds, vengeful growls, and agonized breaths created a strange sort of melody. Part of me wanted to put words to it, a fierce song of retribution.

The pseudo-lumberjack rebounded off the wall, his face swollen and legs wobbling. He looked as though he might have been regretting a few of his life choices. He glanced toward the street at the mouth of the alley as if he was considering turning tail and running.

The guys didn't give him the option. Jett snatched up his helmet from where he'd left it on his parked motorcycle and bashed the jerkwad across the side of his head with it. Kai, who'd hung back a little from the fray while waiting for an opening, held up a rope he'd found somewhere or other. "We're going to need some answers," he said. "Get him immobile and we'll interrogate him."

Nox had just been snatching up a bent fork someone had tossed aside in the alley. He jabbed it into the douchebag's side with a crackling hiss that made the man's body spasm like a marionette that'd been shaken on its strings. Between the sound, the motion, and the faint whiff of burnt meat, I knew the former gang boss had sent a jolt of his ghostly electrical energy into his opponent.

Jett let out a sound that was half whoop, half snarl, and swung his helmet into the guy's face so forcefully the slimeball's head whipped back on his neck. The lumberjack gunman rammed into the wall with a crunch of shattering skull. Several shards of that skull remained mashed into the bricks as he crumpled in a heap on the ground.

Jett looked at the mangled mess on the back of the guy's head and then at Kai, swiping his messy purple-dyed hair back from his face with a slightly apologetic grimace. "Oops. Sorry. I didn't realize I was going to hit him quite that hard."

"He was trying to kill Ruin," Nox growled, his broad shoulders flexing. "He deserves what he got."

Ruin bobbed up and down on his feet with his fists raised as if he was hoping another attacker would come lunging out of the shadows for a second round. His hazel eyes gleamed with excitement. "That was a workout, all right."

Somehow the guy always managed to look on the bright side of things.

Kai dropped the rope with an exasperated sigh and nudged his rectangular glasses up his nose. "It would have been nice if we could have found out *why* he gave us that workout. I don't suppose he mentioned anything about what he wanted with you before he put that gun to your head?"

"He wasn't after Ruin," I said first, the memory coming back to me of the few words I'd heard the attacker speak before the guys had charged at him. "He thought he was threatening Ansel."

The four guys fell into a momentary silence to consider that fact. The truth was that none of them were exactly the men they appeared to be. A couple of weeks ago, the bunch of them had been among the worst of the tormenters who'd insulted and attacked me at Lovell Rise College. But then those jackasses had been possessed by the former gangsters they were now: my childhood not-so-imaginary-after-all friends who'd decided they needed to show up and protect me.

It was all a little complicated. I hadn't quite finished wrapping my head around the situation.

But it was getting easier to think of these four as the men they claimed to be now rather than the sneering popular guy, the bullying jock, the judgmental brownnoser, and the hostile professor they'd been before. For one thing, their personalities couldn't be more different. For another, their ghostly energies and their own efforts had been gradually transforming their bodies in ways that matched their former selves better.

Zach the jock had never worn glasses like Kai did. Professor Grimes hadn't been anywhere near as buff as Nox was quickly becoming, and he definitely hadn't gelled up his hair into little black spikes tipped with red. Vincent the brownnoser's body had also filled out significantly with Jett in possession of it, and he'd probably have shrieked in horror at the sight of his new purple hair. Golden boy Ansel's hard-edged good looks had softened with Ruin's influence, and his once golden locks were now bright scarlet.

But that hadn't stopped Mr. Lumberjack from coming after him for who he'd once been.

Ruin's eyes had turned briefly distant with thought. He waved his hand as if he needed to catch our attention. "There was some dude who bugged me before! A different guy—he stopped me from a car when I was out grabbing some food and wanted to know…" He knit his forehead as he reached for the memory. "Where I'd been. He said I hadn't reported in when I was supposed to, or something like that."

Nox blinked at him. "Why the fuck didn't you mention that earlier?"

5

Ruin shrugged, smiling contentedly. "It obviously didn't have to do with *me* me. I told him to take a hike and figured that was it—and that if it wasn't, we'd just take care of things. And we did. So it's all good."

"It's not all good." Kai motioned to the dead man. "You said the guy who harassed you before was someone different. So *that* guy is still out there, and thanks to *some* people taking the Skullbreaker name a little too literally, we have no idea who they are or what they want."

"I said I was sorry," Jett muttered.

I rubbed my forehead. "The guy didn't say anything at all about what he wanted—neither of them did? What you were supposed to be reporting about? Who you were reporting to?"

Ruin shook his head. "They mostly just seemed angry and like they wanted to push me around. They had no idea who they were dealing with now." His smile stretched into a grin.

Nox turned to me. "You knew this Ansel guy from before, right? Was he mixed up in anything when you were younger?"

I spread my hands. "I have no clue. It wasn't like we talked about our hobbies and the secret clubs we were members of. The only time he spoke to me when we were kids was to make fun of me for being a loser and smelling like marsh water."

Ruin bristled as quickly as he'd smiled before. "You're not a loser, and you smell much nicer than the marsh. We should know, after all the time we spent in it."

I gave him a baleful look. "I appreciate the vote of confidence. Although I probably did smell kind of marshy back then because of all the time I spent hanging out down there with the bunch of you."

"Time well spent," Nox said.

"No argument here," I replied. "But anyway, all I know about Ansel is that almost everyone liked him and wanted to be his friend, and his parents have quite a bit of money. His dad owns the marina down the lake and a few other properties in town, and he's friends with the mayor too. But the last time I was around Ansel for any length of time, we were both thirteen. I have no idea what he might have gotten into while I was off in the looney bin."

I had been gone for seven years, after all. And Ansel had grown from a pompous just-past-preteen to a fully-fledged adult prick in that time. The possibilities were pretty much endless.

"Well, let's look this asshole over," Jett said, like he was impatient to get past any conversation that might circle back around to how unfortunate it was that he'd killed the guy, and crouched down next to the pseudo-lumberjack. The others went over to join him.

They patted him down with unusual efficiency. After a moment, Ruin seemed to get bored and went over to straighten up his motorcycle, which had toppled over during the assault.

Kai dug a few slips of paper out of the guy's shirt

pocket which he appeared to dismiss as useless and flicked away. Nox pulled a phone out of the back of the man's jeans. He jabbed his thumbs at it with the typical impatience the guys seemed to have for technology that was two decades ahead of what they'd been used to before their murders.

"I can't get it to open up," he grumbled. "This is where the good stuff would be, right?"

"Let me see." Kai held out his hand, and his boss handed it over. But while Kai was incisive enough to frequently give the impression that he read people's minds and to have absorbed two decades of recent events by speed-reading news magazines at a hundred pages a minute, he apparently didn't have the same skills when it came to electronic devices. He tapped at the screen and the buttons, tried pressing the dead man's phone to the same spots, and finally gave it a little zap of supernatural energy which only made the screen jitter briefly.

"Don't break it," Jett said.

Kai shot him a narrow sideways glance. "What, like you broke *him*?" He grimaced at the phone. "I don't know how to unlock it. It needs a passcode. If I still had my old network of contacts... We haven't had a chance to build that up again. I have no idea who could handle something like this."

"It's not that urgent, right?" Ruin said. "So far these people have been no big deal. We can look into what Ansel was up to in other ways."

"And if the phone gets any calls, those should come

through without needing the passcode," I said. "Someone will check up on him eventually, right? We could try to find out what's going on from them."

Kai nodded, aiming an approving smile my way that sent a warm if slightly unnerving tingle through my body. I'd only had any kind of intimate relations with Nox and Ruin, but I'd be lying if I said I wasn't finding all four of these men increasingly appealing in their own ways. Which was probably insane, because they were criminally homicidal and also, y'know, technically *dead*, but I'd decided yesterday that sanity was overrated. So here we were.

At least so far all of the Skullbreakers' homicidalness had been in defense of themselves or me.

My gaze slid back to the dead man. "What are we going to do with him? We can't just… leave him here in the alley by my apartment, right?" He really wasn't an attractive addition to the décor, even when that décor was a grungy alley. And I'd also had the police breathing down my neck just a few days ago.

Nox hummed and then nodded to himself. "We'll take care of it. Ruin, you should finish taking care of getting us all some food. *I'm* starving now."

He paused and touched my cheek with a gentleness so off-kilter with the rest of his cocky, aggressive demeanor that it woke up a heck of a lot more than a tingle inside me. "You go down and wait in the apartment, Lily. We wouldn't want you being seen around the body, and I don't want you off with Ruin when he could be a target."

I wanted to argue, but there wasn't really any good argument to offer. He'd made good points. Gritting my teeth, I dipped my head in acknowledgment.

"Be careful," I said, the caution I'd wanted to give them before seeming only slightly less absurd now. Then I walked down the stairs to the dingy apartment with my stomach sinking even faster than my feet.

I didn't like this. I didn't like it at all. We'd already figured out that my sister was under some kind of threat, probably from a scarily powerful businessman, and now it turned out Ansel had been wrapped up in something dangerous too?

I had to protect Marisol, and I had to protect the men who'd risen from the dead to defend me, as much as they'd let me defend them. And it looked like I was going to need to tackle both problems at the same time if I wanted to be sure that everyone I cared about—the only people who'd ever cared about *me* too—made it through the next few days alive.

two

Lily

Ruin came back loaded with so many bags of Indian takeout that he looked like one of those peddlers in fairy tale illustrations carrying their entire inventory on their backs. My rickety table almost toppled over as he laid out the spread, which involved multiple tiers by necessity. The rest of the guys had returned to the apartment by then, and they all fell on the containers of curry, roti, and biryani rice like they'd been starving for half a century.

I wasn't sure I was ever going to get used to their constant need for fuel. Was that going to taper off as their spirits got more acclimatized to their bodies—and to the fact that they hadn't gotten to eat at all during the twenty-one years they'd been deceased—or were they always going to have the appetite of great white sharks?

My stomach was still knotted up from the most recent conundrum we'd gotten into, but it was almost dinner time now, and I'd been so keyed up from my personal confrontations earlier today that I hadn't eaten much before. I squeezed in to snag a piece of garlic-stuffed naan here and a dollop of butter chicken there. Then Nox let out a gruff sound, and suddenly all four of the guys were assembling a plate for me that held more food than I was likely to eat in a week.

I sank onto my futon to the left of its saggy middle and took my first few bites gingerly. Ruin had a particular liking for extreme levels of spice. Extreme levels of everything, really. But the guys had clearly avoided loading my plate from any dishes he'd ordered for his specific tastes, because my tongue didn't go up in flames. It was actually pretty freaking delicious.

I decided not to worry about corpses or guns or shady old businessmen for a half hour or so while I got a decent meal into me. They'd still be waiting when I finished, after all.

Even though the guys were eating about a hundred times more than me, they finished before I was full. Jett set to work either tidying or artistically arranging the remnants on the table—possibly both—and paused to smear a little vindaloo sauce on one of the thick pages of paper he'd picked up with his other painting supplies. He cocked his head at it and then crumpled it and tossed it in the trash with a wrinkle of his nose.

Ruin dropped onto the broad wooden arm of the futon right next to me so he could sling his arm across my shoulders and stroke my hair. I let my head tip toward him, enjoying the affectionate but undemanding touch. We'd made out once, and he gave out hugs and kisses like there was a fire sale, but I never felt like he was unhappy with how far we'd gone—or hadn't gone. There was something kind of miraculous about the sense that he adored me exactly as I was.

Nox sat at the other end of the futon, and Kai pulled a chair over to what was becoming his usual spot across from us. He swiped his hand over his face, where his skin had darkened to a golden tan from Zach's previous peachy pale, and studied the rest of us.

"We can't just sit around and wait for that phone to ring. We need to come up with a plan of action."

"For figuring out who's after Ruin—Ansel—and for protecting Marisol," I filled in.

He nodded, and Ruin perked up. "We can add it to the list!"

I raised my eyebrows. "The list?"

Nox motioned at Kai, who retrieved a folded piece of paper from the pocket of his jeans. "That night you stayed out," the Skullbreakers' leader said, "we came up with a list of our next steps toward reestablishing ourselves with the respect we deserve."

Of course they had. Why wouldn't they? It was probably full of items like, "Smash all their heads in," and "Hang them in a tree by their toenails."

Kai tapped his lips with a pen he'd also produced.

"Find out who has it in for Ruin's host. That should get pretty high priority, don't you think?"

Nox made a noncommittal sound. "We did put that idiot in his place pretty fast, and it isn't *really* anything to do with us. I think figuring out who offed *us* way back when is more important. Better to deal with them before we make an official return and they realize we'll be gunning for them."

I reached up to curl my fingers around Ruin's. "We can't ignore the problem with Ansel. What if someone comes at Ruin someplace he can't count on you guys for help?"

Ruin leaned over to nuzzle my hair. "I could have handled him on my own. I was just giving him a chance to get confident before I taught him a thing or two."

Kai's gray-green eyes glinted menacingly behind his glasses. "And there are a lot of other people who need their lessons delivered." He sighed. "Well, we've got no other responsibilities at the moment, and both might take some time. I think we can follow two threads simultaneously."

"Good." I ran my thumb over the back of Ruin's hand. The image of him squashed against the bricks with the pistol jammed to his temple rose up in my mind, making my pulse lurch. I weirdly felt as if I'd known him forever and also only a couple of weeks. Maybe both of those things were true, but however weird it was, the thought of losing him after all that time or so little sent a stab of panic through my chest.

I tucked myself closer against his side, and Ruin let

out a pleased hum. Without warning, he adjusted his position so he could scoop me up and hop off the futon arm simultaneously, landing on the cushion with me tucked onto his lap.

"You don't need to worry about me, Angelfish," he told me, tipping his face close to mine. "I'm not going anywhere, not when I can be here with you."

My heart skipped a beat in a totally different way, and then he was kissing me, tenderly but eagerly, drawing it out until every nerve started to thrum with building heat.

More heat pooled between my thighs. Ruin's hand stroked down my side, and the urge to grind against him gripped me. I tensed up to hold myself back, thinking of the other guys sitting all around us.

Ruin drew back from the kiss and studied me with obvious concern. "Too much?"

"No, I— I mean, it was fine—it was good—I just —" I clamped my mouth shut for a second while I got my thoughts in some kind of coherent order. Then I dragged in a breath and peeked around at the rest of the resurrected gangsters.

"Maybe we should talk about this. About… about what exactly this is. I don't know what you all were expecting. *I* definitely didn't have any ideas of getting involved with you like this back when I was younger. I mean, I didn't even think of you as being actual people…" I trailed off again and bit my lip.

Nox looked vaguely horrified. I had another momentary panic that he was offended I'd even brought up the subject before he said, "*We* weren't thinking like that either back then. For fuck's sake, you were a kid." He paused, his dark blue eyes holding a tumultuous mix of envy and desire as he took in the sight of me on Ruin's lap. "You're not a kid now. I look at you and see the woman you are, not the girl you used to be. And now that we *are* 'actual' people again—you know how I feel about you."

Yes, I did. The memory of his worshipful words and equally ardent hands and mouth set a lick of fire over my skin.

"But we don't want anything to happen that doesn't make you happy too," Ruin said emphatically. "We're here for *you*, not the other way around."

"And we're *all* here for you, or not, however you like it," Nox added, with a flick of a glance toward the two men who hadn't spoken yet. "None of us is going to be staking any separate claim on you, including me. You mean the world to all of us. No one can say you're more theirs than the others."

Jett had gone a bit rigid where he was still standing near the table. He held up his hands, his jaw flexing. "Lily's my muse," he said, his voice a little stiff too. "I'm not going to ask for more than that from her. I'll share a hell of a lot with you guys, but orgies aren't really my thing." He tipped his head to me, his expression softening. "It's a lot harder to find the right muse. You're something fucking special, Lil."

If I'd felt any unexpected twinge of disappointment

at his dismissal of orgies, those last words swept it away. I smiled back at him and glanced at Kai.

The brainiac of the former gang shifted on his chair awkwardly. "I'll admit I'm not *unaware* of your appeal," he said in his usual matter-of-fact tone. "This body… Fucking teenage hormones. I should have picked an older host." He let out a huff. "But I wouldn't expect you to return that sort of interest, and I think at this point it's really more of a distraction than anything else." His gaze flicked to Nox. "For me. By all means, you two give Lily whatever you'd like to. She sure as hell deserves better after the shit she's had to go through before now."

Nox caught Ruin's gaze. "Just the two of us then. I think we can manage to keep our woman's needs satisfied."

A blush flared in my cheeks. Ruin gave a pleased chuckle and kissed my cheek. "I'm sure we can," he murmured happily, but for now he only gave me another hug. "But we have gotten distracted. You need to help your little sister too."

"Yes," I said, latching on to that change of subject with relief, even though I was the one who'd brought up the previous topic. Now that the air had been cleared and everyone knew where everyone stood when it came to getting handsy with me, I'd rather not dissect my exact "needs" in any more detail in a group setting.

"We know the Gauntts are involved," Kai said, looking equally eager to get onto a new topic. "Or at least Nolan Gauntt, the patriarch of Thrivewell Enterprises."

"Yes, he's the one my stepfather mentioned." Under extreme duress. I rubbed my mouth. Kai had done some preliminary research into the business mogul whose company seemed to employ half of Lovell Rise as well as the surrounding towns, his home city of Mayfield, and who knew where else. None of it had explained why he would have been at all involved in my or my sister's life. Other than that Wade had undoubtedly found it very hard to say no to whatever Nolan had asked for. My stepdad liked to lord his authority over people he knew he could beat up on, but he cowered before anyone who was a real big dog.

"It'd be hard to go at this guy head-on," I said. "We can't just find him on the street and intimidate him into talking. He probably has, like, a gazillion bodyguards. And whatever happened with him—as much as I plan to make sure he pays for it—it was seven years ago. Marisol seemed nervous *now*. Before we do anything else, I'd like to check whether she has a good reason to worry or if it's just leftover nerves. I don't want to do anything that could put her in danger."

"How are you thinking you'd check?" Nox asked.

I worried at my lower lip, considering. "I can keep an eye on her from a distance when she's going to and from school—and wherever else she goes between there and the house. Or, not so much keep an eye on her but check whether I can see anyone *else* monitoring her. I should be able to cover a lot of that time in between my classes, now that I'm out of a job."

I winced inwardly at the thought of my manager's last words to me outside the grocery store. It hadn't been a pleasant firing, and it didn't bode well for future job prospects. Basically, I'd made too much trouble for him simply by existing—and by other people having a problem with me existing.

"We can help too," Ruin volunteered. "Watch for any shady characters lurking around."

I immediately pictured the former gangsters barging up to random strangers on the street who happened to look at Marisol sideways for a split-second and pummeling them as punishment. "Um. Sure. But you have to let me take the lead with this one, all right? We'll talk about how you can keep watch, but I don't want you going near Marisol or taking any other kind of action until we've talked about it first."

Jett grunted in a way that suggested he felt being reined in was unnecessary, but Nox was already nodding. "Your arena, you call the shots. Unless she's under attack. Anyone lays a finger on her, we aren't going to stand by."

I gave him a skeptical look. "More than a finger. Tapping her on the shoulder to get her attention doesn't deserve a beatdown."

"It depends on the tap," he said, and waved off my glower. "All right, all right. We'll work it out." He rubbed his hands together. "It sounds like it's time to get busy."

three

Ruin

In some ways, Lily's bed was less comfortable than the air mattress and sleeping bag that were technically mine in the living room. For one, her mattress was kind of lumpy. For another, it was only twin-sized, which was barely big enough for *one* person to stretch out, let alone two.

But it had Lily in it, and as long as that was the case, it was my favorite place in the world.

I hadn't been able to resist slipping in here a little earlier than usual and squeezing myself between her and the wall with my arm looped around her waist, spooning her. She was used to my presence enough by now that she'd simply given a sleepy murmur, scooted a little closer, and gone right back to sleep. I'd drifted back off too with her watery wildflower scent in my nose.

When I woke up again, she was still sleeping, her breaths soft and even. I trailed my fingertips up and down her bare arm that'd tucked over the blankets, delighting in the smoothness of her pale skin.

She rolled toward me onto her back, her eyes still half-closed. I let my fingers glide across her shoulder and over her collarbone just above the neckline of her baggy sleepshirt. Lily squirmed a little and opened her eyes wider. "Tease," she muttered.

Who was teasing who was really debatable after the way my dick had jerked to attention at the brush of her thigh, but I had no interest in arguing. I leaned closer and nuzzled the side of her face, letting my lips brush her cheek as I spoke. "If you want more than what I'm doing, I'm perfectly happy to keep going."

She tipped her face toward mine, and I caught her mouth for a perfect kiss, waking from drowsy tenderness to heated alertness as our mouths moved together. My hand drifted lower, displacing the blanket in its wake, and traced the curve of her breast through the thin cotton of her shirt.

Lily let out an impatient sound that made me even harder and pressed into my hand. I smiled against her mouth, joy lighting me from the inside like someone had set a flame to a fuse.

Nox had told me before that we needed to be careful with Lily. We didn't want to hurt her more than she'd already been hurt, to take anything she didn't want to give when she'd already lost so much. But she'd made it very clear since then—and especially last night—that she was fully on board with receiving all the affection we were dying to offer.

Still, it couldn't hurt to make sure. I nudged my nose against hers and skimmed my fingers over her breast again, grinning as her nipple pebbled at my touch. "Would you like more of this, precious?"

"Fuck, yes," she grumbled, and tugged my mouth back to hers.

I rolled her nipple until it was taut and straining against the fabric and she was whimpering against my lips. Then I eased my hand to the other side with a glimmer of mischief. "And how about here?"

Lily gave a little growl that electrified me and pressed into my touch. I slipped my tongue between her lips as I flicked my thumb over the peak of her breast, mimicking the same movement. Her hands came up to grip my hair, her fingernails striking sparks across my scalp. I restrained a groan, my cock aching, and slid down to nibble her neck.

"Are you enjoying this, Angelfish?" I murmured.

She sputtered a laugh. "What do you think?"

"I want to hear you say it. Just to be sure."

She swatted me lightly and then dug her fingers into my hair again. When I swiped my tongue along the column of her throat, her voice turned breathless. "Yes, I'm enjoying it a lot. Please don't stop. Full speed ahead."

I hummed my approval and moved even lower,

tugging up her shirt at the same time to bare her perfect pert breasts. When I flicked my tongue over one of her stiffened nipples, she gasped and clutched me tighter.

"That's right," I mumbled as I nuzzled closer. "I love hearing all the ways you let me know what you like. And I'm going to make sure you get all the goodness you deserve."

I closed my mouth around her breast with a swivel of my tongue, and a full moan tumbled out of her. Her thighs were rubbing together, the scent of her arousal lacing the air. I dipped my hand lower and almost moaned myself at the dampness of her panties.

"So happy already," I said, and licked her other nipple. "Should I do something about this, do you think?"

I curled my fingers against the dampness as I asked, and Lily arched up to meet me, her breath stuttering. "Ruin," she muttered impatiently.

I beamed at her. "I'll take that as a yes."

As I delved my hand beneath her panties, I returned the attentions of my mouth to her neck. I wanted to leave her mouth unoccupied so I could hear all the delicious sounds she made as I worked her over in her most sensitive places.

My fingers slipped easily into her slick channel. She rocked with my movements as I pulsed them deeper and deeper. Her pussy quivered around me. If she was aching even half as much as my cock was, I shouldn't leave her hanging much longer. We could have plenty more fun after she'd gotten her first release from the torment.

I massaged the heel of my hand against her clit while I plunged a third finger into her. Lily yanked my head up and kissed me so hard her teeth nicked my lip. I savored the brief sting, leaning into the kiss, thrusting my hand faster. And then she came, with a choked little cry and a shudder that ran through her whole body against mine, making her pussy clamp around my fingers.

As she sagged into the mattress, panting, I brought my hand to my mouth and licked her tangy juices off my fingers. A renewed hunger flared in Lily's eyes as she watched. She reached to pull her panties right off—

And just then Nox walked in, as usual not bothering to knock.

He took us in and simply sighed, heat flickering through his own eyes at the same time. "I'm glad someone's having a good morning," he said. "But we were going to get over to that prick Ansel's house before Lily has to get to her morning class. So put *your* prick away and let's get going."

Lily gave a huff, but he was already leaving, not offering a chance for debate. I dipped my face close to hers.

"Soon," I said. "You have no idea how much I want you too. But I can wait until we don't have anyone breathing down our necks."

A wicked little smile crossed Lily's lips. "Maybe it'd be even more fun if we made him watch."

I didn't know if it was that this new body of mine was high on all the sensations I hadn't gotten to enjoy in decades or if this woman's appeal was just that potent, but I nearly came in my boxers simply hearing her say those words. I swallowed another groan and stole one last, quick kiss before pushing myself off the bed. "Soon."

Even though I'd been left wanting, energy thrummed through my body with the knowledge of the pleasure I'd given Lily. I bounded into the living room, tossed on some clothes, took those off and pulled on some different clothes when Kai pointed out that I needed to look as Ansel-ish as possible, and gulped down about five pounds of bacon drenched in hot sauce until at least one kind of hunger was totally quiet. For the moment.

Kai was already dressed in fairly posh clothes—a collared button-up and dark jeans that didn't have any wrinkles—which was typical for him. He was coming along with us so that he could observe the situation the way only he knew how. I was totally aware that some subtleties would go straight over my head.

Especially since Lily was joining us as well. She'd pointed out that since she'd known Ansel at least a little and she was more familiar with the recent state of the town than we were, she might be able to pick up on clues the rest of us wouldn't realize were relevant. Her presence was definitely going to make the trip much more enjoyable. Unlike Kai's.

"If we run into anyone from his family, don't talk

too much," he ordered me as we got into Ansel's car. Unfortunately, Kai had also insisted that showing up on our motorcycles would raise too many questions. "And try not to be so happy about everything while you're there. We don't want them suspecting anything."

"I've got to be totally Ansel," I said with a bob of my head. "No problem!"

"Yes, problem," he grumbled. "You don't sound like some arrogant golden boy at all."

"They're going to notice *something's* different," Lily pointed out, reaching forward from the back seat to ruffle my hair. "He has had a bit of a makeover."

Kai sighed. "Tell them it was a dare," he instructed. "A hazing ritual for a club at school. Maybe we should splash a little alcohol on your clothes so you'll smell like you're drunk. That could explain a personality shift."

I patted the polo shirt that'd been left over from Ansel's wardrobe, pre-makeover. "I thought you wanted my clothes to look *nice*. Or are we going to make this a game? What crazy things can we trick them into believing! Ha."

As I started the engine, Kai rolled his eyes skyward. "That wasn't exactly what I had in mind."

Technically I had Ansel's home address from the driver's license in his wallet, but Lily knew exactly where that section of street was. She gave a few directions and sat perched in her seat, peering out the windows. It occurred to me that she might be nervous about running into other people—the kind of people who'd been hurling insults and garbage at her since she'd come back home. I flexed my hands against the steering wheel and made secret plans for running *over* anyone who attempted to harass her.

We didn't pass any bystanders who seemed to notice her, though. When we got to the house, I fished the keys that had also come with Ansel's packaging out of my pocket and then contemplated them as we ambled up to the front porch.

There were several different keys on the ring, and I had no idea which one fit the front door. Kai would probably nag me that it looked weird to go through different tries to find the right one, but I wasn't going to suddenly become psychic. Maybe I should exclaim loudly about how very drunk I was.

But it turned out I didn't need to try any of the keys. I was just playing a silent game of eenie meenie miney moe to decide which to lead with when the front door swung open. A woman with feathery blond hair, smile lines etched around her mouth, and a pearl choker at her throat peered out at us. At the sight of me, she blinked and did a double-take. The smile she gave me looked awfully stiff.

"Ansel!" she said. "I— Well. This is an interesting look. You haven't been home in a while. At least not while I've been here." She gave an awkward twittering sort of laugh.

I beamed back at her and then, remembering what Kai had said about being too happy, reined it in to what I thought was a reserved smile. Ansel obviously knew this woman. She was too old to be his sister, right? Probably mother?

It seemed risky to open by calling her "Mom," just in case he had some atypical family situation going on, so I gave her a quick nod and said, "The hair was a dare. Hazing for a club. I kind of like it, though! Just needed to pick something up from my room. Oh, and hang out with a couple of my friends."

Kai made a quietly strangled noise like he was considering dying on the spot, but I didn't see how anything I'd said was all that bad. A guy like Ansel must have been reasonably upbeat about coming home, right? It was a nice house, all high ceilings and polished floors, if you went for that kind of thing. I had a brief image of myself sliding along that front hall in my socked feet and caught the goofy grin that wanted to spring across my face just in time.

The woman's gaze slid past me to the "friends" I'd mentioned. Kai didn't seem to have any effect on her, but her eyes narrowed slightly when they focused on Lily.

"You're the Strom girl," she said in a clipped tone full of disdain.

I bristled automatically, my shoulders coming up. Kai snagged my wrist, which might have been a good thing as annoying as it was, because I was already tempted to take a swing at her. I guessed that definitely wasn't how Ansel would have responded to his mother. Even if she was being incredibly judgmental and bitchy.

Lily's jaw tightened, but she gazed straight back at the woman. "I am. Ansel and I go way back."

I knew from what she'd said before that they hadn't been at all *close*, but I realized she was just needling the woman for the exact reaction she got. Ansel's mom—or whoever she was—widened her eyes and then let out a dry little chuckle. "Well." She turned back to me. "Whatever you need, be quick about it. The cleaners will be here in a few minutes. And don't bring any of your hazing or what-have-you into the house."

"Absolutely," I said, and gave her a brisk salute that made Kai's grip on my other wrist clench. Then I remembered the other thing we'd talked about that I should check. "Has anyone come by or called asking for me?"

The woman knit her brow. "Not that I can think of. I'm sure they'd reach out to you on your own phone— you haven't broken it, have you?"

"Oh, no, it works just great," I said, patting my pocket. "Well, thank you!"

Her smile turned even stiffer, but she gave us a little wave and walked onward.

"Charming," Lily muttered under her breath.

"Maybe you just have to get to know her," I said. Or maybe she actually did deserve a fist to the face. Or, even better, we'd find what we needed today and not have to worry about which it was.

"I suppose we know where Ansel got his stunning personality from," Kai said, striding up the stairs. "If he was into anything questionable, it'll be in his own room, not in the common areas. It wouldn't make any sense for him to stash things where the family could find them."

I hadn't drawn that conclusion yet myself, but as usual, what Kai said made sense. I nodded and bounded up the stairs two at a time.

It wasn't hard to figure out which room was Ansel's. The big bedroom at the front of the house with a bay window and a wedding photo on the wall was obviously his parents'. Next to it we came to a guest room without a single personal touch, like a blank canvas before Jett had his way with it. Then there was a doorknob that jiggled but wouldn't open.

"He's locked it," Lily said, her eyebrows rising. "From his own family. I guess that's a good sign for there being secrets inside."

I got it to open with the third key on Ansel's ring, and we stepped inside. The space was about three times bigger than Lily's cramped bedroom in her apartment, with a queen-sized bed, a sleek wooden desk, and a TV with a massive stereo system set up by a narrow sofa. My eyes bugged out at the sight of his game system. "Why haven't I been here before? These are all mine now!"

As I dove down to check out the titles, some of which were weirdly sequels to games I'd played way back when I was alive before, Kai clucked his tongue chidingly. "We're not here to play around. And you can't bring that stuff with you. The family will probably assume it's been stolen—and the mom saw Lily with you. It'd be a bad scene all around."

"But it's *mine*," I protested, at least, as much as I was Ansel, which I did have to admit wasn't very much, thank God.

"Hey, you still have access to the asshole's bank account," Kai reminded me with a pat to my arm. "You can buy yourself a new one."

My smile came back at full force. "Right. Of course." I rubbed my hands together. "Now where would a popular jerk keep his secrets?"

Lily was already poking around under the bed. She dragged out a suitcase, opened it up, and made a gagging expression. "Okay, that was one secret I didn't need to see."

I peered over her should and caught a glimpse of stacks of creased magazine covers all featuring naked women… wearing diapers? One had a pacifier in her mouth. I snorted a laugh. "I'm definitely not him when it comes to my tastes in that department."

"Praise the heavens for that." Lily shoved the suitcase back under the bed. "Nothing else under here but some dirty clothes and a bottle of cheap rum." She looked it over. "I don't think having bad taste in alcohol is a murder-worthy crime."

I went back to the video games, because even if I couldn't play them, there might be something interesting tucked away in there. Kai looked over the bookcase. By the time I'd determined that nothing was hidden away among the game cases—but that they

really did keep making new editions of *Street Fighter*—
he'd moved to the desk.

I poked around the speakers and patted the walls,
because sometimes people in movies turned up secret
compartments and shit that way, right? Then Kai tugged
a scrap of paper from between the pages of a novel from
one of the desk drawers.

"Ah ha!" he said as he looked it over.

"What?" I dashed to his side. Lily dropped the
mattress she'd been peering under to come join us.

Kai waved the paper like a pennant. "He was
keeping very close track of Lily's schedule. Look at this."

She snatched the paper out of his hand and stared at
it. "Those are my class times and the buildings they're
in. What the hell? Was he stalking me or something? I
don't remember seeing him around *that* much."

"His friends could have all contributed," Kai
pointed out.

I frowned. "What does it mean? Was that guy with
the beard trying to kill him for following Lily?"

Kai knuckled me in the chest. "No, you dork. I
haven't found anything that explains the whole
murderous stalkers thing." He grimaced and lifted his
chin toward the paper. "It just means Ansel was a lot
more invested in bullying Lily than we realized.
Tracking her movements instead of just targeting her
when he happened to cross paths with her."

"But that doesn't matter now, does it?" I said
hopefully. "I mean… he's not around anymore. And

Lily doesn't mind *me* following her around." I shot her a grin.

She elbowed me in response. "Most of the time." But her expression stayed pensive.

"We'll have to keep a close eye on his friends," Kai said. "We cracked down on them hard, but we need to be sure it was hard enough." He glanced around at the room. "I think the rest of this place is a bust. If he kept any evidence of what he'd gotten into, it wasn't here."

As I followed his gaze, my mood dimmed. Not only was I in the body of a jerk who'd been trying to make Lily's life even more hell than we'd realized, I hadn't turned up anything useful myself.

What was the point in being here for her if I couldn't come through when she needed it the most?

four

Lily

Sitting in the second-story café looking out over the street, I felt like a character in a spy flick. I had a felt hat pulled low on my head to shadow my face, with most of my hair tucked up under it so the pale blond strands wouldn't catch anyone's notice. I'd even put on makeup when I hadn't usually bothered since I got back in town, so my face wouldn't look exactly like me at a glance.

There was only so much I could do to disguise myself, but I didn't want anyone catching a glimpse of me and immediately thinking, *There's Lily Strom.*

The café gave an angled view toward the high school my little sister currently attended. The students were due to get out in five minutes. I sipped my caramel latte, rolling the bittersweet liquid across my tongue, and willed myself not to fidget with nerves.

Besides, I had to concentrate before Marisol even left the building. If someone *else* was spying on her, monitoring her movements and making her feel she couldn't trust her surroundings, they were the ones I wanted to catch. I needed to know whether I could go over and talk to her again without bringing a heap more trouble down on her head.

I'd been carefully watching what I could see of the street for almost half an hour now, since I'd gotten out of my last class at the college. I hadn't seen anyone lingering by the school looking suspicious, but I assumed a creep keeping tabs on her wouldn't walk around wearing a neon sign saying *Stalker*.

I had to consider everyone, no matter how innocuous-looking. The elderly man shuffling over to the bingo hall across the road. The perky woman in a pastel jumpsuit who emerged from a house farther down the street. The toddler jumping along as he clutched her hand—okay, maybe not him.

My phone vibrated with an incoming text. *No one's been sticking around by this end of the school*, Jett reported. *Anything over there?*

Not so far, I wrote back. *Hold your post and keep watching*. I'd given all four of the guys *very* specific locations to stay in, with strict orders not to budge one step from those places unless I explicitly said so. Short of someone coming at Marisol with a gun or dragging her into a car, I didn't want them to do much more than breathe and keep their eyes open.

Not that they couldn't have helped in other ways. The problem was that once they started helping, they sometimes got caught up in the momentum and ended up solving problems I really hadn't thought needed tackling… at least not by literally tackling anyone.

One by one, the others texted to report the same thing. Then I made out the peal of the final bell distantly through the windowpane. I shifted a smidge forward in my seat. Any second now…

Teenagers started pouring out onto the sidewalk, some stopping there in clusters, others walking off toward home or afterschool jobs or whatever else they got up to. One couple were so glued at the lips they nearly walked into a telephone pole. I alternated between scanning all of them for Marisol's golden hair and checking the streets nearby for any sign that some lurker had emerged with similar interests.

I didn't spot anyone other than typical pedestrians, and my phone didn't chime with notifications from the guys of threatening figures they'd spotted. They had much more of a hair trigger than I did, so if *they* weren't worried—

There she was. I caught sight of her bright, wavy hair amid the crowd. My heart skipped a beat with a painful pang. I wanted to be down there hooking my arm around hers and telling her I'd make everything all right, not way up here separated by glass and a whole lot of distance.

She wove through the mass of her peers like she had the first time I'd come out to the school, when I'd tried to talk to her: shoulders hunched, head low. She didn't wave at or speak to anyone. Just tramped through their midst and drifted on down the street.

It looked like she was heading in the same direction as before. That made my job easier. I didn't have to follow as closely to still know where she was going.

I stayed braced by the window as she came almost to the storefront beneath me and then turned the corner. A few other students rambled along a similar route, but none of them appeared to be paying any attention to her. A couple headed up to the coffee shop without a glance her way. A few shoppers walked by from another direction, but no one who'd tailed her from the area of the school.

It didn't seem like she was being followed. Quite possibly she was just worried that it *could* be happening.

I sucked my lower lip under my teeth and then left behind my half-full mug to hustle down the stairs so I didn't lose her completely. As I stepped out onto the sidewalk into the brisk September breeze, a small green form sprang past my feet. I glanced down.

A frog—what else could I have expected? It took another few hops forward and then peered back at me as if wondering what the holdup was.

I'd come to realize that Lovell Rise wasn't simply a town infested with frogs. They had a particular affinity for me, something to do with the weird powers I'd apparently picked up during my near-death experience half-drowning in the marsh as a kid. The guys had said I must have brought some of the marsh back with me when I'd reclaimed my life, and the evidence did support that conclusion.

Frogs and water—my superpowers. Get me tights and a cape and call me Swamp Woman.

Actually, no, definitely don't do that.

I trotted down the street with the frog keeping pace next to me as if we were out for a casual jog. When I caught a glimpse of Marisol a few blocks ahead, I slowed and pretended I was deeply fascinated by the shop windows next to me. Really, I was studying their reflections for any covert moves people nearby might make when they thought no one was watching.

Nobody twigged my concerns, as much as I was trying to stay alert to the slightest hint of suspicious behavior. Nothing unsettled me at all until my phone buzzed in my purse.

I jumped, startled, and then pulled it out. It was a text from Nox.

Saw a guy walking across the schoolyard who didn't have a good reason for being there. Following him now.

Oh, fuck. *Was he anywhere near Marisol?* I asked, jabbing my keys across the phone frantically.

No, but he's heading your way. I don't like the look of him. Followed by a scowling emoji. Of course he'd already figured out those after just a couple of weeks' exposure to modern phones.

My heart started thumping twice as fast for reasons that had nothing to do with my sister. I darted across the street, still keeping an eye out for hazardous strangers but mostly heading to intercept Nox. *I told you to stay in position unless someone actually went after her.*

He COULD be going after her. I won't know if I don't keep an eye on him, will I?

I made a face at the phone. *Where are you now?*

Coming up on Hyacinth St.

I dashed down a side-street so Marisol wouldn't notice me charging over from behind her and then loped up to Hyacinth. I reached it just as a man in a slightly oversized suit with sweaty armpits strode past me—and immediately ducked into a dentist's office on the opposite corner. Through the window, I saw him greet the receptionist, who was clearly expecting him.

I spun around to glower at Nox, who was just slowing down where he'd been storming down the street after the guy. He looked from me to the dentist's office and back and raked his hand through his spiky hair.

"He was weird," he said as he reached me, before I could criticize him. "In a suit but kind of shabby-looking, walking through the yard outside the school."

"He was probably just taking a short cut," I said. "It's public property, you know. I'm going to bet you've taken plenty of short cuts in your life, probably a bunch of them through places you weren't really allowed to be at all."

Nox grinned as if this were a point of pride rather than a reminder of his wrongdoings and pushed on down the street, bumping his shoulder companionably against mine. "Where's the kid now? You didn't lose her, did you?"

"If I did, it's because I had to go make sure you didn't hoist anyone up a flagpole or drop them down a manhole," I muttered as I hurried along beside him.

"Hey, what are they called 'manholes' for if you're not supposed to drop a man down them when you need to?"

We made it back to the street my sister had been ambling along and spotted her a couple of blocks farther down, standing by a street display of cartoonish sketches. A guy with a limp ponytail was sitting on a stool with an easel, nodding as she asked him a question.

Nox bristled immediately. "What does *he* want?"

I put my hand on his shoulder and gave him a firm nudge in the opposite direction. "Um, he's trying to get paid to draw pictures of people, obviously. It's not his fault she stopped to look."

Nox's eyebrows drew together. "Is that what he calls art? Jett would figure those doodles are criminal right there. Definitely sketchy."

He didn't appear to notice the inadvertent pun, pushing against my hand until I shoved him back. Marisol was already wandering onward, and the guy didn't even glance after her, focusing instead on a middle-aged couple who must have looked like they'd have deeper money pockets.

The woman in the couple abruptly bent down and then ran after Marisol. My pulse skittered only for a second, but Nox leapt forward with a growl as if he was going to go all medieval on the lady's ass right now.

"Nox!" I hissed, and flung my arms around him. My heels skidded on the sidewalk before he jerked to a halt. He wasn't willing to fight me, but he frowned down at me. Thankfully, he came along when I hauled him back into the relative shelter by the building on the corner before anyone noticed the human volcano in their midst.

"We're trying not to get noticed," I hissed at him, and waved toward the woman.

She was just holding out something that glinted to Marisol. "I think you dropped this, hun."

"Oh!" Marisol grabbed the cheap bangle and slipped it back over her hand onto her wrist. "Thank you so much."

The woman walked back to her partner, who appeared to be haggling with the sketch artist over exactly how much a cartoon version of himself was worth.

"There was no way I could have known she was only handing that over," Nox said.

I gave him a pointed look. "Yes, there was. The way we just found out."

"She could have been about to kidnap her. Or knife her. She still could be. Just gaining the mark's trust." He nodded sagely.

I resisted the urge to punch him in his massively muscular chest. It probably would have hurt my hand more than him anyway. "I don't think so. Anyway, we're

41

supposed to be watching for anyone who's *observing* her, watching what she's up to. If someone was trying to hurt her, they'd have done it in the seven years before I got back in town, don't you think?"

Nox paused and rubbed his chin. "I guess you might have a point there. Have you seen anyone like that?"

"No," I admitted. "Have you? Or should I assume if you had, their intestines would be strewn all over Main Street already?"

He looked down at me with an amused but affectionate gleam in his eyes. "You know me so well, Minnow." Then he cocked his head, gazing up the street again. "Where's she going now?"

Marisol was just slipping into a store toward the end of the street. I decided it was safe to venture a little closer, squinting at the sign.

"Oh, it's the bookshop," I said, coming to a stop. Not a place she'd ever been interested in going into when we were kids. Did she prefer looking at other people's pictures to drawing her own now?

We eased closer, me keeping a tight grip on Nox's arm in case he made any sudden moves. I peered through the window.

Marisol didn't appear to have any official reason for coming to the store. There was already a woman stationed behind the counter by the cash register. It took me a few moments to spot my sister way at the back of the store, her shoulders still hunched and head low as if she was trying to be as invisible as possible, turning the page of a book she'd picked up.

My stomach knotted. "She must hang out in there, reading or whatever, until closing," I murmured to Nox. "So she doesn't have to be around Mom and Wade any more than necessary." She didn't feel all that safe out here on the streets, but she felt better than in her own home. That just wasn't right.

Nox jerked his chin toward the window. "Why don't you go over there and get her? Bring her home with you. You said you didn't see anyone watching her, right? None of the other guys have called in any problems, have they?"

They hadn't. Hopefully that meant they'd kept their cool and not that they were now busy stashing bodies. I nibbled at my lower lip again. "I mean, we can't be absolutely sure…"

The former gang boss folded his arms over his chest. "What's going on, Lily? You know you want her away from those deadbeats. You know you can take on anyone who comes at you or her. You've got nothing to be scared of anymore."

As he said those words, the breeze rippled past me, bringing a faint whine into the air as it whipped across a nearby metal awning. A car rumbled past, and a doorbell jingled, and the thumping of my pulse combined with all those sounds into a patchwork of a musical harmony. It rang through my limbs and brought back the image of the water I'd summoned gushing from the walls in my old kitchen to terrorize Wade into answering my questions.

It was true. I was queen of frogs and commander of H2O, it seemed, and that should get us pretty far. What did I really think anyone could do to Marisol that I couldn't defend her from with those new tricks up my sleeve?

I dragged in a breath, and the answer tumbled out of me. "I've just—I've been worried that I hurt her, that I could hurt her again, for so long. I don't want to mess anything up. I don't want to be the reason she ends up in danger."

Nox considered me for a long moment. "It sounds like she's already been through plenty when you *weren't* around to take care of her. I don't think there's a single chance you'll make her life worse."

"You can't know that for sure," I said, but at the same time, I raised my chin, holding on to the harmony humming through me. "But maybe I should trust me and her more. I'll make sure I've really got a handle on my powers, and then I'll have another talk with her."

If I was going to put myself forward as her protector, I'd better make sure I knew what the hell I was doing with myself.

five

Nox

"Do things usually change this much in twenty years?" Ruin asked, shooting a puzzled glance at the antique shop that'd once been the headquarters of another local gang, the Wolverines.

The crystal chandeliers, ornate china plates, and brass candlesticks displayed in the store window definitely didn't fit that ragtag bunch of miscreants. Five minutes in that place, and there'd have been nothing left but chunks of glass and ceramics mixed in with some melted metal. Even without further investigation, I felt comfortable concluding that the guys we'd once squabbled with were no longer operating out of this place.

Maybe they'd completely disbanded. You couldn't expect much consistency out of a bunch of dudes who named themselves after a comic book hero.

"Twenty-one years," Kai corrected automatically. "And you have *no* idea how much has happened in that time." He shook his head as if jostling all the pieces of information he'd consumed in the past couple of weeks into order. He'd stuffed so much into his brain I was kind of surprised he could even hold the damn thing up.

"The guys we knew would all be old now," I said. "Like—as old as our parents were when we got started." A smile tugged at my lips. "Bald spots and crow's feet."

Jett's mouth twisted into a rare smirk. "Dad bods and beer guts."

Ruin snickered and bounced on his feet with eager energy. "Then we'll have no problem taking them down if they're the ones who did us in. How are we going to find them?"

I rubbed my mouth, considering. The towns like Lovell Rise and those around it weren't big enough for more than one gang to stake a claim for long, so we'd owned the Rise, and various other operations had lorded it over its neighbors, like this shabby collection of buildings.

Our killers must have come from one of those other towns. I was tempted to simply barge from main street to main street, smashing windows and battering doors until someone coughed up the information we needed, but that might only give the pricks a chance to make a run for it.

It was better if they didn't know we were back and looking for vengeance until we had them in our grasp. All it'd take was a little restraint. We could pretend we had a more... academic interest in the murderous history of this area. In Kai's case, that wasn't even totally untrue.

"We know all the gang signs," I said. "And we know what looks like one even if it isn't a logo we recognize from before. Let's just cruise around until we find an indication of who's still pretending to be in charge around here and where they're hanging out these days."

The other guys nodded, and we all revved our bikes' engines. I adjusted my position in my seat, soaking in the reverberation that ran through the powerful machine I was riding. My old Hog hadn't boasted anywhere near this much horsepower. Thank the Devil for modern innovations and a professor's bank account.

It didn't take much cruising before we spotted a hastily spray-painted tag on the wall of a tattoo club, which was currently closed up, probably because it'd take about a week to tattoo the entire population of this area who actually wanted to get inked and then you'd just sit around twiddling your thumbs until the next generation came of age.

I'd been wanting to replace some of my ink, but I wasn't turning to a place that had any affiliation with dorks who used a jagged claw symbol that a three-year-old could have drawn as their calling card. Jett was the artist around here, but I did have *some* standards.

There was a dingy curtain hanging over the window on the second-floor apartment, but it only covered half the pane, letting through the faint yellow glow of an electric light behind it. I parked my bike and motioned to the others to follow me.

We marched around back, noting even more of the Wolverines' tags in the lane and one sprayed right across the rear door. It didn't look like just a drive-by tagging. And if I was wrong and we burst in on some startled family, well, we'd say sorry and leave again. No real harm done.

Anyone living around here could probably use a little more excitement in their lives anyway.

I tested the lock with my hand, judged it wanting, and slammed my heel into it hard enough to snap the latch. It swung open on squeaking hinges, and we hurtled up the stairs to the apartment.

"What the—" some young guy said as we charged into the main room, and then Ruin was crashing into him, knocking him to the ground on his stomach. As he planted himself on the guy's back, grinning as he mashed his victim's face against the ground so the guy couldn't speak any more, two more men, a little older, barreled out of another room. Jett toppled one with a punch and a smack of a chair he snatched up, and I rammed the other right into the wall with my hand around his throat.

"Stay right there," I told him, not like he could go

much of anywhere when I pinned his arms over his chest and tightened my grip on his neck at his first feeble kick. Then I took a proper look around the place.

It sure didn't look like the home of any kind of family—other than the halfwit gang type. A ratty sofa stood in one corner, a card table with four dented chairs in the other, playing cards and a few chips still scattered across it. The air stunk of cheap alcohol and weed. Someone had tacked a couple of Playboy centerfolds to the wall next to the oven, I guessed in case you wanted to jack off while you were making a pot roast.

"You're the bunch that calls yourself the Wolverines?" I asked in a growl, turning my attention back to my captive. This guy looked like the oldest of the bunch, but he still couldn't have been much over thirty. At best, he'd have been a teenager when we'd kicked the bucket. That didn't mean he wouldn't know anything, though.

He let out only a faint gurgling noise, which suggested I should loosen my hold a little. I allowed his feet to touch the ground but kept my fingers firmly in place. "Try again."

"Yeah," he rasped. "We're the Wolverines. Who the fuck wants to know?"

"None of your goddamn business." I gave him a vicious smile. "We're here to tie up some loose ends. What do you know about an attack on a gang hangout over in Lovell Rise twenty-one years ago?"

"Twenty-one years ago?" the guy replied. "Fuck, I

was in middle school then. What the hell are you talking about?"

But the guy Jett was currently using as a chair cushion made a sound. Jett prodded him. "What's that?"

The guy wheezed and then said, "I heard about that. Dirk mentioned it a couple of times."

Dirk—that'd been one of the dicks who'd run with the Wolverines when we'd known them. I glared at the guy over my shoulder. "And what did Dirk say about it?"

"Just that—that we should watch our backs around the Silver Scythes out in Rushford. I guess they had something to do with getting that whole gang wiped off the map."

My lips pulled back from my teeth in a silent snarl. "The fucking *Silver Scythes*?"

My men looked as disgusted as I felt. It was one thing to name yourself after a comic book, and another level way lower to go for a wimpy-sounding title like Silver Scythes. Like they wanted to be *pretty* about their life of crime or some shit. Maybe they figured people would write poetry about them.

But the name resonated with me with even more horror than just that. The thing was, I'd known the Scythes had it out for us. They'd made a stab at robbing the site where we stashed our stolen goods for fencing, but *because* they'd seemed like such wimps, not much more than a bunch of snot-nosed kids with visions of grandeur they'd never live up to, I hadn't put bullets in their brains. I'd let them off with a few bruises and a firm threat about what they'd face if they messed with us again.

And instead of shaping up, they'd stewed on the situation for six months and then come at us with guns blazing? The fucking bastards. I didn't know who I wanted to rip to shreds more—them or myself for giving them a second chance.

If I hadn't, we might never have died. If I'd laid down the law as hard as they'd obviously deserved, I'd have been there for Gram, I'd have watched the Skullbreakers grow in prestige and power…

Anger and guilt wrapped around my gut like barbed wire. I hurled the guy I'd pinned toward the window, where he cracked his head against the glass. Then I spun around, my hands clenched.

We would build ourselves up again. And we had Lily now. We never would have had her if we hadn't been through all this.

But I still should have fucking known better.

"Move out," I snapped at the other guys. Jett and Ruin got off their human seating. We all stomped down the stairs to our bikes.

"Over to Rushfield?" Kai asked as we mounted. "It sounds like the Silver Scythes are still active." Disbelief laced through his tone. He found the idea that they'd gotten the better of us even more ridiculous than I did.

Jett was frowning. "It *couldn't* have been them," he said.

"They've sure been spreading the story that it was." I

gunned my engine. "Let's see what they've got to say for themselves now."

Rushford lay on the opposite side of Lovell Rise, a little bigger but also a little more rundown. It was like someone had cloned our town but ended up with an expanded, grainy copy. They didn't have the lake right there to draw tourists out to the marina, and they weren't quite as close to Mayfield for the city pricks to come looking to get some "country air." As far as I could tell, they didn't have much of anything. Maybe that was why they were such dickheads about everything.

The Scythes hadn't been on my radar enough for me to have memorized the location of their headquarters, if they'd even had one back then, but it wasn't any harder to find them than it had been with the Wolverines. We roared into town and tore up and down a few streets, observing a tag in silvery metallic paint that might have been supposed to look like a curved blade but really bore more resemblance to a limp dick, which fit better anyway.

There were more tags around a dumpy-looking board game shop than anywhere else. We marched in, strode right past the counter into the back room, and found a couple of idiots lounging on sofas with cartoons on the TV and Cheeto dust smeared on their jeans.

"Are you the fuckers currently calling yourselves the Silver Scythes?" I demanded, wrenching the nearest guy out of his seat and into the wall in the middle of the question.

As he sputtered, I noted the crummy tattoo peeking from beneath the collar of his shirt and the scar across his forehead. I was pretty sure this prick had been part of the Scythes back in my day, as one of the runty high school seniors that made up most of their numbers.

Jett and Ruin had shoved the other guy to the floor. Kai picked his way through the empty junk food bags and opened a cookie tin on a shelf. "They're dealing coke," he reported. "Either that or using so much their noses should be falling off any day now."

"What the fuck—" the guy I was holding spat out. "You can't just—"

"I can do whatever the hell I want," I interrupted. "And I'll take that as a yes, you are the shitty Silver Scythes. You're going to explain to me what went down between you asses and the Skullbreakers twenty years ago, and you're going to explain it to me fast, or I will personally break your skull. Slowly, into many very small pieces."

I might do it anyway, but there was no point in mentioning that upfront. I sure as hell wasn't going to be generous with these imbeciles again.

The guys were clearly still wimps, whatever else they'd done. The one I had pinned shuddered in my grasp. His voice took on more of a whimpering tone. "We didn't really— It wasn't us. We only— They were so full of themselves, and they acted like they owned everything around. But we barely had anything to do with it."

"That's not what you've been saying around town," Kai said in his usual nonchalant tone.

"What exactly *did* you have to do with it?" I asked, yanking him back for just long enough to slam him against the wall again.

"We just—it wasn't even *me*, it was Tony's idea, and he's dead now, so—"

"What the fuck did *Tony* do?" I growled.

"He put out word to one of the big dogs in Mayfield that the Skullbreakers were talking shit about them and making moves to steal ground in the city," the idiot said with a hitch of breath. "I guess he convinced them really well, 'cause they acted on it. *I* had nothing to do with it. I said it was a bad idea getting mixed up in—"

I didn't want to hear his lame-ass excuses. I tossed him on the ground and kicked him in the side hard enough to fracture a rib or two. As he lay there groaning, I exchanged a glance with my comrades.

I had fucked up. My leniency with the Silver Scythes two decades ago had set us up for our fall. But if we wanted to deal with the villains who'd actually mowed us down and dumped us like week-old trash, it sounded like we needed to head to Mayfield.

Before I could say so out loud, a guy came bursting through the back door, gun in hand. The new arrival was pointing it straight at me.

My body reacted instinctively, whipping out a punch even though he was at least a couple of feet beyond my reach. But as I moved, the electric sensation

I'd felt when we'd kicked the asses of Lily's bullies in the grocery store crackled through my limbs—and seemingly out of my hand. *Something* walloped the guy across the jaw, sending him careening to the side.

Kai was there a second later, ramming his knee into the prick's wrist and retrieving the gun. He shot the guy in the side of the head without so much as a blink and glanced at my fist as our attacker crumpled. "That's never happened before, has it?"

I looked down at my hand, flexing my fingers. "No. Looks like there's a little more to our superpowers than you'd already figured out."

six

Lily

"Do it again!" Ruin crowed, applauding his heart out.

Nox chuckled and swung his fist toward another low branch on the hunched sapling he'd been battering. His knuckles didn't even come close to hitting it—he smacked the empty space about a foot from the bark. But the air shimmered faintly, and the branch split in half as if it'd been struck. The former gang leader raised his hand triumphantly, grinning.

A cool wind swept off the lake and licked over the back of my skin. I wasn't sure how much it was the chill and how much the supernatural energy in the air that raised the hairs on the back of my neck.

After a broken plate, a shattered glass, and a dent in

the front door, I'd finally convinced the former Skullbreakers that if they were going to insist on an experimentation session, we really should do it someplace where I didn't have a security deposit hanging over my head. We'd driven out here to a particularly secluded section of the marsh, Ruin opting to ride in my car with me and the others zipping along on their new motorcycles. They made quite the entourage.

And they'd make even more of one if they all developed fancier powers like this one of Nox's. Playing around some more, he reached up and twisted his fingers—and a nearby twig snapped from its branch.

Jett took a few swings at another tree, but he didn't seem to be able to manipulate his lingering ghostly energies in the same way. Ruin and Kai hadn't managed it either, although Ruin seemed content to simply watch Nox work his powers anyway. Right now, Kai was rubbing his chin with a pensive expression.

"It obviously isn't a general effect of our previously free-souled state," he said. "Then we'd all be able to do it. Physical violence has always been one of your primary ways of getting things done, so the energies may be adapting to your specific skill set or focus. We might find that different effects emerge for each of us."

"Let me guess," Jett muttered. "You'd get the power of being a total know-it-all. No, wait, you've already got that."

"Jett, you'd have to get something to do with art," Ruin said gleefully. "And Kai will have to have something smart." He paused, tilting his head to one side. "I'm not sure what would make sense for me."

Nox cuffed him in the arm. "Maybe you'll start literally beaming sunshine out your ass like you already do metaphorically."

Ruin laughed. "I guess that'd be handy in the dark."

Kai had ignored Jett's remark. He nudged at his glasses and contemplated his friends. "We'll have to stay alert to shifts in the energy moving through us and new manifestations of it. It's important that we're aware of our capabilities so we can work to our full potential."

Nox cuffed him next. "Now you sound like a self-help guru." He turned to me. "What about you, Siren? Didn't you say you wanted to play around with your powers some more, see what *you're* capable of?"

I had, and I'd been thinking about that ever since we'd come out here. But somehow, now that I was faced with a stretch of the reed-choked water that'd almost swallowed me up fourteen years ago, an immense sense of hesitation gripped my mind. Some part of me would rather dunk my head in that cold marsh water than try to manipulate it again.

I'd used my powers two times so far—well, two times on purpose. There was also the time when I'd splashed the girl who'd been one of the ringleaders of my bullies, Peyton, with water that'd jumped right out of its bottle in her hands. And the time when I'd frightened my stepdad and possibly my mom too by throwing water around the house after I'd discovered

Nolan Gauntt with my sister... doing something. That incident was still a total blank in my mind.

That fact unsettled me too. I had to take Wade's word for what had happened. His babbled, terrified words, which suggested he'd been scared into honesty. But who knew how accurately he even remembered what'd gone down seven years ago?

The underside of my arm itched in the spot where I had a birthmark-like splotch, one I'd only discovered after I'd started my stay at the looney bin, like the stress had caused even my skin to freak out. I scratched at it as I gathered my resolve.

"I do need to experiment—and get better control over what I can do," I said. "I'm just not sure where to start. I don't want to destroy anything out here."

Ruin shrugged with a smile. "You've got marsh magic, and we're at the marsh. I don't think you can mess it up by making it marshier."

He might have had a point there. I dragged in a breath and tried to tap into the feelings that'd surged through me when I'd used my unexpected powers before.

A humming sensation had risen up in my chest and expanded through my whole body. And—listening to the sounds around me, forming a rhythm with them, had helped me focus the power. I squared my shoulders and willed something to happen... but no hum rushed up inside me. No tingling spread to my fingertips.

I wiggled my fingers, but that didn't summon anything. Frowning at my hands didn't help either.

"I don't know how to get it started," I admitted. "Before it always just… happened."

"Something provoked you," Kai suggested. "What were the circumstances when you tapped into it before?"

That question was easy to answer. "I was angry. Or upset, at least. And feeling under threat, some of the time." I had no idea how I'd been feeling when my strange power had first emerged at age thirteen, but I obviously hadn't been *happy*.

"Hmm," Nox said with a teasing lilt to his tone. "So we need to piss you off to let you get some practice in."

I glowered at him. "I'd really rather you didn't volunteer. Maybe if I just *think* about situations that would bother me…"

I tried imagining scenarios from the past, like a bunch of the guys from school showing up at my work to frame me and then trying to beat up Kai. Or Peyton and her friends shoving me into the school's basement utility room. Or Wade complaining that the mental hospital hadn't "fixed" me.

Little whiffs of anger flickered through me, but they didn't provoke the hum I was looking for. Maybe it wouldn't get riled up when I already knew how those situations had been resolved. I rolled my neck, stretching the tension out of my muscles, and imagined up new encounters that hadn't actually happened but could.

What if Wade went back on his word and tried to move Mom and Marisol away from Lovell Rise? I could show up at the house and find them and all their stuff gone…

Picturing walking up to the empty shell of a home brought out the first strains of the hum reverberating up from my gut. I imagined seeing the car driving off, Marisol screaming my name from the back window, and my blood quivered in my veins.

I held on to those taut emotions and drummed my fingers against my thigh, feeling the beat all through my body. Lacing it through the hiss of the wind through the cattails and the chirping of a nearby bird into a minor orchestration. Any other time, my throat would have tickled with the urge to put words to the melody. Now, I was reaching for something else.

The first time I'd used my power on purpose, I'd called in an army of frogs on Peyton. My lips twitched with the memory. Could I do that again, just by wanting it?

Thinking back to that moment, I did my best to send out a call to those jumpy creatures who seemed to follow me around so often of their own accord already. *Come on, slimy green friends*, I thought into the void. *Nothing so urgent today. Just want to see whether you can hear me.*

It wasn't like the other day with Peyton. The reeds rustled, and there was a pattering of soft thumps as one and another squat body leapt from the marsh water onto the grass to join me. They came. But when I opened my eyes and looked down, only a couple dozen were clustered around my feet.

I'd brought at least a hundred down on Peyton, and I'd been miles from the marsh when I'd accomplished that.

"Hey," I said to the ones who'd answered my call. "Good to see you. I guess you're the overachievers, huh?"

Ruin crouched down and let one hop onto his hand. He stroked its sleek back and grinned up at me. "They're cute!"

"Not exactly going to put the fear of, well, me into anyone, though," I grumbled. "Two dozen frogs—just enough to be very weird, not enough to send anyone running."

"That's not what you unleashed on your stepdad," Nox reminded me.

"It's not." I eyed the span of tangled reeds that stretched at least a quarter of a mile out before thinning into open water. I'd called to the water running through the pipes in my childhood home. Conducting the marsh water to my will, if it was where I'd gotten these powers in the first place, should be a piece of cake. But I already felt tired. Why was this so hard?

"You're worried," Kai said, evenly but quietly, answering the question I hadn't voiced out loud. "Your powers make you nervous. You're still afraid you'll hurt someone."

My hands balled at my sides. "Yeah."

"You *can't* really hurt us," Ruin pointed out, straightening up. "I mean, we've already been dead. I guess if something happens to these bodies, we'd just… find new ones?" He cocked his head at Kai.

The other guy lifted his hands. "I'm not sure, but that'd be my best guess."

I *really* didn't want to think about that. When the guys had first barged into my life, without me really understanding who and what they were, I'd wanted nothing more than to get away from them. But now, just weeks later, the thought of losing them might as well have ripped me down the middle. An ache swelled around my heart.

They'd been the first people who'd really supported me and been there for me when I was a kid, and they were the only people I'd been able to turn to since I'd gotten back into town. They'd recognized the strength I had in me, both supernatural and otherwise, and helped me bring it out. I didn't know what I'd do if they vanished and I was left to deal with this insanity on my own all over again.

The pain of that possibility sent the hum roaring through me with twice as much force as before. A shiver ran down my back, and I gulped the damp air. Then I fixed my attention on the lake and beckoned.

A warbling sound filled the air and rang through my nerves. A taste like algae crept into the back of my mouth. Then a surge of water swept up over the bank and rippled across the grass to kiss my feet.

More, I thought, leaning into that warbled harmony. Twisting the melody in my mind into a shape I wanted to see.

The water slipped back toward the marsh—and then shot upward in a thin but towering wave.

My control wasn't perfect. Little droplets rained down on us as the wave held its rigid loom. Jett looked up at it and gave a low whistle, lifting his hands as if he were framing the image with them for a future painting.

This time, Nox was the one who applauded, with an emphatic slow clap. Ruin let out a joyful little whoop. I inhaled shakily, a smile crossing my lips, and shooed the water back toward the marsh.

The wave flipped over and crashed down into the reeds, splattering the tree trunks along the shore.

"What do you think?" Nox asked me, his eyes smoldering with appreciation. "Ready to take on the world?"

An unsteady giggle tumbled out of me. "Maybe not the entire world quite yet. But I think it's time I talked to my sister and found out exactly what she's scared of. Because whatever it is—whoever it is—they're going down."

SEVEN

Lily

When I'd parked a couple of blocks down from the bookstore and gotten out, the guys converged on the car.

"Are you sure it's still safe to drive this thing?" Jett said in a doubtful tone, tapping the rust-speckled hood. "The engine was making more noise than a woodchipper."

"We're getting her a new ride," Nox said before I had a chance to answer. "We already decided that."

"*I* didn't decide it," I protested. I'd fully admit that the car—which I'd affectionately named Fred—was a junker, but it was *my* junker. Bought with hard-earned cash I'd scraped together during the work placements that St. Elspeth's Hospital had let me take on in the past year as I'd proved my mental stability.

Okay, so maybe the melodies Fred's engine produced were more in the vein of heavy metal screeching than I'd generally prefer. And the front passenger door was a thread from falling off its hinges. And an occasional plume of smoke emanated from beneath the hood. But only occasionally! I could live with that.

Ruin slung his arm around me. "You don't need to decide," he said with his usual buoyant optimism. "We'll take care of everything for you. We're taking care of *you*."

Jett made a rough coughing sound and muttered something under his breath that might have been, "Some of us more than others." But then he nodded in agreement with the overall statement.

"It would be better if you were driving a vehicle that wasn't quite so… on the verge of breaking down," Kai said.

Nox fixed me with a firm gaze. "It isn't an argument. You can keep *this* car if you really want it, but we're getting you another one." A slow, cocky smile curved his lips. "I mean, we do owe you, right? It's kind of our fault that you lost your job. What kind of men would we be if we didn't make it up to you?"

I could have pointed out that the men who were more responsible for me losing that job had done shit-all and still seemed to consider themselves manly enough, but I didn't really want my ghostly avengers thinking I saw my bullies as a suitable model of behavior. Instead, I let out a huff of a sigh. "I don't want you stealing Fred away in the middle of the night. He's doing his best." I patted the hood. "If he actually breaks down, then you'll have a point."

Nox let out a noncommittal grumble.

"Are we going to get to meet your sister too?" Ruin asked, beaming in the general direction of the store. "I don't really remember her that well from back before."

The guys had never really joined in with the games Marisol and I had played together back when I'd thought they were my imaginary friends. I'd assumed it was because it hadn't made sense in my mind for them to interfere when I already had company. I guessed that'd been essentially true, except it'd been them deciding it of their own accord.

I eyed the four of them with a twist of my mouth. "Um... Maybe it's better if we hold off on those introductions until she's totally comfortable with *me* being around again. I mean, your situation is a whole nother level of crazy." I waved my hands in their general vicinity.

That statement was so undeniable that none of them bothered to argue. "Next time!" Ruin said cheerfully, like everything was going to be sorted out that fast.

"We can keep an eye on things out here while you're talking with her," Nox said. "I haven't seen those pricks who had it in for you making any moves lately, but we've got to make sure it stays that way. How long until she should show up?"

I was pretty sure the beating the guys had given my tormenters up and down the aisles of the grocery store had driven the message home pretty solidly. People at school were looking at me like they were afraid I'd randomly decide to stab them, but they'd already been doing that. At least they weren't also making snarky comments and tossing garbage at me anymore.

I checked the time on my phone. "About ten minutes. I'll go into the store in a moment so I'm already in there. Hopefully she'll feel safer talking to me where there'll be less chance of prying eyes."

As I finished speaking, an alert sounded from Kai's pocket. He got out his own phone and peered at the screen.

"I've been tracking any new mentions on the internet about Thrivewell Enterprises and the Gauntts," he informed us, answering the question before it'd been asked as usual.

My heart skipped a beat. "Anything interesting?"

He shook his head. "Unless you consider the fact that they're looking for a new mailroom clerk damning evidence of anything other than high employee turnover at the grunt level, nope. I'll let you know as soon as anything comes up."

"Okay." I rolled my shoulders and bounced on my feet to loosen myself up, like I was about to go into a boxing ring rather than a bookstore. "I'll see you all in a bit. Wish me luck."

Ruin gave me one last squeeze before letting me go. "It'll be fine. She loves you."

His words sent a little pang through me. Marisol had *used* to love me. She was practically a different person now than she'd been back then. Sixteen was leagues away from nine. And she hadn't seen me or spoken to me in those seven years except for our brief conversation last week.

I walked over to the bookstore and pushed inside. A waft of crisp, vaguely lemon-scented air washed over me.

It wasn't one of those cozy bookshops full of old wooden bookcases and tables, ancient volumes bound in fabric and leather, and the smell of dust and old paper. The shelving units shone so starkly white I could make out a glimmer of my reflection, and they were lined with brightly colored spines of what were obviously mostly new releases.

But there was nothing wrong with that. I could imagine taking a kind of comfort in the shiny freshness of the place, especially if other parts of your life felt awfully murky.

As I walked down an aisle of travel guides and biographies to the back of the store, I trailed my fingers over the smooth spines—until I noticed the woman behind the counter narrowing her eyes in my direction. Jerking my hand back to my side, I ended up in the back corner in between the picture books and children's novels. I pretended to be fascinated by a neon-hued cover for a story about an octopus that was sad because it didn't get to wear shoes.

Actually, I kind of did want to know what the moral of that story could possibly be.

I debated flipping through it, wondering if browsing that avidly without buying might bring the wrath of the counter lady down on me. Then the door squeaked open again, and Marisol walked in.

"Hello, again," the woman said in a dry voice that wasn't exactly friendly. I guessed Marisol hadn't usually been buying whatever books she'd been looking through in here either. I'd give the woman credit for having a *little* patience with her.

Marisol slunk to the opposite end of the back and sank down on a stool in between Science Fiction & Fantasy and General Fiction. She contemplated the titles but didn't pick anything up, just hugging her backpack on her lap.

Did she usually not even let herself steal a chapter or two of reading while she holed up in here? It looked like no. After a moment, she pulled a book out of her backpack instead, one that I assumed had been assigned in class based on the dreary cover, and opened it up.

I could think of all kinds of reasons why she wouldn't want to hang out at home. But why here? I guessed it was getting chilly to hang out in the park, and the nearest library was a twenty-minute walk farther from the high school, so there might not have been any other options. But still, something about the image before me was so pitiful it made my heart ache.

My sister shouldn't have needed to resort to hiding away in some random store to feel any kind of security.

She'd turned her back mostly to me, not even noticing I was there in her attempt to make herself as unnoticeable as possible. I eased over and spoke quietly. "Marisol."

Despite my efforts, she startled and jerked around. When she saw me, her gaze immediately darted around the store, giving me the same impression I'd gotten before that she was worried about someone seeing us together.

"Hey," I said quickly, crouching down so we were at the same eye level and setting a careful hand on her arm. "No one's in here who'd hurt you. And I talked to Wade a few days ago—I made sure he isn't going to get in the way of us seeing each other anymore. Talking to me won't get either of us in trouble with him or Mom."

Marisol dragged in a shaky breath. "Okay." She stared at me, her eyes nearly round.

I had to ask, as much as the possible answers scared me— "Do *you* not want to talk to me? Because the last thing I want is to be harassing you."

"No!" she said hastily. "No, it's—it's really good to see you." Her tone was still nervous, but after she'd spoken, a smile touched her face, soft but bright enough to convince me she meant it. "It's been such a long time," she added.

A lump filled my throat. "I know. I'm so sorry. I *wanted* to call you or send you letters, but Mom and Wade put a ban on that. It was never because I didn't want to be here for you. And now that I'm back, I'm going to do whatever I can to have your *back*, like always."

Marisol's shoulders came down, but her gaze flicked to the store around us again. I had to ask the next tough question.

"Mare, is there someone else you're worried about? Has anyone been giving you a hard time or following you around?"

She hugged her backpack, her mouth twisting. "I—I don't totally know."

"Wade mentioned something about Nolan Gauntt," I prodded gently.

Marisol blinked at me, her expression vaguely puzzled, not horrified the way I'd have expected at the mention of her probable abuser. Had I been wrong in my assumptions?

"Him?" she said. "There's nothing… I mean, I'm not sure…" She rubbed her forehead. "I just—a long time ago, after you got taken away, I thought I saw people hanging around who seemed to be watching me. I got it in my head that they might take *me* away too. But then… nothing ever happened. So maybe I just imagined it." She frowned. "But every now and then I still get the feeling like someone's watching me. And it's not a good feeling."

I wasn't sure if that was a good or a bad thing. It sounded like her current meekness was more a result of living under Wade and Mom's roof with no one to stand up for her than any other villain's involvement. But on the other hand, her instincts could be right.

"Has anything at all happened that would prove someone's keeping an eye on you?" I asked. "Or has anyone mentioned anything about me?"

"Only Mom and Wade," Marisol said. "And no. I couldn't prove it. I never even mentioned it to them because I knew what they'd say. But because it happened right after you left... And I always had this feeling it was somehow connected, like they had it out for me *and* you... That doesn't really make sense." She looked at me beseechingly. "I'm sorry for taking off on you the other day. I *wanted* to talk to you."

I risked leaning forward and giving her a quick hug. To my relief, Marisol leaned into my embrace with a ragged little sigh that broke my heart. When I pulled back, she'd relaxed even more.

I hated to ask this last thing, but I had to. "I know things got pretty crazy the day I got taken away. I don't remember exactly what happened, but I know I saw something that made me upset. Maybe something to do with you. Mr. Gauntt was there at the house, wasn't he? Did he or someone else... do something to you?"

The puzzled look came back. Marisol's gaze went distant as if she was trying to remember. Her jaw tightened. "I don't— He just wanted to talk to me. They do some kind of special placements for kids. He thought maybe..." She knit her brow. "I didn't want to anyway. I think that was all. Then he left. And you got mad at him. It's kind of jumbled up in my head. I thought you were upset because you figured he was going to make me go with him or something?"

It sounded like the craziness of the situation and my emerging powers had rattled her so much she'd detached herself from those memories over the years. I didn't buy that I hadn't seen anything other than Nolan Gauntt suggesting Marisol take some extra classes. I hadn't been an aggressive person—I still wasn't one—and I couldn't picture myself flying off the handle over that. The bullies on campus had done way worse before I'd finally unleashed my powers on them.

No, what made the most sense was that something worse had happened, and the Gauntts were spying on Marisol while also keeping tabs on me to make sure neither of us spoke up about it.

But that meant that Marisol might not be really safe talking to me. At least not until I sorted everything else out. I squeezed her shoulder and held her gaze.

"I'm going to make sure that no one's taking you or me anywhere, all right? We don't know yet whether that was just your imagination or something real, and it's better to be careful. And then I'm going to set things up so you can stay with me instead of Mom and Wade, for as long as you'd like. If you'd want that."

A wider smile stretched across Marisol's face. "That would be amazing."

The sense prickled over my skin that I might have already put her at risk by talking with her for so long. I straightened up. "I'll get everything figured out as quickly as possible and keep you in the loop. Have you got a phone so I don't have to keep going all stalker on you?"

Marisol managed a quick laugh. "I don't mind when it's you. But I do."

As we exchanged numbers, my mind whirled with the challenge ahead of me. Somehow I had to figure out if the Gauntts were keeping tabs on my sister—if they were still invested in her situation at all. Wade had certainly seemed to think so.

An idea sprang to the front of my mind like a frog out of the marsh. That... that might be crazy, but so far crazy had been working pretty well for me.

I left Marisol to her reading and went out to regroup with the guys by their motorcycles.

"Everything went according to plan?" Nox asked.

"Yep," I said. "And now I've got a new plan." I turned to Kai. "I need to get that mailroom job at Thrivewell. It's time to take our mission straight to the source."

eight

Lily

I never really thought about how small Lovell Rise was until I went someplace else. Standing on the busy street in downtown Mayfield with glossy high-rises looming all around me, my chest constricted. It wasn't like I stood taller than the houses or stodgy college buildings in town either, but for some reason this place in particular made me feel very small.

Kai took in my expression and slipped his hand around mine to give it a quick squeeze. The brief gesture felt like something bigger coming from the detached, analytical guy, the equivalent of a hug from Ruin. He could probably read my nervousness just looking at me.

He confirmed that a moment later with his next remarks. "You'll be fine. Everything's set up to work in your favor. The interview is only a formality so they can show they checked off all the boxes."

I focused on the one particular glossy high-rise up ahead, the shiniest and highest of them all: the headquarters of Thrivewell Enterprises. Nolan Gauntt's main workplace.

"I'm the goddaughter of Harmon Kitteridge," I said, going over the story Kai had coached me on one last time to shore up my courage. "He told me *all* about what a great place Thrivewell is to get started at. I know he's looking forward to doing more business with them and knowing he's got family there now."

"Exactly." Kai smiled, his gray-green eyes gleaming behind his glasses. "Thrivewell has a bunch of contracts with Kitteridge, some of them coming up for renewal soon. They won't want to risk pissing him off. I've already laid the groundwork with a few phone calls and well-placed documents. You just have to show up and be your sweet self, and they'll be glad to get the position filled that easily."

I dragged in a breath. "And if someone mentions Harmon's goddaughter to him?"

Kai's smile grew into a smirk. "Oh, I've laid the groundwork with him too. He knows that he'd better continue having a goddaughter named Lily Strom, or his business partner might receive certain files that show Harmon's been screwing the guy's wife for several years now."

"The Gauntts would probably suspect something. They know at least a little about my family."

"They're not likely to be paying much attention to new hires at the mailroom level. And if they do, it's unlikely Kitteridge ever mentioned to them that he specifically *didn't* have a goddaughter. If any problems come up, we'll deal with them as they do."

The confidence in his words steadied my nerves. Kai had managed to arrange all this—what *couldn't* he do?

"Who are you a secret relative of to get your job?" I asked. Kai had decided he was going to interview for another open position—something a little higher up in the offices doing market research. He'd pointed out that it'd be easier for us to find out what we needed to with both of us there coordinating our efforts.

Kai rocked on his heels with an eager energy I wasn't sure I'd ever witnessed in him before. "Oh, I'm not going to need that. I've done my diligence on the hiring staff. All I've got to do is walk in there, read the room, and I'll have them eating out of my hand in a matter of minutes."

I'd never seen him fully in his element before, I realized. Nox came totally to life in a fight, Jett did when he was immersed in his art, and Ruin found joy everywhere he looked. Kai was lit up by working his machinations on the world around him. His body, though it still held some of Zack's footballer muscle, didn't exude physical might the same way the others' did, but right now, the air around him hummed with his own kind of power.

There was something magnetic about it. I had the urge to grab him by that collared shirt and find out what it'd feel like to kiss him in this state. But I held myself back, because I'd never kissed Kai in any state. When we'd had that group discussion about my relationship with the guys, he'd seemed reluctant to pursue anything like that. He'd said it'd be too much of a distraction.

It wasn't like I was getting a shortage of action from his friends, anyway.

He peered down at me, and for a second I thought I might have caught a flicker of interest in his gaze too. Then it vanished, leaving only measured concern. "Are you completely sure you're okay with this? I mean, giving up your studies and everything?"

There was no way I could hold down a fulltime job at Thrivewell while also attending classes at the college. But as soon as I'd realized that, it'd been relief that'd hit me, not regret.

"All I've got from campus is a bunch of bad memories," I said. "I still think I might want to go into sociology, but that can wait. A few of my courses let me transfer to the online option, so I'll still be working toward it anyway." And Kai had worked his persuasive magic there too, convincing the admin office that they really needed to refund me for the courses I couldn't continue on the basis of the hostile environment their school had provided.

Marisol needed me. That was more important than any of the bullshit I'd put up with from those asshats.

"Good," Kai said. "Ready to head in there?"

"Absolutely," I said, raising my chin. "Let's do this."

As we set off down the sidewalk toward the Thrivewell headquarters, my phone chimed. A text from Ruin had popped up. *You're going to knock them dead, Waterlily! Not the way I knock people dead, but that wouldn't work out so well for getting a job anyway. Anyone with eyes will be able to see how amazing you are.*

The corners of my lips quirked upward at his overboard enthusiasm. *About to head in now*, I texted back. *Thank you for the cheerleading.*

Kai caught my eye and nodded to me with another small smile of encouragement. Then he strode ahead of me so we didn't come in together, which might look odd if anyone noticed and thought about it later. His host had only been nineteen, and I'd gotten the impression that the Skullbreakers had all been in their early 20s when they'd died, but in the business casual suit with his dark brown hair carefully styled, self-assurance radiating off his stance, he could easily have passed for ten years older.

So, yeah, I might have checked him out as he ambled into the building half a block ahead of me. Sue me.

I tugged my blouse straight and zoned out for a second into the rumble of the passing cars and the clacking of my heels against the pavement. A battle chant of a song rose up in my chest. *Here I go to take my stand. Defend my sister and stick it to the man.*

By the time I reached the building's immense lobby, Kai had already passed through. A skeletal man behind a huge marble reception desk studied me as I approached.

"Hi," I said, willing my voice to stay steady even though he looked like he might be sizing me up for his stew pot. "I have an interview with Ms. Fuller at ten o'clock."

He consulted his computer, which apparently contained all the things, because a moment later, he said, "Miss Strom?"

"Yes, that's me."

He pointed to the elevator alcove just past the desk. "Third floor and to your left."

The short elevator trip took me to an open-concept office area full of cubicles and fronted by another polished reception desk half the size of the one downstairs. When I introduced myself to the woman there, she motioned me to a row of chairs outside one of the smaller office rooms that actually had doors.

Ms. Fuller's office had a window, but the blinds were drawn. I was the only person sitting outside. I clasped my hands on my lap, and then dropped them to my sides, and then folded my arms over my chest, and started worrying I'd look too fidgety for a job in this place.

Would she know about my past—about my stay at St. Elspeth's? I couldn't see how, but word had certainly gotten around Lovell Rise at lightning speed.

I only had a few seconds to worry about that possibility, my pulse kicking up another notch, before the office door swung open.

A petite woman in a beige dress suit bobbed her head to me. "Miss Strom? Please come in."

With her curly, white-blond hair swept into a fuzzy ball on top of her head, her big dark eyes, and her bulging nose, she could have passed for a sheep without needing a costume. It was hard to be all that scared of a farm animal in human form. I managed a smile that didn't feel totally stiff and followed her into the office.

"Well, now," she said, sitting down at her desk and shuffling some papers there. "You come with glowing recommendations. I understand your godfather, Mr. Kitteridge, is particularly approving of you joining our team."

Getting right to the nepotistic point, were we? "Yes," I said, smiling brighter. "He says Thrivewell is a great place to work."

"Oh, we are. We certainly are." She gave a soft little laugh with a faint *baa* to it and looked at her papers again. "You don't have any previous mailroom experience?"

"No," I said quickly. "But I've done a bunch of retail work, which I think has pretty similar skills. Making sure everything goes in the right place, getting things to people who need them."

I'd rehearsed that pitch for my skills beforehand. Ms. Fuller didn't look particularly impressed, but she didn't look concerned either, so I guessed that was a win.

"It is an entry level position," she said. "And I'd

imagine fairly easy to pick up the details as you go. You'd have a senior assistant there to advise—oh!"

Her eyes widened, and she jerked back in her chair. The frog that had just leapt onto her desk let out an inquisitive *ribbit?* and hopped over to her pencil holder.

"Er." I panicked for a moment before it occurred to me that my interviewer wasn't going to assume the frog had anything to do with me. How ridiculous would that be? People didn't go walking around with frogs trailing after them. Ha ha ha.

I let out a little of that laughter, hopefully more convincingly than it'd sounded in my head, and acted like I was surprised too. "Would you look at that. Where did it come from?"

"I have no idea!" Ms. Fuller exclaimed. She waved her hands vaguely at the frog until it hopped off the side of her desk and then scrambled to grab her phone. "I'll have… the maintenance staff see about it. They must have some idea what to do."

Yeah, I'm sure they deal with invading frogs all the time, the snarky voice in my head remarked.

As we waited for a janitor to come scoop up the frog, I sat straighter in my chair, feeling the need to demonstrate in every way possible that I was an upstanding citizen who definitely wouldn't bring random amphibious creatures into the workplace. "You were saying about the job being entry level. I'm a fast learner—I'm sure I can get up to speed quickly."

"Yes, yes, excellent." Ms. Fuller shuffled her papers again, clearly flustered. I found myself picturing a kitten curled up in the fluff of her hair. The absurdity of the image calmed me down just a little.

A man hustled in, muttered at the frog as he retrieved it, and hustled back out again. I resisted the impulse to call after him to be gentle with the poor thing. Were there any ponds in the city where he could deposit it?

Maybe it was better not to think too hard about that.

"And you're living in Lovell Rise at the moment," my interviewer said, seeming to relax once our unexpected visitor was gone. "You won't find the commute too long?"

I shook my head. "To get a chance to work here, it's worth the drive. And I'm planning on looking for an apartment in the city too."

I hadn't exactly been planning that until the moment the words came out of my mouth, but as soon as they did, it sounded like a brilliant idea. There was no room for Marisol in my current place, and it'd be hard to find a better apartment in town, where there wasn't a ton of selection. And everyone saw me as the psycho girl there now. Maybe I could find a place at the end of the city that was closest to Lovell Rise and drive her out to school and back... or she could even transfer to a high school here in Mayfield. A fresh start might be just what she needed too.

Ms. Fuller cleared her throat and broke me out of that daydream. "Excellent. Well, I'm sure you realize that an entry-level position comes with a corresponding level of pay and benefits. But there will be opportunities to work your way up if you apply yourself."

"Of course," I said, putting my smile back on. "I hope to do just that."

It seemed like a perfect note to end the interview on, except just then another note pealed out—from my phone. I'd gotten another text. And another, and another, in quick succession. I peeked at my phone just long enough to turn it off—why hadn't I done that to begin with?—seeing that Ruin had just sent me a bunch more cheerleading plus questions of whether I was done yet.

I shoved the phone back into my pocket, my cheeks flushing. "Sorry, I should have shut it off before."

Ms. Fuller's eyebrows had arched slightly. "Is there a problem?"

"No, not at all." Then a brainstorm hit me, and for a second, I felt like I was channeling Kai. "It was just Uncle Harmon. That's what I always call him. He wanted to know how the interview went—I told him I was coming in this morning."

"Oh!" My interviewer flushed in turn. "I suppose you can give him good news, then. You're the best candidate we've had, and we'd be happy to have you start on Monday. If that sounds good to you."

I beamed at her, my fluster falling away. One step closer to finding out what was up with the Gauntts. "Yes. Thank you. I'm looking forward to it."

I texted Ruin back on my way out of the building. By the time I reached Fred where I'd parked him, the guys had already roared up on their bikes. Kai joined us a moment later with a satisfied smile that said he'd landed his job as easily as he'd expected.

"Hurray to being gainfully employed!" I said, and Ruin wrapped me in a hug. "Did you guys find out anything?" They'd taken the opportunity to prowl around the city searching for information on which of the urban gangs had decided to come after them decades ago.

Nox frowned. "Nothing solid. But we'll get there. They can't hide for long." He looked me over in my business clothes and gave me a smile just short of a leer. "We don't have to worry about that right now. You deserve a celebration."

He patted the back of his motorcycle. I hesitated for a second and then clambered on, deciding not to think about the way my skirt rode up my thighs, just tucking my arms around his well-built frame.

I was on my way to tackling the most powerful man in the city, and just for the moment, victory felt like it was already within my grasp.

nine

Kai

"If you could have those leads sorted out by the end of the day?" my supervisor said as he paused by my desk.

"Not a problem," I replied with an ingratiating smile, not bothering to mention that I'd already worked through all my assignments for the day. I would put the files on his desk before I clocked out, and in the meantime, he could think I was hard at work making his life easier while instead I looked into making the Gauntts' lives harder.

Most of those efforts were going to need to be centered on the woman with the largest desk at the far end of the room. Her fortress guarded the private elevator that was the only one to ascend to the top floors where the high executives—including, of course, Nolan and Marie Gauntt—had their offices. They all had their own personal admin assistants... and Ms. Townsend played gatekeeper to those PAs.

I guessed you knew a business was at the top of the food chain when even the secretaries had secretaries.

Ms. Townsend didn't look all that impressive. She was slight with a head a bit too big for her slim frame, like a living bobblehead, and her voice was so soft you had to be standing within five feet of her to make it out. In the few days I'd been here, I'd noticed she touched up the pearly polish on her fingernails regularly—to hide a bad habit of nibbling on them, most likely.

But despite all that, she seemed to have no problem sending people off with that soft voice, refusing appointments and other attempts to reach the bigwigs on the top floors. She did get her job done.

One of the most important things I'd figured out in my old life was that people's biggest weakness was usually other people. So I'd spent most of my investigative time so far observing how the secretaries' secretary interacted with her various colleagues. A couple of interesting facts had become clear.

Ms. Townsend had a thing for a woman in the accounting section, who she called "Alice" rather than by her last name and blushed a little about—not while they were talking but as Alice walked away. Possibly Alice would have been receptive to that interest. She seemed awfully smiley during a simple conversation about whether the budget could accept a third brand of coffee added to the breakroom.

This was all bad news for Mike Philmore, one of my colleagues in market research, who found some excuse to talk to Ms. Townsend about three times a day, always looking like he was just barely holding back his drool. She didn't appear to have noticed that he wanted anything out of her other than small talk, but then, I'd also figured out early on that I picked up on a lot of things others didn't.

That was why I was here and the rest of the Skullbreakers weren't. *I* could help Lily in ways none of the others were even capable of. That knowledge left me with a weird ache in my stomach that was probably partly the ever-returning hunger but with at least a little guilt and irritation mixed in.

If they'd *all* been able to work at my level, we might have solved her problems by now, not to mention our own.

This wasn't the time to dwell on that thought, though. I had a gambit to work here, and Lily was waiting to do her part.

I got a text ready to send and slipped my phone into my pocket. Then I ambled over to Ms. Townsend's desk, having confirmed that she wasn't occupied by anyone else at the moment.

Although she had a computer on her desk, she seemed to do most of the scheduling part of her work using five immense agendas that lay across her broad desk, one for each of the executive assistants. I'd already determined that the one at the farthest right was for Nolan Gauntt's assistant. That was my goal.

But first, I might as well dig up what I could out of the woman herself. I stopped at the distance from the desk I'd noticed she appeared most comfortable with and shot her a smile. "I hear you're the woman with all the power around here."

I'd also observed that she enjoyed having her status acknowledged, even if she acted humble about it. She let out a little laugh and swiped her hand across her mouth, though her eyes stayed professionally focused.

"You're the new one in market research," she said, tapping her pen on the cover of one of the agendas. "What can I do for you?"

I ducked my head as if I were feeling awkward about the subject, still smiling. "This might sound a little strange, but I have a cousin, a lot younger than me —she's ten this year—who was really impressed when she heard I was starting at Thrivewell. I know the company's been involved in a lot of different initiatives. I don't suppose they do any outreach involving kids?"

I hadn't found any clear evidence of that in my own research—a few workshops at schools here and there, but nothing ongoing. Nothing that would confirm what Lily's sister currently believed Nolan had been visiting her about. But it couldn't hurt to check right at the source.

Ms. Townsend tilted her head in thought and brought up something on her computer. "We do have a few initiatives that involve school visits," she said. "But those are only on an occasional basis, not anything longer-running."

"Fair enough," I said. "Is that something Thrivewell has done at all in the past—a more involved program— or should I let her know she'll just have to wait until she's employable age?" I added a little chuckle to show I wasn't overly invested.

"I can't think of when we've done anything intensive on the educational side, but I've only been here nine years, so it's possible farther back, that was a thing. I can't say I'm aware of any upcoming plans, though. It's sweet that she's interested." The secretary smiled back at me.

I had her eating out of my hand now, but I needed to land the second part of my gambit before her work interrupted us. "Oh, well, she's old enough to understand that she can't always get everything she wants. If the company decided to launch something like that, they'd obviously need to get you involved. Alice from accounting was saying to me how impressed she is by the way you go above and beyond to help the rest of us."

I didn't hammer the point home, just gave Ms. Townsend a brief lift of my hand in farewell as I took my leave and walked away leaving that last statement wriggling through her brain. While her attention shifted to her crush and the joys of the second-hand compliment, I sidled over to Philmore by the water cooler.

"Heard you were having some trouble with the new

photocopier," I said, which was completely true, although only because I'd been eavesdropping like a champ for the past day.

The other guy sighed. "Yeah. Programming that thing to do what you want is a nightmare. I swear it's possessed."

I had to restrain a chortle at the idea of a spirit taking over that hulking machine. Where would you even fit? What would be the point? But of course, Philmore had no direct experience with possessions to inform his perspective.

I made a vague motion toward the secretary's desk. "Townsend was just telling me how much she appreciates the new features." Actually, she'd been telling Alice that yesterday, but it amounted to the same thing. "You should ask her to give you a tutorial. She seems like she'd be happy to help anyone who needs it."

Philmore brightened like I'd lit a candle up his ass and headed right over to the secretary's desk without so much as a thank you. That was fine. His acting on my advice was thanks enough.

He said something to Ms. Townsend, and she got up immediately and ushered him over to the photocopier room, shooting a glance toward the accounting department and walking slower as she passed it to make sure Alice noticed her being her helpful self.

I restrained a smile. It was almost too fucking easy. Like most people, I just gave them a little nudge, and they hopped to my command like a bunch of puppets.

That left Ms. Townsend's desk—and her precious agendas—unguarded for at least a few minutes. I surreptitiously sent off my prepared text without taking my phone from my pocket and ambled back over.

Before I'd quite made it there, Lily came bustling into the office area with a cart of envelopes and packages. Conveniently, she had actually gotten a package for one of the employees who had a view of the secretary's desk from theirs, which she'd simply held on to until it could be put to optimal use. We'd arranged some surprise mail for the other main potential witness. She went to that woman's desk first.

"Mail for you," she said cheerfully, not even glancing my way.

The woman cocked her head at the padded envelope, ripped it open, and immediately hustled off to the bathroom where she could examine the... provocative contents more carefully in the privacy of a stall. Lily pretended not to notice her reaction as she headed over to the man who'd gotten a proper package. She placed herself right where she was in between him and Ms. Townsend's desk and made a production of offering it up.

"It seems pretty important," she said, lifting it slowly. "I wanted to make sure it got to you safely. Do you need help getting the tape off? There is an awful lot."

Because she'd added two extra layers.

The man struggled with the packing tape and ultimately accepted Lily's offer to cut through it with a utility knife that she then spent a minute searching her cart for. In the meantime, I darted behind the secretary's desk and flipped open the agenda for Nolan Gauntt's assistant. My gaze whipped over the pages, absorbing the dates and notations so quickly the data might as well have been uploaded into my brain. By the time the guy finally had his package open, I'd taken in the entire year's schedule and set the bookmark ribbon back in its correct place.

At the same moment, Ms. Townsend's voice reached my ears, much closer than I'd anticipated. She'd obviously sped through her little photocopier tutoring session with Philmore. I hustled from behind the desk, needing to get well clear of it without drawing attention. No doubt she'd wonder why I was over there at all. My throat tightened with the thought that I might have jeopardized my standing in the company this early on—

And then Lily collided with me as if she'd backed up her cart without seeing I was there.

She didn't hit me hard, but I caught the concerned gleam in her eyes and knew what she was trying to do. So I let my feet slip from under me as if she'd knocked me right over, grabbing her as if for balance and tugging her with me for extra effect. I landed on the linoleum floor on my ass with Lily in my lap.

For just a few seconds, I had her entire, softly toned body pressed up against me. A startling heat swept through my veins as all my nineteen-year-old host's hormones sprang to attention.

"Oh my God, I'm so sorry," Lily started babbling, scrambling up. Ms. Townsend was hurrying over, and I realized I had something different to cover up now: the bulge of my overeager dick, aching at the loss of contact. I shoved myself onto my feet at a crouch, bringing to mind the best cold shower of an image I could summon—Lily's asshole of a stepfather dancing around in the shower to the tune of the Macarena—and willing down my sudden erection.

By the time I could safely stand, Ms. Townsend had reached my side. "Is everything all right here?" she asked, and I could tell from the fret lines on her forehead that it was. Lily's trick had made the secretary worried about me rather than suspicious about my location in the office.

"Yes, totally fine," I said, brushing myself off and smiling at both Ms. Townsend and Lily. "No harm done. Those things are pretty tricky to maneuver. Glad it's not my job!" I nodded to the mail cart.

Lily poured out several more apologies and then hightailed it out of there, and I went back to my desk to contemplate the months of data I'd taken in… and definitely not the feel of Lily's ass against my groin.

We'd planned to meet up with the rest of the gang at a bar several blocks from the office after the end of the workday. I stayed a few minutes late to put on the appearance of a dedicated worker and then walked fast enough to catch up with Lily halfway to the bar. She grinned at me, and even without any part of our bodies in contact, that smile and the sight of her windblown hair sent another flare of lust through me. Damn it if I didn't want to pin her up against the side of the bank we were walking past and kiss her brains out.

More than just kiss, if I was being totally honest with myself, which I did attempt to be.

I mentally shook myself, as if that would calm the teenage hormones I'd technically outgrown six—or twenty-seven, if you counted my body-less time—years ago. Would it be so horrible if I just acted on them? I knew I didn't have to worry about Lily demanding more from me than I could give her. She'd always accepted me exactly as I was, even when she'd thought I was a figment invented by her imagination.

"Did you find out anything?" Lily asked, and I yanked my attention back to more important matters.

"First steps," I said. "I know when Nolan's executive assistant is regularly away from her desk. Now I just need to get up to her office and take a look at *his* schedule when she's not around to stop me."

Lily knit her brow. "That sounds risky."

I shrugged. "I'll figure it out. I managed just fine today, didn't I?" I shot her a smile more genuine than anything I'd aimed at my coworkers today. "You were brilliant with that last-second save. Thanks for that quick thinking."

She laughed. "It was the only thing I *could* think of to do in the moment. Hopefully they don't all figure I'm a horrible klutz now."

"Hey, getting that kind of reputation can be useful in unexpected ways."

We walked into the warm, boozy-smelling air of the bar to find the other three guys clustered in a booth in the front corner, looking vaguely panicked as they stared at a phone in the middle of the table. A phone that let out a peal of a ringtone a second later.

"What's going on?" I demanded, dashing over.

Ruin waved toward the phone, his body bobbing with an erratic mixture of excitement and uncertainty. "The guy's phone! The one who attacked me. It's finally ringing."

"So answer it!"

"I don't know what to say," Ruin said, wide-eyed.

"Just ask whoever it is what the fuck they want with you," Nox growled.

"No." I held up my hands before this turned into a total disaster. "That'll be too obvious. Play it cool. Talk vaguely, use the same kind of phrasing these people did when they came after you before. The guy... he had kind of a gruff voice, right? So try to talk like him. And hurry on and pick it up before it goes to voicemail!"

Ruin snatched up the phone and jerked it to his ear as he hit the answer button. "Hello," he said in a voice so gravelly you'd have thought he was auditioning to play the new Batman.

I winced, but whoever was on the other end must have had a bad enough connection that it didn't sound too weird to them. Ruin nodded. "Yes, I was just taking a bit of a break."

Oh, sure, that'd sound just wonderful. I tugged the

phone from his grasp and set it on speaker so I could hear what the other party was saying too.

"—the hell are you taking breaks for? That's not why you get paid. Did you set the Hunter kid straight or not?"

Ruin gave me another pleading look. I nodded sharply. "Uh, yeah," he said. "He knows what's good for him now. Won't be giving any more trouble."

"What's the latest report on the target's movements, then?" snapped the man on the other end.

"Well, he's been going to class and hanging out with his friends—"

"Not *Hunter's* movements. The girl he's supposed to be keeping an eye on."

Ruin's eyebrows leapt up. He gestured wildly toward Lily, as if we all couldn't figure out instantly who the speaker had meant, and seemed to forget about the fact that he was still in the middle of a conversation.

I jabbed my finger toward the phone and mouthed the words, *What do they want?*

Ruin frowned at me, which I didn't understand until he repeated what he must have thought I'd been prompting. "What a cunt."

"Excuse me?" the voice on the other end said, and I pressed the heel of my hand to my forehead.

"That's what he said," Ruin improvised. "I mean, he's kind of an asshole himself. Anyway, she hasn't done anything all that interesting either."

I restrained a groan. Before I could coach the other guy any further, the caller made a disgruntled sound.

"Fine." And he hung up without so much as a good-bye.

Ruin beamed at us. "That didn't go so badly." A shadow crossed his expression a second later. "But why did these people want Ansel to follow Lily around?"

"That's what I was trying to get you to ask them," I said, keeping my voice low despite my frustration.

There'd always been a place for me in the Skullbreakers. The guys had appreciated the talents and knowledge I'd brought to the table, and I'd appreciated having the three of them around to enforce certain types of plans way better than I could on my own. But sometimes… sometimes I wondered why I bothered working with anyone at all.

"It doesn't matter," Nox said firmly, shoving the phone back toward Ruin. "They'll call again. Ruin knows what to ask about next time. Are we going to go do some ass-kicking now or what?"

Ruin slipped his arm around Lily and gave her a peck on the temple. "Shouldn't we spend a little time with Lily before we go charging off? She's had to put up with those office people all day."

"Hold on." Lily managed to put her hands on her hips without displacing her admirer. "If you guys are going off to find out more about who attacked you, I want to come along. I'm mixed up in this now too. I should have some idea what we're up against."

Nox and Jett both looked doubtful, but admiration flickered up through my chest. The guys might be on the dim side sometimes, but I couldn't complain about

Lily. She was right there with us, ready to face anything, despite everything she'd already been through.

I set my hand on her shoulder—the one Ruin wasn't hanging all over. "Sounds good to me. You're stronger than all those pricks anyway."

And I wasn't sure I really wanted to let her out of my sight for any longer than I absolutely had to.

ten

Lily

The helmet Nox had gotten me so I could ride with him on his motorcycle rather than dragging Fred's sorry fender all over town muffled the roar of traffic around us. The cacophony blended into a wavering melody that seemed to match the steady thump of my heart. I kept my arms wrapped tight around Nox's torso, as much terrified that I'd topple off as enjoying the heat that seeped through his new leather jacket into my chest.

These guys would never hurt me on purpose, but they hadn't shown the soundest judgment when it came to risk assessment.

I wasn't sure where we were going—and maybe neither were the former Skullbreakers. All at once, Nox raised his hand and pointed, and the four guys swerved their motorcycles down a side-street.

We'd come into a grungier part of town where the buildings were covered in grubby brick and concrete rather than glossy glass. Litter tumbled down the street in the breeze. The streets were narrower, the smell of car exhaust thicker, and someone a couple of blocks away was yelling at someone else loud enough to wake the dead.

And now I had to wonder if that was a real method of resurrection, seeing as it turned out the dead could actually be woken.

A few guys were hanging out on the more secluded side-street, slouching in hoodies and baggy jeans, one of them taking a drag from a cigarette. As we roared toward them, a couple of girls in garish makeup approached and started gesturing like they were talking as much with their hands as their mouths.

Nox jerked to a halt with a screech of the tires. He and the others leapt off their bikes so fast the girls took one look at them and paled.

"Beat it," Nox snapped, and they took off with a clatter of tapping heels.

"What the fuck, man," one of the hoodie guys protested as the Skullbreakers converged on them. "We were trying to move some product there."

"What makes you think we give a shit about your product?" Jett asked, and punched the guy who'd spoken in the stomach hard enough that he smacked into the wall behind him ass-first.

Obviously my guys were still subscribing to the hit first, ask questions later school of thinking.

I stayed perched on the motorcycle as the four of them batted their prey around a little, more like cats playing with mice than tigers going in for the kill. They didn't have any specific vendetta against this bunch, at least not yet. They were just... loosening them up, as Nox would probably have put it.

The thump of fists against flesh made me a little queasy, but I didn't let myself look away. This was what I'd signed up for when I'd thrown my lot in with these guys. And I had no doubt the guys they were beating down would have happily done the same to anyone weaker they thought they'd get something out of.

When the three drug dealers were all slumped against the wall, groaning and grumbling, Nox loomed over them with his hands still fisted. "What do you know about a hit that went down a couple decades ago?" he asked. "Some pricks from Mayfield took out the entire leadership of the Skullbreakers out in Lovell Rise. You ever hear about that?"

"Who the fuck wants to know?" one of the drug dealers muttered.

"The king of Constantinople," Kai said sarcastically. "So you'd better cough up what you've heard, or the royal guard will chop you up."

When the dealers just stared at him in bewilderment, Nox rolled his eyes. "*We* want to know, you idiots. We can keep going if you need more help jogging your memory." He waggled a fist.

"Twenty years ago, I was two," the second guy whined. "How the hell should I know?"

Nox glowered at him. "People talk on the street. People brag."

"No one in our crew," the first dealer said. "I've never heard of the Skullbreakers. You—" He cut himself off abruptly, his mouth pressing flat.

"We what?" Kai demanded, his eyes narrowing.

"You should suck my dick," the guy shot back in a brief show of bravado.

Ruin twirled a knife he'd snatched off one of them and grinned. "It'd be more fun to cut it off."

Bravado vanished. All three guys staggered to their feet and dashed down the street as fast as they could go.

Nox glanced at Kai. "You believe them?"

Kai nodded. "I didn't see any sign that they recognized our name. Whatever the guy was going to say that he stopped himself from, it didn't have to do with us."

"It had to do with *something*," Jett muttered.

Ruin bobbed on his feet, grinning away as usual. "Let's go find out what! So many outfits in this city; so many heads to crack." He let out a laugh that was as close to a maniacal cackle as I'd heard any real person produce. Somehow, on him, it was cute.

It was getting late, the sun nearly sunk, the shadows stretching long. We tore through the city for another several minutes until Nox spotted a building marked up with gang tags that he wanted to check out.

We stepped inside to amber lighting that might

have been purposefully dim to disguise the worn patches on the velvet-cushioned chairs and benches. A crooning jazz orchestration wove through the room from a band up on the little stage at the far end of the space. It was some kind of dining club, with little black tables placed between the seats. Apparently, the kind of crowd this atmosphere appealed to dined late, because only a few of the tables were occupied this early in the evening.

My body started to sway with the music automatically. Nox ran his fingers lightly down my back. "We'll need to get you to compose a battle song for us," he said, playful but not entirely teasing, and directed us all toward the back of the room, where a narrow door stood next to the stage area.

As we reached it, a woman stepped out on stage. She might have been middle-aged under the foundation caked on her face, but in the hazy light, she looked ageless, almost ethereal in her gauzy white dress. She leaned toward a microphone on a stand in the midst of the musicians and started to sing.

It was another language—Spanish, I thought, or maybe Portuguese—and I didn't understand the words. But the emotion that rippled through them grabbed me by the heart in an instant. The woman used her voice as just as much of an instrument as the men with their guitars and keyboard and saxophone. Any chatter in the room fell silent. The hairs tickled along the backs of my arms.

We ducked through the door into the back rooms,

but the song followed us, filtering faintly through the walls. The sensation around my heart solidified into an ache.

If I was being totally true to myself, I knew that my ideal future didn't involve year after year going over case files in an office or trying to mediate couples and families into making a better life for themselves. I wanted to help people, sure, but more than anything, I wanted to touch them the way that woman out there could with the simple lilt of her voice. My throat tingled with the urge to join her right now with my own.

Was that even possible? Since I'd gotten dragged off to the psych ward, I hadn't let myself sing other than briefly, while Nox and I were having sex. It hadn't felt like I deserved to take joy in music. But he'd reminded me that other people's judgments didn't have to weigh me down. I knew now that I hadn't really hurt Marisol —that I'd at least believed I was defending her. Why should I punish myself?

Why shouldn't I chase the dream I really wanted?

This obviously wasn't a good time to start making career plans, though.

The guys barged ahead of me into a large room that stunk of nicotine. An old steel desk stood in the back corner and a long wooden table ran down most of the rest of the space, with a bench on either side. Five men were sitting around it, a few of them with bottles of beer, a couple with their phones out. From the tone of their voices, they were haggling over some decision when we burst in, but the second they saw us, they leapt to their feet.

"Who the hell are you?" one of the men snarled.

"Your worst nightmare," Nox retorted, springing at him. "Up to you how soon you wake up."

I hung back by the door, my pulse thudding faster as all four of the guys sprang into action. They were outnumbered this time, and the men they were up against were clearly more experienced than the drug dealers they'd taken down before. The men dodged as many fists as hit the mark, and one of them whipped into a maneuver that sent Kai stumbling backward, clutching his glasses to keep them from falling.

A few of the others yanked out guns. Nox whacked one pistol aside with one of his ghostly punches that didn't quite make contact with the guy's hand, leaving the dude startled and blinking for a second before the former gang leader flipped him heels over head and stomped on his neck. Jett managed to send a little jolt of electrical energy through another guy's arm as he tackled him, making his opponent's fingers spasm and drop the weapon. But the one who aimed at Ruin didn't have anyone close enough to stop him.

The now-familiar hum rang out inside me, swelling through my whole body in the space of a breath. "Ruin!" I shouted, and in the same moment, a gush of beer sprang out of the nearest bottle on the table.

The dollop of sour liquid smacked the guy right in the eyes. As his lips parted in surprise, another splash socked him right in the mouth. He choked and sputtered, swiping frantically at his eyes, and Kai dashed in there to wrench the weapon from his hand.

Ruin didn't seem to care that there were still a few men not yet incapacitated. He flung his arms around me in a bear hug with a victory cheer. "That's our woman. You can't find anyone better." He let go of me to swing around and slam his fist into the jaw of a guy who'd just lunged at him. "And no one's going to convince me otherwise," he added.

A weirdly delirious smile spread over the guy's face as he swayed on his feet with the punch. "You're right," he said. "She's pretty amazing. All of you are something to watch."

Ruin gave him an amused but puzzled look. "Thank you for agreeing." He looked down at his fist, and then pummeled another of the men who were still standing. This time, I heard a faint hiss of electricity with the impact. "You should all bow down before us," Ruin declared at the same time. "Anyone who messes with us will end up shitting their pants in terror."

He didn't even appear to hit the guy that hard, but his opponent immediately crumpled on the floor, hugging himself and shivering. "Please, just leave us alone. We'll do whatever you want. Just don't hurt us anymore."

A radiant grin stretched across Ruin's face. He let out a whoop and spun around. "I think I've found my special power!"

"He hits them with his happiness," Jett muttered. "Or whatever else. Oh, joy."

But whatever the others might have said about Ruin's newfound ability to impose his feelings on others, it did help turn the tide. Ruin seemed to have used up all his current emotion-warping ability on his first two targets—his next few punches didn't have the same impact—but the colleagues of those two were distracted enough by the weird effects and their friends' bizarre reactions that they faltered.

In a minute or two, the former Skullbreakers had tossed the rest of their opponents into a heap next to the desk. Ruin declared himself the king of the mountain and perched on it, jabbing and kicking anyone who started to stir. He watched with avid interest as the other three closed in on the two he'd infected, one of whom kept smiling giddily and the other cowering in fear.

"All we want to know is what you've heard about an attack on the Skullbreakers twenty years ago," Nox said, glaring at them. "From the looks of you, you were all well out of diapers by then."

"Skullbreakers, Skullbreakers," the happy guy murmured to himself. "What a great name. Never heard it before."

"I'd tell you if I knew anything," the frightened dude whimpered. "Please, I've never heard anything about that."

"Do you know anyone else who might have an idea?" Kai asked, stepping forward with his arms folded over his chest.

The guy shuddered. "I—I mean—there's the

Skeleton Corps. They've got a hand in almost everything. But even they aren't as scary as you."

Someone in the heap under Ruin let out a hiss as if he thought his colleague had made a mistake. Nox glanced at Kai. "Why hasn't anyone mentioned the Skeleton Corps to us before if they're so important?"

Kai shrugged. "We didn't ask about that."

"Where can we find them?" I asked, wanting to get to the point before any more guns came flying out. I didn't think the sole remaining beer bottle would be enough for me to save anyone.

"Around... all different places." The scared guy cringed. "They move their headquarters all the time."

"You want to hang with them, just put word out on the street," the happy guy said cheerfully.

"Great." Jett wrinkled his nose at them. "I wonder how long these two are going to be stuck like this."

"Their problem, not ours." Nox spun on his heel. "We got what we need out of these dorks."

Ruin scrambled down his human mountain to join us. As we walked out through the club, Nox grasped my hand.

"You *were* amazing in there," he said. "I didn't know you could throw beer around like you can with water."

A giggle tumbled out of me. "Neither did I. I guess it's *mostly* water."

"Let's get some more beers!" Ruin declared. "Lily deserves a toast."

A quiver of triumph ran through my chest. I'd helped Kai with his plan to get at Nolan Gauntt today, and tonight I'd saved one of my guy's lives. I was Lily fucking Strom, and I wasn't letting anyone mess with me and mine anymore.

That fact felt like it deserved more than a toast.

My gaze caught on a pharmacy down the street. A spark of inspiration lit inside me. "There's something I want to pick up first."

eleven

Lily

I stared into my apartment's chipped mirror, combing my fingers through the waves of my hair. Some of them looked like actual ocean waves now. I'd streaked in blue dye last night that'd turned out even more vibrant than I'd expected against my usual flaxen blond. I looked like… some kind of mermaid. Like I really could have emerged from the marsh with watery magic inside me.

Like a siren, as Nox called me.

The memory of the first time he'd said it, of the hungry huskiness in his voice, sent a pulse of heat low in my belly. I hadn't been thinking of that when I'd bought the dye, only of finding a visible way of manifesting the strength that now hummed through me. Turning myself more into the woman I could be, just like the guys had recovered some of their former looks. And every time I caught a glimpse of my reflection, it'd remind *me* what I was really capable of.

I swept my hair behind my ears, shot a quick smile at myself, and went back out into the cramped living room.

It was less cramped at the moment because only two of my four new roommates were present. Kai and Jett had gone out to pick up "supplies," which from them could mean anything from news magazines to art supplies to a mountain of food. Nox and Ruin were lounging on the sofa, Nox currently squinting at something on his phone's screen. He'd gotten more comfortable with the modern device over time, but he still seemed to consider its multitude of features an annoyance rather than a bonus.

"There's a place we should check out," he announced to Ruin. "Fast, before anyone else nabs it." He shifted his attention to me. "Now that we're getting ready to deal out some vengeance, it'll be better if we have a temporary clubhouse to operate out of. I don't want to have any pissed off thugs coming around here."

"I thought you were going to get your old place back," I said, remembering the Dishes for Dollars store he'd pointed out to me, which had been built on the spot where the Skullbreakers' original clubhouse used to stand. The guys had seemed to take the existence of the discount shop as a personal affront.

Nox nodded. "We'll get our real home turf back.

But that's going to take a little more time, and we need to settle the score with the pricks who offed us before they know we're back in town." He cracked his knuckles and smirked with a fierceness that provoked another heady tingling inside me.

"We'll find Lily a better place than this too," Ruin piped up, beaming at me. "Something much nicer. You were thinking you could move into Mayfield, right?"

"For now," I said. "It seems like that would be easier than trying to get Lovell Rise to like me again."

Nox scoffed. "They should be worried about *you* liking them."

I gave him a baleful look. "It's still not fun being the resident 'psycho girl,' even if I don't care as much anymore. And it'd be a fresh start for me and Marisol." And if I did want to pursue some kind of musical career… that would be easier in a larger city too, wouldn't it?

I hadn't mentioned that part to the guys yet. The idea felt too fragile to say it out loud.

"We can definitely get a place that's fresh," Ruin said, bounding onto his feet.

"Not this place tonight," Nox said. "It's definitely clubhouse, not house-house, material. But I'll find an apartment too. I think Kai's already been scanning the listings." He got up and motioned to Ruin. "Come on. The guy said we can take a look now as long as we're out by ten." Then he extended his gesture toward me as well, with a warmer smile. "And you should join us, if you want. After you pitched in with the tussle last night, you're basically part of the gang."

A sense of mingled relief and pride washed through me, more than I'd expected. I'd been dreading the thought of being left on my own in the dingy apartment, even though I hadn't intended to ever share this place with anyone, let alone four kind-of dead gangsters. They did grow on a person.

And it could be that I'd been craving friendly company for longer than I'd let myself acknowledge.

I also still wasn't sure about my part in the gang battle last night, but it had felt pretty awesome being able to protect my men like they'd protected me so many times, if not always in ways I'd wanted in the moment. I didn't want to be just some pathetic creature they had to defend at every turn. The new Lily, the Lily who didn't care about being sane or polite to people who crapped on her, could hold her own with the former Skullbreakers.

Maybe I'd end up breaking a skull or two myself if the people deserved it.

I'd swapped my office-appropriate blouse for a more relaxed sweater and stripped off my tights, but I'd left my skirt on. As I followed the guys up to the alley, the evening breeze tickled over my bare legs. Nox glanced at me, his gaze lingering for a moment on my naked calves, and then motioned to Fred. "We'll take your car. Better if the owner doesn't realize exactly what types he'd be renting to." He winked at me.

So I ended up driving, cruising along the highway

into Mayfield and then weaving through the streets following Nox's somewhat haphazard directions. He kept turning his phone around as he looked at the map in a way that wasn't particularly reassuring. I think we circled the spot we were trying to reach five times, like a dog getting settled to sleep, before we actually came to a stop outside the building.

The building itself was a narrow restaurant with the front window shuttered, squeezed between a sushi place and a brunch spot. I didn't pay much mind to the crown symbol painted onto the faded sign until Nox had tapped in the code on the key box and we walked into the main space.

The former tenants had gone all-out with their Medieval theme. The dusty wooden chairs and tables had fake coats of arms printed on them. Suits of costume armor, axes, pikes, and surprisingly sharp-looking broadswords decorated the walls. And at the far end, one larger table that I guessed was for special events stretched most of the width of the room, with the central chair behind it a full-out throne, gleaming with gold-tinted paint.

"This is fantastic!" Ruin enthused, roaming through the space. He grabbed a sword off the wall and swung it experimentally, laughing. "No one better try to take us down in here. It comes with all this stuff?"

"Yep." Nox strode toward the banquet table at the back. "The old tenants couldn't be bothered to take their shit with them, so we inherit it if we want it." He stopped across from the throne. "Fit for a fucking king."

I wandered over to join him, taking in the space and noticing all the extra details that added to the vibe, like the fortune teller's orb on a velvet-draped stand in one corner and a rearing brass horse statue next to the entrance to the kitchens. My brain couldn't quite decide whether this was all horribly cheesy or impressively horrible.

"I know you want to rule the city," I said, "but don't you think it's a little on the nose?"

Nox snorted. "No such thing. We didn't call ourselves the Skullbreakers because we like to gently nudge our enemies."

Okay, fair enough.

He ambled off to the side, where a King Arthur themed pinball machine stood. He rubbed his hands together in anticipation, but when he pulled at the levers, nothing lit up or made any sound. Nox gave the machine a smack, but that didn't wake it up.

"Maybe you need to unplug it and plug it back in?" I suggested, since that seemed to be the standard tech support advice for all electronic equipment.

He muttered to himself and crouched down by the base.

Ruin grabbed my hand and tugged me over to the throne. He set his sword on the table before whisking me up and onto the seat. The wood was actually comfortably worn and smooth, high enough that my feet dangled off the ground.

Ruin let his hand linger on my knee, grinning at me. "If we're the kings of the city, then Lily is our queen." A sly glint lit in his hazel eyes. "And we should worship her the way she deserves."

He knelt before me and slipped his hands around one calf, raising it so he could press a kiss to my shin. Heat rippled up my leg and flushed my cheeks. "Um, are you sure this is a good idea?" I asked.

Ruin just kissed the inside of my knee, in a sensitive spot that made my core clench with need and went a long way to convincing me all on its own. Nox abandoned the pinball machine at the sound of this new game, which apparently appealed to him even more.

He came around to the other side of the throne, his gaze heated. "I think it's a good start, but I can think of plenty of ideas that are even better."

"That wasn't exactly what I meant," I protested half-heartedly, and then he'd captured my mouth with his, and I didn't really want to protest in any way after all.

I wasn't exactly a master of sexuality. I'd only had two partners before these guys, and not at the same time. Feeling both of the guys' mouths on me in unison set off a flare of hunger that blazed in my chest and pooled between my legs.

I was embracing the insanity of our situation, wasn't I? Why shouldn't I enjoy every bit of the craziness?

Nox eased back to trail his scorching lips along my jaw to the crook of my neck. "We didn't thank you properly for stepping up last night, Siren. If this is going to be the Skullbreakers' new hangout, then we definitely need to break it in with the woman who kept our spirits alive and brought us back."

Ruin hummed against my leg where he'd switched to kissing the side of my other knee. His hands slid up under my skirt, his fingertips teasing across my thighs. "We have lots of time, don't we?" he asked Nox. "No interruptions? I want to make my first time with our Angelfish something to remember."

Nox chuckled. "The owner said it was ours to look around until ten. We've got a couple of hours. And I locked the door." He nibbled his way down my neck, with one slightly sharper nip that made me gasp with a spark of painful pleasure. "Such a good girl. We can show her just what a queen she is."

A very un-queenly whimper of need crept from my throat. Ruin responded to it by dragging me closer, yanking down my panties with the same motion. He shoved up my skirt and buried his face between my legs.

The first swipe of his tongue across my sex brought a jolt so thrilling I gasped. Nox swallowed the sound with the crash of his lips against mine. He devoured my mouth as Ruin savored my clit.

I dug my fingers into their hair, one hand fisted in Nox's short spikes, the other in Ruin's tousled locks. All sense of the room faded away. My awareness narrowed down to the heat of their bodies next to mine and the bliss surging through my nerves.

If this was what being queen of the Skullbreakers meant, then engrave my name over the fucking door.

I rocked with the deft movements of Ruin's mouth. He sucked on my clit so hard I moaned and flicked his tongue right into my opening.

Nox kissed me again and eased back with a feral grin. "I love watching you go wild as you're coming undone. You can take even more, can't you, Siren?"

When he stroked his hands across my chest to fondle my breasts, all I could do was gasp my agreement. I gripped his shirt, tugging him closer for another kiss, and his chest thrummed with his approval. "That's right. You manhandle me all you want. Everywhere you touch me, you set me on fucking fire, baby."

"So fucking precious," Ruin mumbled against me, and teased his teeth over my clit. I cried out against Nox's mouth, my body quaking. Nox's demanding kiss, his thumb sweeping over my taut nipple, and Ruin's fingers delving in to join his tongue against my sex all swelled together into a maelstrom of pleasure that burst inside me.

I felt myself gush with my release and Ruin lapping it up. Nox kissed my cheek and my jaw, murmuring more praise, and then glanced down at Ruin with hooded eyes. "I think we should give her something even more special. Make full use of the wonders of our new headquarters."

I was too dazed from my orgasm to totally follow the silent exchange that followed. The next thing I knew, Ruin was stepping back and Nox was lifting me onto one of the throne's broad wooden arms. My legs splayed over the edge.

Ruin grabbed the sword he'd left on the table by the guard and waggled the hilt. He glanced from it to me and then cocked his head with a momentary flicker of concern. "We don't know who else was touching this before."

Nox tossed a couple of foil packets at him. "Good thing I have extra. Suit it up."

"What—?" I started to ask in bewilderment, and Nox's palms swiveled over my breasts as he leaned against me from behind. The friction and the giddy rush that came with his touch knocked the words from my mind.

"Feels good, doesn't it?" he murmured, kissing my neck again and then across my shoulder. "We're going to make you feel even better. Like no one ever made you feel before. Just trust us, and we'll take care of you."

I did trust them, I realized with a little flash of shock. Sometime over the past few weeks, I'd gone from wary to welcoming to utterly committed, without even totally realizing it.

I was safe in their hands. More than safe. I was ecstatic putty, and I didn't see any reason to get off the ride before it'd reached its final destination.

Ruin had opened one of the condom packets and stretched its contents over the hilt of the sword. The grip wasn't particularly larger than the average dick, as far as I knew from the few examples I'd encountered, but it was tapered toward the guard where he was holding it and rounded at the pommel, a little wider there than anything I'd taken inside me before.

My lungs gave a nervous hitch as he brought the sword closer, but he didn't try to thrust the hilt right into me. He rubbed the rounded end over my slick sex, dampening it with my arousal, twisting it against my clit. As little quivers of pleasure built up between my legs, the cool surface warmed. Ruin watched my responses avidly.

Nox kept stroking my chest and marking my neck with his mouth. "Are you ready, baby?" he asked, and my hips canted toward the sword of their own volition. Nox let out a low laugh. "That's right. I can't wait to see you ride it." He tipped his head toward Ruin. "Nice and slow."

Ruin grinned and dipped the pommel to my slit. My channel stretched to admit it with a heady burn that made my breath shudder in a way that was all delight. A whine tumbled out of me as he slid it deeper, his free hand massaging my thigh in tandem.

I was fucking a sword. I was Lily Strom, getting off on a deadly weapon, and it felt absolutely amazing.

I groaned and clutched at Nox, arcing toward Ruin at the same time. He leaned in to claim my mouth as he started to pulse the hilt in and out of me. The heat of his mouth burned into mine and the swell of the pommel brushed against the most eager place deep inside me, and the wave of bliss started to sweep me higher all over again.

My groping hand slipped down Ruin's muscled chest. My fingers brushed the substantial bulge behind his jeans, and his breath stuttered where our mouths were still melded together. My sex ached for release, but suddenly the metal shaft between my legs wasn't enough.

I tore my lips from his. "I want *you*," I said firmly, squeezing his groin for emphasis. From the first morning when he'd snuck into my bed and we'd ended up making out, I'd been dying to know what the full experience would be like. Ruin seemed like the kind of guy who could, well, ruin a woman. I didn't know how anyone could ever top his blend of enthusiasm and devotion.

Ruin let out a choked sound that somehow also sounded cheerful and tossed the sword aside, condom and all. As I fumbled with the fly of his jeans, he spun me on the throne arm so I was facing forward instead of sideways. When my hand delved into his boxers, he bucked into my hand.

"That's right," Nox said with only a tiny edge of envy. "You look after him too. Look at how hard he is for you already."

Ruin's eyelids had drifted to half-mast. Now he opened them all the way to shoot a determined look at his boss. "You keep taking care of Lily," he said, apparently deciding he got to give orders now too. "She should get everything we can both give her."

"No arguments there," Nox murmured, and nipped my earlobe as he teased his hands down my torso. He dipped one between my thighs, inhaled sharply at the feel of my wetness, and spread my legs even wider for his friend.

I leaned into his embrace, tilting my head to kiss

him where he knelt beside me while yanking Ruin closer. My fingers wrapped around the redhead's erection and gave it a few encouraging pumps.

Ruin groaned and gripped my hips to tug me right to the end of the wooden arm. He wrenched open another packet, readied himself, and plunged into me in one smooth movement.

"Fuck," he murmured breathlessly when he was fully embedded in me. My channel throbbed around him, hungry for more. I tucked one arm around him and tore my mouth from Nox to kiss Ruin instead.

Our mouths collided, all harsh breath and dueling tongues. Ruin withdrew halfway and then thrust in even deeper. A soft keening emanated from my chest at the giddy sensation spreading through me from my core.

"This is paradise," he mumbled between eager kisses, drinking in every sound I made. "You're all the heaven I need, Angelfish."

When he plunged even deeper, I gasped. I kept clutching Ruin as I turned back to Nox, not wanting to leave my other lover neglected. The Skullbreakers' boss pinched my nipples to ignite electric shocks of pleasure and kissed me so hard my head spun.

This didn't feel like enough either. I wanted *both* of them, as fully as I could have them. I wanted to feel how much we were all in this together.

I managed to focus enough through the tingling pulses of bliss that came with Ruin's quickening thrusts to reach for Nox's jeans. He was hard too, his cock straining against his fly. When my knuckles grazed him, he growled.

"Oh, baby, just keep doing that," he muttered.

"I could do even better," I said raggedly.

He caught my gaze, passion blazing in his eyes, and eased up onto his feet on the seat of the throne beside me. "You want this, Siren?" He ran his hand over his groin and licked his lips. "I bet you can handle it. You're bold enough to take both of us, aren't you?"

I yanked at his jeans in answer. He unzipped his fly and freed himself. When he brushed the head of his erection across my lips with a shaky breath, I flicked out my tongue to lick it.

"Oh, *fuck*, yes," Nox said with a groan. "That's so good. You're fucking perfect."

I responded by parting my lips and drawing him right into my mouth. He rested his hand on my hair, his fingers tangling with the strands but not forcing me faster or closer than I was ready for.

Ruin let out a pleased sound and bucked into me faster. The ecstatic burn of our connection sizzled through my veins. I bucked with him and tightened my lips around Nox, swirling my tongue at the same time. Nox pumped into me, matching the rhythm of my mouth.

In that moment, it didn't even seem crazy. It only felt like a culmination of all the affection and passion they'd been showering me with from the beginning.

I was one of them now, and we could make a beautiful symphony of bodily bliss together. Every grunt and gasp and hum twined together into a buoyant melody. I was careening higher and higher on the thrill of it all—

My second orgasm exploded through me, whiting out my mind with a hail of shooting stars. I sucked hard on Nox instinctively, and he swore as he emptied himself into my mouth.

"So precious," Ruin mumbled, pounding his last few joyful strokes into me. "Our Waterlily. Oh, Lily." With a half-swallowed cry, he stiffened as he found his own release.

Nox sank down beside me, kissing me before I'd even finished swallowing his cum. He didn't seem to care about his taste on my lips—maybe that made the kiss even hotter for him. He pressed another to the side of my head and tucked his arm around my shoulders in an iron embrace. "Our queen. Couldn't have earned the title more thoroughly."

A giggle spilled out of me. Ruin leaned in as he softened inside me and hugged me too, and right then it was hard to imagine why anyone *wouldn't* want their very own gang of semi-ghostly lovers.

"So this is the place, then?" I said.

Nox let out a laugh. "I think it'd better be after all that. Now all we need is to find *you* a real home."

twelve

Lily

The moment I spotted the envelope marked *CONFIDENTIAL* with Nolan Gauntt's name on it, I ever-so-carefully tucked it into a spot I'd already scouted out between two of the mailroom shelves. If my supervisor noticed it, he'd tell me to take it up right away. But unfortunately for him, doing my job efficiently was a lower priority to me than getting a better scoop on the man in charge.

Kai had found out when Nolan's admin assistant would be away from his desk for half an hour today. I had no idea what the big boss himself would be doing during that time, but at least I'd have an excuse to go up to his floor and hang around the assistant's desk for a minute. I didn't have Kai's manipulative skills or speed-reading ability, but an ordinary gal could figure out a thing or two.

I hoped.

I was queen of the Skullbreakers, I reminded myself as I sorted a bunch of other envelopes that'd arrived and slapped labels on a stack of packages that were supposed to go out this afternoon. I'd held two powerful gangsters in my sway last night. I had the power of the marsh inside me and marked into my hair.

I was a force to be reckoned with, and the Gauntts and whoever else would regret the day they'd messed with my sister.

My supervisor, a pasty-faced man named Rupert, marched through the room and let out a faint huff when he glanced my way. He'd been doing that ever since I'd turned up yesterday morning with the blue streaks in my hair. *His* hair was the faded, yellow-brown hue of dying marsh grass, so I didn't think he was in much of a position to criticize. I satisfied my annoyance by picturing a miniature heron stalking around the combed strands, pecking at imaginary bugs.

"Make sure you line up the labels totally straight," he sniped at me a minute later. "We have an image to maintain, you know."

I stared down at the package I'd just applied the mailing address to, unable to see how it could get any straighter. Did he have a ruler stuck up his ass to make him so anal?

"I'll be more careful," I said, resisting the urge to grit my teeth.

When he picked up his cup of coffee, a small hum tickled through my chest. I let just a little of it loose, flicking a tiny splash that he could believe was a slip of his hand onto his shirt collar.

A giddy shiver ran down my spine when it worked. Rupert grumbled and dashed off to dampen a tissue to wipe at the stain.

It seemed like anything liquid—at least, liquid that was mostly water—I could command. Although water on its own was pretty handy. Every modern building had plumbing. There were sewers and water mains under every street in the city and back in town.

And the frogs appeared to have no problem with long distance travel. A faint croaking caught my ears, and I ducked down by the table to find another green friend perched on a plastic crate.

"You should go home," I whispered to him. "No good flies here." I didn't figure I was going to come at anyone in Thrivewell with a frog army. Somehow I didn't think the head honchos here would be quite as easily intimidated as Peyton had been.

Lucky for me, Rupert stepped out for his break a few minutes before Nolan Gauntt's assistant was due to take a hike. I retrieved the prized envelope from its hiding place, tossed a few other recently arrived pieces of mail into a satchel so it wouldn't look like I was making the trip up there just for him, even though I really was, and headed to the elevator.

I had to go past the woman on Kai's floor who guarded the more exclusive elevator first. But I'd already texted Kai about my plans, and he was over by her desk exchanging some quick remarks with her when I breezed up.

I flashed the envelope at her. "Confidential mail for Mr. Gauntt."

The secretaries' secretary was distracted enough that she didn't scrutinize me super closely, not that I thought I'd given her any reason to deny me regardless. *No point in making it harder for ourselves than it has to be,* Kai had said. She waved me on to the elevator and tapped in a code that opened the door for me.

The mirrored doors boxed me in. Then I was soaring upwards in the metal box, closer than ever to the man who'd started the catastrophe my life had become seven years ago.

There were actually four Gauntts in the building. Nolan and Marie had offices on either side of the top floor, and their son and his wife had offices below them, in whatever roles nepotism had bought them. When I stepped out into the vast, high-ceilinged hall on the penthouse level, I realized that was a bit of a problem.

Nolan's admin assistant had abandoned her post, but Marie's was still staked out at his desk at the opposite end. Granted, with the hall being as palatial as it was, that meant he was still thirty feet away from where I stood as I came to a stop outside Nolan's office, but he wasn't blind. If I started poking around on the other assistant's desk, he'd notice.

I tapped the envelope against the desk and glanced around as if searching for the desk's expected occupant, my nerves prickling in anticipation of the other assistant telling me he'd handle the letter. Could I reasonably insist that I needed to deliver it to Nolan or his representative directly?

But it seemed that Marie's assistant didn't give a shit about his boss's husband's business. I stood there for about a minute without the man saying a word, and then his phone pinged. He ducked into Marie's office, and all at once I was on my own.

My pulse stuttered. I dashed around the assistant's desk, my gaze darting over the objects I'd already noted there. No paper agenda for this dude, only a computer, the monitor currently asleep. Otherwise there were just a few pens and a box of tissues, which weren't likely to offer up much intel.

"Wake up, wake up," I sang under my breath in a reverse lullaby to the computer, tapping the space bar. Thankfully, the monitor blinked on. Less helpfully, a password box appeared.

I glowered at it as if I could intimidate it into filling in the correct combination of characters myself. "I could drench your circuitry," I muttered at it, but the computer remained impervious to my threat. I decided I was better off checking out other avenues rather than continuing to try to bully the machine into compliance.

I spotted a postcard tucked partway under the tissue box and tugged it out to check it. The glossy announcement was for some special benefit dinner—at a restaurant full of crystal chandeliers and copious wine, based on the imagery on one side. Some spiffy business association that went by the acronym BLEC. Maybe it was better that they didn't spell out what that stood for.

In any case, the benefit dinner was happening in two weeks on a Wednesday, and tidy scrawl at the bottom of the card said, *Looking forward to seeing Nolan and Marie there!* I didn't know for sure that they were going, but the sender seemed pretty confident, and the assistant had set it aside. I snapped a quick picture of the card with my phone to be sure I remembered the date and tucked it back into place.

The only thing left was the half-full trash can tucked mostly behind one end of the desk. I squatted down next to that, grimaced, and started pawing through it. Desperate times called for desperate measures and all that.

"What've you got for me?" I murmured to the metal bin and its crumpled papers and cellophane wrappers. "Cut me a break here, won't you?"

For all Nolan's admin assistant's high standing in this posh office building, he definitely had tastes that were a little low brow. Toward the bottom of the bin, I found a ticket stub from a theater with three Xs in the name and a wrapper from a pack of... Pokémon cards? Gotta catch 'em all, I guess. Where possibly 'em referred to STDs.

I was just reaching for another postcard that looked like an invitation when the handle of the office door clicked over. My heart lurched to the top of my throat.

I sprang away from the trash can, swiping my hand across my skirt as if I might have X-rated cooties on it now, and jerked to attention with the envelope that was *my* ticket—to being here—clutched in my hands.

The man who was just stepping out looked me over. He wasn't Nolan Gauntt, unless the man had gotten extreme plastic surgery since the photos Kai had pulled up for me to check, but he was obviously someone important enough to have a personal meeting with the big boss.

I waved the envelope and did my best to channel my panic into the appearance of starstruck nerves. "I just—I'm new in the mailroom. There was a letter for Mr. Gauntt. I think it's important. But his secretary isn't here. I wasn't sure if I should knock…"

My cheeks were burning, but at least that fit my intimidated ditz act. As did the fact that I accidentally let the envelope slip from my fingers and had to fumble to snatch it up again. If I kept this up, they'd fire me for having the approximate coordination of a toddler.

"Is Mr. Gauntt still busy?" I added, my pulse thumping with a heady mix of hope and terror. "Can I bring it in to him?"

Would I get to stare my theoretical enemy straight in the face? Did I *want* to? All of a sudden I was scared Nolan would see right through my act to my true intentions.

Well, so what if he did? *He* was the one in the wrong in this scenario, when you cut down to the root of it.

I drew my shoulders back with that surge of defiant confidence, but the man was shaking his head. "I don't think that's a wise idea. Here, I'll hand it over to him. We shouldn't leave it any longer if it's important."

Before I could put my plans of arguing for chain of custody or whatever the right term would be in an office setting, the stranger had already plucked the envelope from my hands. I managed to get out an, "Oh!" and then he'd slipped back into the office, shutting the door firmly behind him. All I caught was a brief glimpse of thick, crimson carpeting and gleaming gold filigree worked into the wallpaper.

So, Nolan Gauntt was an opulent ass. Not exactly a surprise, seeing his place of work. With no further excuse to hang around, I slunk back to the elevator. But I wasn't leaving empty-handed.

In a couple of weeks, that office and the one down the hall would be vacant while the Gauntts attended the benefit dinner. With Kai's help, maybe I could penetrate the inner sanctum of the villain.

thirteen

Jett

As I took in the three-story building, where the beige doorframe clashed with the maroon bricks, my heart sank.

"Kai said this was your best bet," I said to Lily, unable to suppress a frown. The guy knew plenty about a lot of things, but aesthetic analysis wasn't exactly his strong suit. "But if it's bad, I'm sure he can dig up some others."

"Well, let's go up and see the apartment," Lily said, nudging my arm with her elbow.

I did my best not to show any reaction, but inside, I stiffened up against the rush of heat that came with her closeness. I *had* to tense a little, or my arm might have gone slipping around her to tug her even closer of its own accord. As if that was what I wanted to be to her—yet another one of us aiming to get into her pants.

Not that I thought Nox and Ruin had any bad intentions. She had needs, they had needs, and there was no reason they shouldn't satisfy those together. Actually, that was a hell of a lot better than imagining her getting it on with some creep we knew nothing about. But she did have the two of them—and maybe Kai too if he stopped conducting data comparisons for long enough to make a move—so it wasn't like I could offer her something she didn't already have in that area.

I could be totally happy with her just sparking inspiration in me while I ignored the lust that sometimes came along with it.

The rental agent who was a collection of brown, black, and navy blue shapes, many of them long and angular, shifted on her feet where she'd been standing by the door. "Yes. You really should take a look at the space." So we headed in.

There was no elevator, of course. We tramped up the stairwell, which might have been Victorian once upon a time but had been transformed over the ages into a hodgepodge of art deco detailing and modernist fixtures. I managed not to wince when we got to the hallway with its olive-green carpet and lemon-yellow walls. As the rental agent fit the key into the lock of a door at the end of the hall, I braced myself.

The door swung wide—and I froze for a second, blinking and taking in the bright, airy space that was the complete opposite of what I'd been expecting.

Lily strode right inside, her pale hair gleaming in the sunlight that streamed through the main room's two broad windows. The hardwood floor creaked faintly under her feet, but it was *real* hardwood, not modern over-polished stuff. You could see the history of the trees in the knots and whirls of the grain—and the history of past inhabitants in the scuffs and scratches laid over top.

The apartments hadn't been updated with the same regularity as the building's common areas. Art deco had touched this space in the geometric flare to the baseboards and the moldings along the ceiling, but only subtly. The walls had been left white, a total blank slate. My fingers itched with the urge to splash some color over them and see just how stunning we could make the room.

It wasn't huge. Lily wandered from the living room area to where she could set up a small dining table with just a few paces, and the kitchen was walk-in closet sized, with just a half-wall separating it from the rest of the room. But the place was still twice the size of her stuffy basement without even getting into the other rooms yet.

"Since it's one of the corner apartments, there are three bedrooms," the rental agent was saying in her brisk, slightly desperate-sounding voice. "Each of them nice and cozy. And on the top floor, you don't have to worry about noise from neighbors overhead."

One of the reasons Kai had picked out this place was its price. We'd afford whatever Lily needed, but she'd already insisted that she wanted to pay her own way as much as possible, and there was no good in stressing her out with a massive rent bill. The neighborhood was halfway through a surge of gentrification, getting too posh and stuffy and just a little out of reach for the low-income families who might have snatched this place up before. But this particular building must be having trouble competing with the sleek modern apartments going up around it.

No doubt in another few years the owners would want to gut it and start from scratch, if they could come up with the dough. By then we'd just have to be ready to buy the whole building out from under them—if Lily still wanted to live here.

From the looks of things, she did. She drifted from one bedroom to another with a shimmer in her eyes and a quiet smile playing with her lips. I wanted to paint her like that. But then, I wanted to paint her every which way. She'd have set off something in me even standing on her head with her tongue stuck out.

In real estate terms, I knew enough to realize that "cozy" meant "tiny." But each of the bedrooms was big enough to fit a double bed and a dresser, maybe even a small armchair or vanity, without leaving you crushed against the wall. The third had a built-in Murphy bed that swung down from the wall at the push of a button.

"We'd take that one," I told Lily. "You and Marisol should get proper beds."

Lily raised an eyebrow at me. "All four of you on

that thing? You'd be getting awfully up close and personal."

A smile twitched at my lips despite myself. "We can set up cots too," I said. "I definitely don't want Ruin flailing around in my face. And we won't all be here all the time. We'll have a couple of pullout couches set up in the new hangout too."

I also figured that when we *were* staying here, one of the other guys would be sharing Lily's bed at least some of the time. Ruin was already making a partial habit of that.

An image flashed through my mind of lying on that mattress with her tucked against *me*, and this time it was my dick that twitched. I turned away, looking across the main room from the doorway.

The rental agent had gone over to the door to give us some space to settle into the place. Lily came up beside me, still absorbing it all.

"It's nice," she said softly. "I mean, it'd be perfect. But I don't know how long I'll have this job at Thrivewell—I don't know what kind of work I'll be able to get after."

"It's cheap for what it is," I said. "Everyone else wants the fancy fixtures, so skipping this place is their loss and your gain. We'll have plenty of cash soon to tide you over if you need it."

"I know. But you shouldn't have to. It should be *me* looking after Marisol—she's my sister."

The determination in her voice sparked a different sort of sensation in me. Memories wavered up of the kind of treatment I'd gotten from *my* family: my parents' harsh words and harder fists. Family ties had been something to survive and overcome, not anything you could count on for support.

Lily could have learned the same lesson from her own asshole parents. But she'd never lost the sweetness she'd had even as a little kid.

"We're looking out for *you*," I said with a sudden determination of my own. We were her family more than the jerks who'd claimed the official titles. We'd been there for her more than her mom and stepdad ever had. "Whatever you need help with, you can count on us."

"I know. I just…" She bit her lip. I knew how strong Lily was, but in certain moments an inner fragility showed through, and I wanted nothing more than to charge with fists swinging at anyone who brought it out in her.

"What?" I demanded, unable to stop my voice from getting gruffer.

She looked down, her fingers drifting along the doorframe. "I've been thinking… I'd like to do more with music. I always loved singing. If there's a way I could make some kind of career out of that—but I know anything in the arts is a tough road. Maybe I'm being ridiculous."

My heart swelled, and even though I'd been making a point of avoiding physical contact, I gripped her arm. "You have to go for that. Your voice—" I hadn't heard her sing in years, but the delicate strains of the melodies she'd produced had stuck in my memory. I'd bet they wove through my own art even now. She'd always been able to transform the sounds around her into something beautiful, tying it all together with the harmony she created as it spilled from her lips.

The general public should consider themselves fucking *blessed* if she offered that talent up to the rest of them.

"When you've got something like that inside you, you have to let it out," I went on. "I'd be miserable if I wasn't making my paintings and the rest." Okay, I was miserable plenty of the time regardless, but I'd have been more so without the outlet. "You let it out, and you see where it can take you. You can always take on other jobs while you give it a shot."

At my emphatic insistence, Lily's smile came back, if shier than before. But her next words came with a teasing note. "Like you do."

I shrugged. "Hey, I see skull-breaking as more of a hobby than a career, but it does pay the bills too." As long as I didn't let my artistic inclinations take over *too* much...

A spurt of guilt seared up from my gut at the thought of the time I had let too much go. I clamped down on it, willing my expression to stay calm. Lily hadn't been any part of that, and I wasn't going to lay it on her.

She shook her head in amusement and stepped back into the main room. At the same moment, my phone jangled with the stupidly dramatic classical song my nerd host had programmed it with, like getting a call was an epic event. Making a face, I drew back into the bedroom and shut the door for privacy.

The screen just said *Dad*, so I guessed I was hearing from another family today. This one I wanted even less to do with than my own. But it'd been inevitable that we'd have to deal with parents eventually, even with the guys who'd been living on campus rather than at home. I had to give the relatives something so they didn't file a missing person report and create even more of a hassle for me.

From what I'd found out so far about the guy whose body I'd taken over, I wouldn't be surprised if he'd previously been in the habit of sending weekly reports to his family, complete with a spreadsheet breaking down recent fluctuations to his GPA and number of professors' asses he'd kissed. They could forget about that from here on. Their boy Vince had flown the coop.

"Hello," I answered in the most even voice I could produce.

"Vincent!" the man on the other end said, with that stiff kind of enthusiasm people use when they're trying to pretend they're happy but are actually pissed off. "You missed our usual family video chat. Your mother's been getting worried about you."

But the man talking to me hadn't been? I swallowed that sarcastic remark and said, "Classes have gotten me really busy. Term papers, extra credit, group presentations, band practice, you know." Were there any other school terms I could throw in there for good measure? I'd only just graduated high school by the skin of my teeth.

"Band practice?" Vince's dad said, and then seemed to shake himself. "You do have a responsibility to the family as well. I hope you won't get distracted from that. We had an agreement—"

His superior tone was already rankling me. "Look," I interrupted, "I'm 21. Officially an adult in every possible way. I get to make my own decisions about what my responsibilities are now. I'm sure you'll be very proud of what I accomplish."

The man started to sputter. "Now wait a minute here. You can't talk to me like—"

"Funny, I just did. I'll call or video chatter or whatever when I feel like it. In the meantime, let me do my thing."

Then I hung up.

It might not have been the most graceful exit, but if I'd stayed on the line much longer, I might have started describing in detail how he should shove his head up his ass, and that would have gone over even worse.

The phone started ringing again. I jabbed at it until it shut up and smacked my hand against the wall with a growl of frustration.

The electric energy that still tingled lightly through my veins, leftover from my previous ghostly state, zapped through my arm with the impact. The wall beneath my hand flickered... and suddenly I was staring at a fog-blue surface instead of the previous white.

I yanked my hand back, staring. The entire wall had

changed color, just like that. I glanced around to make sure the other walls were still white and it wasn't just that my vision had fogged, but nope, my gloom hadn't gotten quite that literal. Motherfucker.

Was that my special angle on our supernatural energies? Nox could beat people down from a distance, Ruin could infect them with his feels, and I could give a room a makeover?

Actually, maybe I was okay with that.

I flexed my fingers, wanting to see what else I might be able to alter, and heard footsteps coming toward the room. The rental agent's footsteps, from the tapping of sharp heels. Shit. I didn't think she'd appreciate my new paint job on a place we hadn't even signed a contract for yet.

My nerves jumped, and I slapped my hand against the wall again. It blinked white an instant later, just as the agent opened the door. If maybe there was a tiny blue tint to that surface still, she was too busy glaring at me to notice.

"I'm not sure what you're doing, but I'd appreciate it if you didn't damage the plaster."

I held up my hands apologetically. "Sorry! Just testing the walls to make sure they're good and solid."

She kept eyeing me as I strode back out to rejoin Lily. The agent cleared her throat. "We do expect certain standards of behavior: there are noise regulations, and the unit should be left in a similar condition to as it started."

"Of course," Lily said, gazing around her again. I

knew just looking at her that she was taking the place. She arched an eyebrow at me. "I can keep my friends in line."

I was definitely having my way with these walls as soon as they were in our possession, though. And maybe this newfound talent could be useful when it came to a certain other project the other guys and I had been discussing...

Lily got a contract to sign from the rental agent, promised to return by the end of the day with the deposit, and headed back to the street with more of a spring in her step than I could remember seeing since she was a kid. "This could be good," she said. "It could be *really* good. I hope Marisol likes it."

"She will," I told her. "A hole in the ground would be better than staying with your parental units any longer, if you're there with her."

She smiled at me, and my heart gave that weird little hitch it'd never done for anyone else in my life. Either of my lives. Then we turned the corner outside and were swarmed by the rest of the crew, who must have just finished up the other business they'd been seeing to.

"Did you like it?" Ruin asked, grabbing Lily in one of his usual bear hugs. Kai didn't say anything, but his eyes gleamed with intense alertness. He was the one who'd picked out the apartment, after all.

"It's great," Lily said. "I'm going to go for it. It sounds like as long as I put down the deposit today, it's mine."

"We've got that covered," Nox announced, and before she could protest, added, "It's our payback for losing you your other job. No arguments. We owe you. We'll cover any charges from breaking your lease on the basement too. How soon can you move in?"

"Two weeks," Kai said. "I specifically looked for places that would be available quickly."

A smile that was outright luminescent crossed Lily's face. We all basked in it for a few seconds before I turned to Nox. "You got the other stuff sorted out?"

"Yep." He tossed me a pistol, which I shoved into the back of my jeans. A twist of tension I hadn't registered before loosened in my chest with the weapon in my grasp.

I'd always preferred working with my hands directly, but a bullet was an excellent equalizer. Strength and speed barely came into it. After the last gang we'd hit up for info had come at us with firearms to our fists, we'd realized it was time to make some new connections in the black market.

"And we found out more about these Skeleton Corps guys," Ruin said cheerfully.

Kai rolled his eyes at him. "Nothing good. While we asked around, putting out feelers, it got obvious very quickly that no one wants to mess with these people. They were practically pissing their pants just hearing the name. These guys have a lot of sway in the city."

"And they were scared of *us* enough to come after us," Ruin added, still spinning this in a positive light the way only he could.

"The guy who told us about them didn't say they offed us," Nox reminded him. "Just that they were the most likely people to know who did. But if it was them, we have a few different tricks up our sleeves this time." His mouth curved into a cocky grin, and he glanced around at all of us. "Are we ready to pay back the pricks who killed us, no matter what they're going to throw at us?"

My stomach had twisted up again, but I spoke without a second's hesitation. "Hell, yes."

Maybe this city gang was big enough to crush us all over again, ghostly powers or not. But I'd already gotten one life, and I'd fucked up both it and three others with my stupidity. So if any of us ended up going down, it could be me.

At least I'd die the second time knowing my friends were shooting the smirks off the rest of those pricks' faces.

fourteen

Lily

Rupert stormed into the mailroom with a severe case of the Mondays. He stomped this way and that, slapped labels onto the outgoing packages like they'd kicked his puppy, and nearly bit the head off the office worker who came down to deliver a verbal message.

"Are you kidding me?" he said, his eyes bulging, and then drew himself up straighter as if good posture would make up for his unprofessional tone. His gaze cut across the room to me where I was sorting mail into the carts for the different floors. His voice lowered, but not so much that I couldn't make out the words. "Why would they want to speak with her? There must be a mistake."

The guy he was talking to shook his head and murmured something that was actually discreet. Rupert let out one of his trademark huffs, and I gleefully pictured the mini heron on his head taking a massive crap. Then my supervisor turned toward me.

"Miss Strom, you've been instructed to go up to Nolan Gauntt's office. Apparently Mr. Gauntt has something he needs to speak to you about."

I froze, the envelope I'd been lifting slipping from my fingers and bouncing off the assorted mail already in the cart in front of me. Okay, maybe I couldn't blame him for his skepticism when I was totally bewildered myself.

"Me?" I said, like there might be another Miss Strom in the room that I simply hadn't noticed before. "Why?"

"A very good question," Rupert muttered. The messenger had already fled. My supervisor eyed me as if I'd set this whole thing up to undermine his authority, and I decided I was best off getting the heck out of there ASAP.

"I'm supposed to go now?" I clarified.

He gave a sharp nod. "Get a move on. He keeps this entire company running. I'm sure he doesn't have time to wait on a dawdling mail clerk."

I had no idea why Nolan Gauntt would want to talk to a mail clerk at all. As I hurried into the hall toward the elevators, my pulse started pounding.

Had Nolan or his admin assistant realized I'd been snooping? Maybe there'd been hidden security cameras in the hall, or the visitor I'd passed the envelope to had seen more than I realized? Was he calling me in to chew me out?

Or maybe Harmon Kitteridge had spilled the beans and they've realized I'd gotten the job under false pretenses. Kai's blackmail material might not have been enough of a threat.

Either way, did that mean Nolan had also put the pieces together about who *I* was? Would he think of me as simply the sister of a girl he'd done something untoward with years ago, or had he taken a more recent role in my family's lives? Wade had seemed to think Nolan loomed large, but he hadn't actually given any proof of that, and it hadn't sounded like Marisol had seen the man since the incident that'd set me off seven years ago.

My fingers brushed over the outline of my phone in my purse's outer pocket. I had the urge to text Kai and tell him what was happening, like a hiker setting off into uncharted wilderness wanting a record in case they didn't return, but I wasn't totally sure that the former gangster would be content sitting on his butt while I walked into the lion's den. He might insist on barging in or making some kind of commotion in the hopes of getting me out of this meeting, and I wasn't sure that was what I needed.

I'd been wanting to figure out what Nolan Gauntt was up to since the moment I'd heard his name from my stepfather's lips. It was the whole reason I'd applied for this job. Now the man himself had called me in for a chat. How could I pass up the opportunity, even if it might end with me getting booted out the front door?

If he was pissed off at me, nothing Kai could do was going to change that anyway. The brilliant gangster might be able to read and manipulate people based on what they thought and felt, but he couldn't make them think something totally different. If we could get Ruin in here to work a little of his magic of feels, maybe...

No, that would wear off, and then I'd be back where I'd started. The only thing to do was to meet this confrontation head-on.

The elevator took about a century to reach the basement floor that held the mailroom, and then another century to rise up to the fifteenth floor where I had to switch over. I smoothed my skirt straight and checked that my blouse and cardigan hadn't picked up any crumbs or stains, but the assistant to the executive assistants still looked me over with a pinched frown before motioning me on toward the exclusive elevator to the upper floors.

When I reached the top floor and stepped out of the elevator, the man whose desk I'd been accosting a few days ago got up and walked to the door to Nolan's office. "Miss Strom is here," he said, and motioned for me to walk past him into the room.

I slipped inside onto that thick crimson carpet. The gold filigree I'd noticed on the wallpaper gleamed against its midnight-blue background. It should have made the space feel dark, but the ceiling was so high and lit with beaming crystal fixtures, with more light streaming through the windows along the far end of the immense office, that it gave me the impression of a vast, stately expanse instead.

Not just one but two figures were standing just in front of the antique mahogany desk near the far windows. I walked toward them warily, recognizing them both from the pictures Kai had dug up during his research.

To the left stood the man I'd been expecting, although even more imposing in the flesh. Nolan Gauntt must have stood nearly as tall as Nox's massive form. Even in his advancing age, he had the build of a linebacker, broad-shouldered and barrel-chested. His smooth, silvery hair still held a few streaks of blond; his jaw was clean-shaven. He watched me approach with a gaze that felt both flat and penetrating at the same time.

To the right waited the woman I knew was his wife. Marie Gauntt stood almost a full head shorter than her husband, but her hair made up for a lot of that difference, rising in a neat, colorless cone the texture of cotton candy. Her thin lips were pursed. Despite her shorter stature, her presence was no less intimidating. The soft grays of her business suit contrasted with the hard angles to her face and body.

It was easy to tell that both of them had been quite the stunners in their younger days. They were still incredibly striking, although there was a detached sheen to their eyes that made my nerves jitter. It was like they were studying my every move while not really giving a shit what I actually did.

"Miss Strom," Nolan said in a cool baritone, just before I got close enough that I felt *I* had to break the ice. I stopped in my tracks as he went on. "I'm glad you could join us. I'm Nolan Gauntt, and this is my wife, Marie. We run Thrivewell together."

"We're making a point of touching base with the new hires here," Marie added, her own voice quiet but dry.

"Oh," I said, groping for the appropriate words. "That's very nice of you."

I might have felt less unsettled if I could have pictured some bizarre animal tromping around on each of their heads, but somehow my mind jarred when I tried to conjure so much as a trunk or a hoof. It was as if the Gauntts' presence was so potent even my imagination couldn't challenge it.

Did they make all the new hires walk a mile across this office while staring them down like prey they were picking the best caliber of shotgun for? Kai hadn't mentioned any meetings like this, and I'd have thought they'd call in someone at his level before a random mailroom clerk.

They'd gone silent again, just contemplating me. Were they looking for some specific reaction?

They did know who I was. I had no doubt about that now. Why else this whole production? But of course they weren't going to admit it or that they'd had anything to do with my sister. What would they get out of showing so many of their cards?

I shifted my weight from one foot to the other. "Was there anything in particular you wanted to know?" I ventured. "I think I've been getting the hang of things in the mailroom, and I like working here."

"Ah, well, you've only just gotten started, haven't you?" Marie said, her tone light but the words undeniably ominous.

"Yes," I said hesitantly. "This is my second week."

Nolan gave a somber nod and an odd flick of his hand, as if he were brushing a bug off his suit lapel. "We did have some concerns. We understand you don't have any prior office experience. The atmosphere here in the head office can get rather... intense."

"Oh." I was so articulate today. I sucked in a breath and reminded myself that the man in front of me might look like important stuff, but he also apparently needed to mess with little kids to make himself feel big. No matter what front he put on, he was a creep underneath.

"I'm sure I can handle that," I continued, raising my chin. I wasn't in a position to challenge him right now, but I didn't want them to think I was some kind of wimp either.

It'd have been handy if either of them had given away something about their association with my family, but they hadn't even used my first name. Marie tapped her fingernails against the top of the desk with a crisp rattling sound. "I'm not sure you can reasonably assume that's true when you haven't experienced it. That's why we felt we should offer you the opportunity to settle in somewhere that might be more your speed."

My stomach knotted. "What do you mean?" Were they kicking me out after all? So far neither of them had mentioned my investigative activities or my supposed godfather—but could I hope they really didn't know?

Nolan swept his arm toward the world beyond the wall. "We have another, smaller office set up in Bedard. That would be a shorter commute for you, coming all the way from Lovell Rise, and it's slower paced there. Less urgency to the communications passing through. They could use a new mailroom clerk there as well. The pay would remain the same, of course, in accordance with your hiring conditions."

"Oh," I said again, resisting the urge to hug myself. They were trying to get rid of me, but in the kindest-looking way possible.

They didn't want me under the same roof as them. This offer would get me out of the way without giving me any reason for complaint. Who could argue about the same pay for an easier job, after all?

But there was a threat implicit in the talk about how "intense" the company could be too. Nolan drove it home, folding his arms over his chest and fixing his flat blue eyes even more intently on me. "I wouldn't want to see an employee burn out by remaining here when it's more of a trial than they can handle. We have your best interests at heart."

I swallowed hard. Yeah right, they did.

But how would they destroy me if I defied them? I

wasn't so worried about me, but if Marisol ended up paying for my refusal... How could I put *her* at risk over a plan I might not have thought through as well as I should have?

Maybe I could investigate the Gauntts from this other office? Kai would still be here checking up on things... I didn't think they could have connected him to me.

The idea started to feel so tempting that my lips parted to accept. I caught myself, my fingers curling into my palms. A sudden jolt of anger rushed through my chest—anger mostly at myself.

I'd tried running away before. I'd done everything I could to dodge my bullies at the college, and they'd just kept coming down on me harder and harder. It hadn't been until I pushed back that they'd finally eased off.

Something Ruin had said yesterday tickled up from my memory. It'd been his usual turning-an-empty-glass-full style optimism, but at the same time, he hadn't been wrong.

And they were scared of us enough to come after us.

He'd been talking about this Skeleton Corps gang, but it applied to this situation just as well. If the Gauntts hadn't been worried about what I might accomplish while working here, they wouldn't have bothered to try to send me elsewhere. The very fact that they'd gone on the attack meant that they had something to defend.

Resolve solidified inside me. I'd come here to uncover the mysteries around my sister and me, and I wasn't turning tail just because a couple of much bigger bullies had decided they should call the shots in my life instead.

"Actually," I said, willing my voice to stay steady despite my quaking nerves, "I just put down a deposit on an apartment here in Mayfield. And I've been through plenty of high-pressure scenarios in the past, even if not in an office environment." They didn't know the half of it. "I'd really love to stay on here and prove myself. If you find any problems with my work, I'd understand the transfer, but for now, I hope you'll give me a real chance."

I smiled at them tightly, almost a dare. Were they going to try to force the issue and show how much it mattered to them?

They eyed me for a few seconds longer while my heart thudded in my ears. Nolan tilted his head to one side. Marie tugged her elbow back in an odd gesture I didn't understand. Then they sighed nearly in unison.

"I suppose that's fair," Marie said.

"We will keep a close eye on how well you're keeping up here," Nolan said. "There's no shame in working your way up gradually."

I forced Ruin-level brightness into my voice. "I know. But I really think I'm up to it. I won't let you down."

Maybe that was laying it on a bit thick, but Nolan nodded. "I appreciate your dedication," he said in a tone that suggested he really didn't at all. "We won't keep you from your work any longer."

At that dismissal, I turned and hurried back across the expanse of the room. My chest had constricted around my lungs.

I'd won whatever small battle this had been. Now I'd better hope it'd definitely been one worth fighting.

fifteen

Lily

At first, everything was simply dark. Darkness everywhere I turned, and the unnerving sensation crept over me that I wasn't standing but floating.

The darkness rippled around me. The currents rushed faster and stronger, tugging at my limbs. They were dragging me down, down into the even thicker blackness that would swallow me up completely.

I opened my mouth to scream, and more liquid darkness gushed down my throat, choking me. My lungs seized up. I couldn't breathe, couldn't speak, and I was sinking, falling, sucked down and down while the last glimmers of light blinked out overhead—

I jerked out of the nightmare with a gasped cry, my

lungs still straining for breath. Ruin's arms wrapped around me.

"Hey," he said, low and sweet. "Hey, it's all right, Waterlily. I'm right here with you."

Before I'd quite recovered from my panicked daze, three more forms burst into the dimness of my bedroom.

"Is she okay?" Nox demanded.

"What's happening?" Kai asked, fumbling his glasses onto his nose.

"If someone's managed to hurt her here…" Jett said darkly with a smack of his fist against his other hand.

Now I was drowning in concern.

"I'm all right," I muttered, swiping my hand across my eyes. "It was just a bad dream. There's no one to beat up, unless you have some ghostly way of punching my subconscious."

Kai cocked his head as if he was working out the logistics of that maneuver.

Nox frowned, his jaw flexing. "Are you sure? It wasn't a bad dream *about* something shitty someone's done to you?"

I glowered at him. "I'm absolutely sure there's no one whose skull you need to crack to avenge my interrupted sleep. Speaking of which, I'd kind of like to get back to sleep if that's at all possible."

"We should all get some more sleep," Ruin put in cheerfully. "With better dreams."

The other guys wavered on their feet for a moment indecisively, no doubt still searching for a way they could defend me from the products of my inner mind. Then they all tramped back out again.

Ruin stayed, cuddled against me on the narrow bed. I let my head come to rest on his shoulder, inhaling his warm, musky scent. "How long have you been in here?"

He'd been slipping into my room earlier and earlier over the past few days, though always managing to tuck himself against me without waking me up. I hadn't yet definitively determined that he wasn't just a giant housecat in human form.

The impression was only amplified by the purr-like hum he let out as he nuzzled my hair. "Just a half hour ago. It's hard sleeping alone when I know you're in here. But I don't want to crowd you." He let out a happy sigh. "It'll be perfect when you have a proper-sized bed."

"I suppose I'll never get rid of you then," I muttered without any actual complaint in the words.

"Nope!" Ruin declared brightly. But he did adjust himself to give me a tiny bit more space on the mattress, with his back pressed against the wall. He stroked his fingers over my hair. "What *were* you dreaming about? I'll talk your subconscious out of making you think about it again."

My lips twitched with a smile I couldn't completely constrain. "I don't know how well that'll work. It was…" I thought back to the smothering, choking darkness, and my pulse hitched all over again. I swallowed thickly. "I was drowning. Like I almost did in the marsh."

Weirdly, I'd never had nightmares about that

moment before, even though it was by far the closest I'd ever come to dying, so you'd think it should be my most traumatic memory. But my plunge into the chilly marsh-water had ended with finding four new friends I'd thought were imaginary but who'd still been a hell of a lot more company than the nothing I'd had before. In a warped way, my near-death experience had made my life *better*.

So why was my brain tossing the worst parts of that moment at me all over again, fourteen years later?

A tendril of uneasiness wound through my insides. My ghostly guys had helped me save myself back then. They'd stood by me while Wade and my mom had treated me like table scraps. But now...

The image rose up in my mind of Nolan and Marie Gauntt, looming large in their cold, stately authority. They controlled an entire corporate empire. They had bank accounts bigger than everyone in the whole county combined. Was a little watery magic and four former gangsters who were only just getting back on their feet really enough to tackle them?

My guys had been protecting me every step of the way since they'd come back to me in bodily form, and I might have just dragged them into a war that was a thousand times more dangerous than anything they'd faced before.

I shoved those thoughts away and burrowed into Ruin's embrace. His arms tightened around me. "We'll kick the marsh's ass before we let it take you again," he informed me, but this time I couldn't quite manage a smile.

The Gauntts might be powerful, but they were still just people, I reminded myself. If I could get proof that they'd hurt my sister and maybe other kids too, their corporate ties and bank accounts shouldn't matter. I just had to keep at it, even if I wasn't sure how I was going to get that proof yet.

Maybe it'd help if I was sure that the other parts of my plans were completely solid. I'd told Marisol I was going to look after her from now on, but I hadn't laid down the law with the people who considered themselves her current caretakers. If Nolan and Marie decided to come after us, it was better she was with me than our crappy excuse for parents, wasn't it? Wade would probably kick her out the door before Nolan had even asked him to.

That thought lingered in my head through the rest of my fitful sleep and while I showered in the morning. I emerged from the bathroom with a sense of conviction that was only a little shaky.

"Before I go in to work, I'm going to stop by my old house and make sure everything's ready for Marisol to come with me once I have the new apartment."

Ruin perked up. "We'll come with you in case your mom and that jerk make any trouble."

As the others started to stir with agreement, I shook my head. "No, I still think it's better if I handle my family on my own. For now. If we have to force the issue, I'll let you know I need backup. But I don't think it should have to come to that."

Wade had cowered in the face of my powers, and I hadn't done anything more than splash him a couple of times. As angry as I was with him and Mom, I didn't see any point in breaking bones if we didn't have to.

Nox clapped his hands together. "We do have something else to take care of this morning. But all you have to do is send a text if you need us."

I ate breakfast in the car, with Fred sputtering and rumbling as if he wished he could share the meal. I wanted as much time as possible for this confrontation before I was due at work. It wouldn't look good if the day after my lecture from the big bosses, I showed up tardy.

As I drove along the lane that led to the house, I was relieved to see that Wade's car wasn't parked outside. I'd already dealt with him anyway. He didn't hold much authority over what Marisol did, since he'd never adopted either of us—any say he had was through my mom. She was the one I really needed to tackle.

I didn't have to knock. I'd only just parked and stepped out of the car when the door swung open and Mom came out on the front step.

She looked like an even more faded version of a self that'd already faded when I'd been shipped off to the mental ward, like a photocopy of a photocopy. I'd seen old pictures of her where her hair was as brightly gold as Marisol's—now it had enough gray woven in to look like day-old dishwater. It drifted fine and limp across her shoulders. The lines around her mouth spoke of how often she forced smiles for Wade's benefit, but in my presence her lips slumped into a frown. Even her skin seemed to have grayed, more a washed-out beige than its former peachy tint.

"What are you doing here?" she asked.

She didn't tell me to leave, and there was a nervous defensiveness to her posture. I guessed Wade had filled her in on the basics of my last conversation with him. It occurred to me that I wasn't even sure how much she knew about the specifics. Wade had said something about telling Mom to leave when I'd started yelling at them over the thing with Nolan Gauntt and Marisol. Did she have any idea how I'd cowed her husband in the end?

She might soon enough. Just seeing her sent the hum reverberating through my chest as my own inner defenses came up. I squared my shoulders.

"I want to talk to my sister," I said. "And in a little while, she's going to be moving in with me. I'm going to take care of her from now on."

Mom blinked at me, her mouth opening and closing a few times before she found words. "What are you talking about? You can't just run off with her."

"I can if she agrees," I said. *And I can make you allow it if you try to stop me.* But I didn't think it was going to come to that. I lowered my voice in case Marisol was listening inside. "I know you'd rather she was out of your hair anyway. You *never* wanted us around after you found Wade. So let me fix that 'problem' for all of us."

Mom's thin jaw worked. A soft pattering sounded on the patchy lawn beyond us. We both glanced over to see a squad of frogs hopping over from the marsh toward us.

I say "squad" because it definitely wasn't an army on the level of the one that'd descended on Peyton in the college restroom weeks ago. There were maybe two or three dozen of the sleek green bodies leaping along in an off-kilter rhythm. They all stopped several feet from where we were standing and squatted there as if waiting to see if they were needed. A few let out quizzical croaks.

I glanced back at my mother. She took in the frogs and then met my gaze again, and the slightly hysterical light that gleamed in her eyes told me she wasn't totally unaware that I might have connections to powers beyond what a regular woman should. I hadn't called up the frogs on purpose, but now that they were here, I didn't mind having the moral support.

We were in this together, apparently: me and the marsh.

And then—maybe because she knew Wade had already backed down and sometime in the past fifteen years, she'd made him her spine—Mom crumpled. Her shoulders sagged, and she drew back into the doorway. "Do what you want. I can't control either of you, obviously. Just don't come to us for help if it doesn't work out the way you wanted."

As if I'd ever imagined she or Wade would help me

regardless of the situation. I doubted either of them would piss on me if they saw me on fire.

I stepped past her into the house and headed upstairs. Marisol was rustling around in her bedroom, the door open. As I reached it, she zipped her backpack shut for school and straightened up. Her eyes gleamed with a wild sort of light, anxious but eager.

"It's really happening?" she said. "I'm going to move in with you?"

I grinned at her, the tension clamped around my chest subsiding. "Yep. I've already arranged the apartment—out in Mayfield, where I've got my new job. It'll be mine in less than two weeks. We'll have to decide if I need to arrange a way for you to commute or get you transferred to a closer—"

"Transfer," Marisol said before I could finish that sentence. "There's nothing I like about the high school here anyway. And they hardly have any of the more interesting classes."

She tugged at one of the braided strands of her hair after she said that, looking suddenly awkward. My gaze flicked around the room, remembering the sketches that had once decorated it. "Don't they even have art class?"

My sister shrugged. "Sort of. It's mostly about the history and stuff."

"You haven't been drawing in a while."

"I know. It started to seem kind of… silly."

An ache gripped my gut. I reached out to squeeze her shoulder. "I don't think it is at all. I miss your farting unicorns and goofy dragons and all the rest. If you're making people smile, that's something pretty important."

"I guess."

Marisol's voice was so small that I wanted to hit someone—whoever had belittled her love of putting pencil to paper. Obviously, moving her in with me wasn't going to be enough. She'd gone seven years without me here to offset Mom and Wade's disapproval. It could be a long rebuilding process.

Was I even steady enough myself to get her all the way back on track?

A faint honking carried through the bedroom window. It repeated a few seconds later. I followed Marisol when she went over to peer outside.

On one of the more distant laneways beyond the scruffy fields that covered a lot of the outskirts of town, four figures with motorcycles were standing around a car. They must have spotted us in the window, because one of them waved energetically and another simply gave a small tip of his hand and a beckoning gesture.

"Who are *they*?" Marisol asked, raising her eyebrows.

That... was a complicated question to answer. "Friends of mine," I said. "They're helping look out for us too. You'll get a chance to meet them after you've moved in." And after I'd had a *very* firm talk with the former Skullbreakers about acceptable conversation topics around my little sister.

"I'd better go see what they want—and let you get

to school," I said, and gave Marisol a quick hug. "Just remember you're getting out of here soon."

Mom didn't even bother to say goodbye. I didn't force it. I tramped out to my car and drove Fred around to the lane where the guys were waiting. When I got out to see what the welcoming party was for, my stomach flipped over.

The car they were standing around... looked just like Fred. Except not at all junker-y. The boxy exterior didn't show a hint of rust, and the blue paint shone with a recent polishing. Not a single dent marked the bumper. The rearview mirror on the driver's side didn't sag slightly downward.

"What's this?" I asked, blinking as if it might be a hallucination I could clear out of my eyes like a bit of dust.

Nox smiled broadly and patted the car's hood. "Your new ride. We told you we'd see about getting you one. But since you're so attached to the old beast, we figured we should track you down the same model. If we could manage to take over four dorks totally different from our old selves, I'm sure your junker's soul could transfer over to this one."

My throat constricted with awed gratitude. I couldn't imagine how they'd managed to track the thing down—to find the exact right shade of paint even—and this could be a new Fred, couldn't it? Fred 2.0, same old spirit in a tuned-up body. Like Nox had said, why shouldn't it be possible?

I stepped closer and let my fingertips rest on the

smooth hood. The guys all watched me with their varied expressions of eagerness, and I didn't know what to say.

"It's perfect," I managed. "Thank you so much."

It really was. And some part of me couldn't quite believe I deserved the level of dedication that'd gone into this gift.

sixteen

Ruin

Lily returned home from work just as I was heading out of her apartment. I saw her before she saw me. She got out of the new car and paused to glide her fingers along the frame, a small, delighted smile curving her lips.

The smile lit a spark of delight in me too. She'd seemed almost downcast underneath her appreciation when we'd first shown her the car this morning, but she really did like it. While I wasn't sure why she'd hesitated to embrace it at first, all that mattered was that she was happy now.

I loped over and grabbed her in a hug, pressing a kiss to the extra soft spot behind her ear at the same time. Lily let out a perfect breathy gasp of pleased surprise and then relaxed into my embrace. "Hello to you too. Are you trying to give me a heart attack?"

"You're irresistible," I informed her, and eased back just enough to clasp her hand and tug her with me. "I've been put in charge of buying takeout for dinner. Come with me."

She tipped her head toward the car. "We could drive."

"Nah, there are lots of good places around, and I like getting my legs moving." Ever since I'd dropped into this body, my nerves had twanged with a constant need for stimulation.

I would have popped in my earphones too and blared some of the pounding rock music I'd figured out how to download until it rattled my eardrums, but since Lily was with me, I wanted to be able to hear her. Even the tap of her shoes against the pavement—the glossy ones with the harder soles that she wore for work instead of her usual sneakers—invigorated me.

Because I was walking right here next to her. I *could* hear every sound she made with perfect clarity instead of the hazy blur of when I'd been without a body and so without proper ears. It really was a miracle.

I swung our hands together. Lily shook her head at me in exasperation, but she didn't stop me, so I figured she didn't mind my enthusiasm too much. She'd used to love my jokes and excited observations when she was younger... but she hadn't been through quite so much back then. I guessed it made sense she'd gotten more serious, more tense.

But the longer she was with us, the more she'd see she didn't need to be. Everything was going to be all right. She'd never have to worry again.

That cheerful thought was running through my head as we turned the corner toward a couple of my favorite restaurants on the main strip in town. Just as my mouth started watering while I debated between Thai and BBQ chicken, two burly men barreled across the street toward the alley we were passing and bumped into me.

Not just me. The one man's shoulder knocked Lily to the side, and protectiveness flared inside me with a sharp jolt that wouldn't have come at all if it'd only been me getting assaulted. I whipped around, defensive energy crackling through me, and that's the only reason I spotted the gleam of the thin blade tucked in the man's hand an instant before he jabbed it at me.

It really *was* an assault. He was aiming it at my chest, probably intending to stab it between my ribs into my heart, but my sudden movement threw him off. My arm flew up, smacking his hand wide. The blade sliced only the air.

A deeper fury blazed through me. I slammed my fist into the guy's head and yanked Lily behind me so I could act as her shield. The man reeled but swung at us again at the same time. Lily let out a squeak, and I snarled. I rammed my foot into my attacker's gut, electric energy crackling through my veins with the surge of feral emotion.

The other man sprang at me too, reaching for my

throat. I shoved him to the side and whipped around to see the first man growling through bared teeth, his expression twisted with vicious rage.

Oh. Oops. I'd forgotten about my new talent for pummeling my feelings into people around me. Infecting him with the same fury I felt probably hadn't been a great strategy.

I moved to launch myself at him and end his murderous rage before he fully unleashed it, but he spun toward his friend instead of me. He slashed the knife through the air, cutting the other guy's cheek.

Huh. It seemed like I'd transferred the target of my anger along with the anger itself. Maybe that wasn't such a bad thing after all.

"What the fuck, you maniac?" the second guy spat out under his breath, raising his arms defensively. The other man just charged at him with nothing more than a wordless howl.

The second man yelped like a frightened puppy and took off down the street. The man with the knife raced after him, now letting out battle cries that sounded like something out of a civil war movie. I threw myself after both of them, my vision still glazed red, my pulse thrumming through my body.

Even if the one guy was acting in my favor for now, they both needed to pay for coming at me and Lily like this. We needed to know who the fuck they were. Had those overblown Skeleton dudes come at me? Was this about Ansel's whole deal again?

Kai would want me to batter that information out

of these dudes, and I'd be only too happy to deal out that beating.

Down the street, the first guy dove into a car parked by the curb. The second man flung himself at the door, yanking it open even as the first set the engine roaring. The car tore off down the road with the man with the knife still hanging halfway out. Curses and thumps emanated from within. But it was still going too fast for me to catch them. It swerved around a bend, dangling legs and all, and vanished from view.

My heart thumped with the urge to chase them down somehow or other. But a chill flashed through me at the thought of Lily and how I'd left her behind. What if some other prick came at her?

I spun around and dashed back toward the alley where we'd been attacked. Lily had ducked into the mouth of it, mostly hidden in the shadows. She was looking down at her arm. As I reached her, my gaze caught on the streak of red showing through her sweater's sleeve, and rage blared through me all over again.

"He hurt you!" I said, grasping her wrist. The knife had cut right through the fabric and into her flesh. More blood was seeping out as I looked at it.

My teeth clenched. That knife had been meant for me. I hadn't taken the men out quickly enough—I hadn't managed to take them out at all. And Lily was hurt.

For a second, I felt torn down the middle, half of me wanting to rampage after the getaway car and smash the assholes' heads under my heels like busted jack-o-lanterns, the other half desperate to fix the damage done to my woman. She was bleeding right here in front of me.

The second urge won out. I ripped at my own shirt and wrenched the sleeve off from the shoulder seam.

"It's not that bad," Lily said, though I could hear the pain in her voice. "I don't think it cut that deep."

"I'll cut him into a billion fucking pieces," I promised, wrapping my sleeve around her forearm in some kind of bandage.

But how was I going to keep that promise? I didn't even know where those fuckers had come from, let alone where they were now. I wanted to tell Lily it'd all be okay, that all was good in the world again, but I didn't really believe that.

I raked my hand into my hair and stalked from one end of the alley to the other. It was a short walk, but I couldn't seem to stop myself. I smacked the toe of my shoe against one wall, swung around, paced over to kick the other, back and forth, like one of Nox's pinballs. So many emotions churned inside me that I had the sense that if I punched one of those walls right now, I'd send the whole thing tumbling down.

Probably on Lily's head. *That* wouldn't help anything. A groan of frustration reverberated out of me.

"Hey," Lily said. "Ruin, it's all right. It looks like the bleeding's already stopped. And you're okay, aren't you? Those asswipes were trying to *kill* you." Anger rippled through her voice. "I should have summoned a wave of sewer water to knock them over. I was so startled—"

"It's not your fault," I interrupted, still ping-ponging back and forth through the alley. "I should have realized—I should have taken them down faster—I shouldn't have let them *get away*—shit."

"It isn't your fault either," Lily said defiantly, but her eyes had widened with obvious worry. For *me*. When she was the one who'd actually been hurt here.

I had to get control of myself, find the upbeat attitude that'd gotten me through so much in life. But I couldn't seem to get a handle on it, and that only made me more pissed off with myself.

"Just—just stop," Lily said. "Stop and talk to me. People have done crap like this before. A couple weeks ago, a guy had a gun to your head. I almost got pirate-walked off a dock. What's different about this?"

I didn't exactly know, but I slowed and then came to a halt as her appeal sank in. She grasped my arm, and I bowed my head over hers, trying to sort through the thoughts ricocheting around in my head.

"They hurt you," I said, "and I couldn't even make them pay. And I can't make it better. I can't even cheer you up, because I can't cheer myself up, and that's the only thing I'm really good at normally. Being happy. Making people happy. If I can't manage that, then I'm just making things worse."

Even when I could cheer people up, that didn't necessarily stop the world from going to hell. Back when Lily was a kid, I'd brightened her days every way I could, but everything had gone horribly wrong anyway. I'd promised her I was there for her, and the pricks in her life had managed to rip her away from us anyway. All the hope I'd offered her had been a *lie*.

Lily's arms came up to wrap around me. She tucked her head against my shoulder. "You're not making things worse. And you don't have to be happy all the time. No one is."

"It's the only way I can make sure no one can bring me down," I said. "It's how I stop the guys from getting too low—it's how I keep you from getting too sad. But… you don't really like it anymore, do you? So it doesn't even work."

Lily hugged me tighter. "It does," she said fiercely. "I'm sorry if I haven't shown it. I—I don't always know how to react to how positive you are about everything usually, and maybe I get a bit grumbly about it, but it doesn't mean it bothers me. I like you the way you are. I like that you can see the good side of everything and that you make me notice the good sides too. Okay?"

Gradually, the clenching sensation inside me let go. I drank in Lily's watery floral smell and let out a ragged sigh. Then, with a glimmer of lightness inside me, a smile curled my lips. "You like me."

Lily snorted with amusement. "As if *that* hasn't been pretty obvious already. I wouldn't put up with you stealing half my bed otherwise."

"A quarter," I argued. "I leave most of it for you."

"Maybe a third, then," she said in that grumbly voice, but I could hear the thread of affection running through it. "You can't protect me from everything, Ruin. None of you can. I wish I could protect *you* better. But this is all new territory, so we'll just muddle through it the best way we can, right? And it's easier muddling if you're looking on the bright side for the rest of us. At least, I think so."

"Okay." The light inside me brightened into a glow that filled my entire chest. I pulled back to kiss Lily on the lips, reveling in the contented noise she made and the softness of her mouth. Then my stomach growled.

Lily laughed and poked me in the belly. "We'd better go get that dinner." She eyed my torn shirt. "If they're not going to look at us too weird."

I shrugged, barely feeling the chilly air on my bared arm. "It's a new fashion statement," I announced.

"If anyone could make it one, you could," Lily muttered through her smile.

I tucked my arm through hers and leaned close to murmur in her ear as I ushered her back onto the sidewalk. "We'll go get dinner, and when we get back to your apartment, I'm going to devour *you*."

The flush that colored Lily's cheeks made me want to bring her to moaning pleasure this very instant, but I couldn't get that distracted out here. The pricks who'd come after me were still lurking around.

If I got eyes on them again, I'd make them pay until they needed to be scraped off the sidewalk. And then I'd kill them a little more, just because.

seventeen

Lily

The first sign that something wasn't quite right at work was the envelope labeled *URGENT* that was sitting in the middle of the packing table when I got back to the mailroom after a trip through the building with my cart. Rupert was standing over it with his arms folded over his chest.

"Why didn't you bring this one with you?" he demanded. "It was supposed to be in Horace Sanders' hands an hour ago!"

I stared at the offending envelope, which was a total stranger to me as far as I could remember. "It wasn't here an hour ago."

Rupert let out one of those huffs I was starting to think he should trademark. "Of course it was here an hour ago. The delivery manifest indicates it was delivered at ten this morning."

"Well, it wasn't *here* in the—"

"Stop making excuses," he barked at me. "You obviously weren't paying enough attention, and it got missed under the other mail. Just get it to Mr. Sanders now!"

I imagined his head heron pecking him hard enough to split his skull as I snatched up the envelope and hustled to the fifth floor to deliver it.

I might have thought it really had been a mistake on my part—that I was still kind of rattled from the attack on Ruin last night and the stinging scratch that was bandaged and hidden under the sleeve of my work blouse, and so had let something slip—except it happened again right after my lunch break. When I returned to the mailroom after my hasty meal, a small box was perched on one of the shelves in plain view, with big letters stamped on it saying, *To be received by noon.*

It was almost one.

Surely I hadn't missed seeing that package too, especially after I'd been on high alert because of my previous oversight? I got the distinct impression it was thumbing its nose at me... somehow, without having a nose or thumbs.

But there wasn't anyone to argue with about it, since Rupert had gone off to eat his own lunch. I just grabbed the package, muttered, "I hope you're happy with yourself" at it, and hightailed it to the eleventh floor as fast as my feet could take me. The woman I handed the box off to glowered at me as she took it.

Today was not going well at all. So much for proving to the Gauntts that I could handle the pace of the head office.

As soon as that thought crossed through my mind, I froze in place.

That was it, wasn't it? They didn't *want* me to be able to handle things here. They'd clearly hoped to push me out. When I hadn't taken the direct bait, they'd decided to force the issue rather than asking nicely.

Someone was messing with the mail to make me look incompetent. Unfortunately, they were succeeding.

I didn't have much time to dig into that problem, or I'd fall behind on the duties I actually could keep up with. The Gauntts hadn't been lying that this was a busy workplace. I spent a few minutes searching the mailroom for any tucked away letters or packages or, hell, secret passageways, but when I didn't turn up anything right away, I had to get back on the everyday mail sorting. There were a whole bunch of glossy laminated envelopes that needed to be out of here within the hour.

Rupert returned while I was doing that, gave me a vaguely disgruntled look as if I were slacking rather than doing the basics of my job, and puttered around for several minutes before heading off with a small cart.

Was he involved in the plot to screw me over? He definitely didn't seem all that happy about me being here, but that'd started before I'd talked to the Gauntts.

I had no idea how to tell whether he was actively sabotaging me on their instructions or just being a sourpuss about the fact that I had a fashion sense he didn't totally approve of.

I was just finishing with the batch of mailings when a slim man with brown hair combed forward so straight you could have used it as a ruler marched into the room. When he spotted me, he kept marching right over to my table.

"I'm admin assistant to Casper Dodds. He was supposed to have an important package delivered this morning, but it hasn't been brought to his desk. The instructions should have been *very* clear."

A chill trickled down my back. I recognized Dodds as one of the bigwigs who had their offices on the upper floors. I'd never met this admin assistant because all his communications went through the woman who was secretary to the secretaries.

I waved vaguely at the shelving units and empty carts around me. "All the incoming mail has already been distributed through the building. This stuff is outgoing. I can't bring up what hasn't arrived."

The assistant drew his chin up higher, as if that would make him taller than me instead of the same height. "We have confirmation from the sender that it was shipped out, and confirmation from the delivery service that it arrived at this building. I hope you aren't suggesting that you *lost* it."

"No, no, of course not," I said quickly. I definitely

couldn't accuse the owners of the company of having hidden it away to make a lowly mail clerk look bad.

Gritting my teeth, I crouched down to check if any packages could have fallen to the floor beneath the tables or shelving units. Wouldn't it be nice to get a solution that easy? But there was nothing down there except a few scraps of paper the janitor would sweep up and a worn spot on the linoleum where Rupert liked to pace.

Oh, and a frog. It hopped over to me from the other side of the table, like I'd ducked down here to have a chat. Perfect.

"I'm *waiting*," the admin assistant said in a voice that was freezing over. "A lot of business is riding on Mr. Dodds receiving this package in a timely matter. If you've dropped the ball on it, I'll have to report the matter higher up."

Shit. And that might be enough of an excuse for the big bosses to kick me to the curb. I wet my lips, scrambling for an answer. What the hell could be in this package that was so important anyway? A scroll holding the secrets of eternal life?

The Skullbreakers might have been able to help advise on that one.

The frog hopped closer, but it wasn't carrying any errant packages. It was only hanging out here making me look crazy.

I paused, letting that thought sink in. A sliver of a smile tugged at my lips.

I set down my hand and surreptitiously scooped up

the frog and set it on my shoulder—at the opposite side from where the assistant was standing. Then I straightened back up with my arms at my sides, paying no attention to it at all.

"I'm sorry," I said in an even voice. "My supervisor should be back soon—it's possible he took the package with him on his last delivery run. In the meantime—"

The assistant's gaze had zeroed in on my shoulder. Or rather, the friendly amphibian currently perched on my shoulder. His eyes bugged out. "Why are you carrying around a *frog*?"

I blinked at him, knitting my brow as if I didn't understand what he'd said. "Pardon me?"

He flicked his hand toward my shoulder. "There's a frog sitting on your shoulder! Where did that come from? What are you trying to pull here?"

I glanced over at my shoulder and gave my best impression of seeing only the fabric of my sweater. Then I gave the assistant an even more puzzled look. "What are *you* trying to pull? I don't have anything on my shoulder. And how could I have a frog with me?"

I must have been convincing enough in my disbelief, because the man grimaced and rubbed at his eyes. "It's right *there*," he said, and motioned at me even more briskly, as if to poke my slimy companion.

I couldn't let him touch it and feel that it was really there. I flinched as if I thought he was going to smack me, and the frog went leaping away to who knew where. Hopefully somewhere far out of sight. But the other outcome of my reaction was that the assistant's fingers swiped over my chest instead of my shoulder.

He jerked his hand back as if he'd been burned, but I'd already urged my eyebrows to shoot up as far as they could go. "Whoa!" I said, summoning all the offense I could. "You come down here threatening my job and then try to grope me?"

His face stiffened in an expression of horror. "It was an accident—the frog—" His gaze darted around searching out the little green animal and clearly didn't find it.

I set my hands on my hips with all the bravado I could muster. "That's a pretty crazy excuse for feeling me up. What is it with you and this frog?"

"Crazy," he murmured to himself, and shook his head as if trying to clear it. "It was *there…*"

"Sure," I scoffed. "Like I wouldn't be able to tell if I had a freaking *frog* sitting on me. I think I should be the one putting in a complaint to HR."

The man blanched. He held up his hands and backed away from me, all his previous haughtiness vanished. "No. There's no need for that. I've just—it's been a tense day—I promise you I didn't mean to touch you at all."

He spun around and hustled out of the mailroom without another word about this super special package. Probably more worried about what was going on inside his head than inside any cardboard box. I exhaled with only a small sense of triumph. I still had to *find* that package before someone else came around demanding it.

I stuck my current batch of envelopes into the spot for outgoing mail and glanced around. The mailroom didn't lead directly outside. Delivery trucks parked by an entrance around the back of the building and unloaded their shipments there, and some worker or another carried the loads of mail into this room, just as they periodically came by and picked up the outgoing bins before one or another truck was due.

Anything coming in could be intercepted along that short route, by the workers themselves or someone coming by under the pretense of overseeing them.

I darted out into the hall and over to the back doors. There was nothing to see outside except a stretch of gloomy asphalt with a currently empty lane and rows of cars parked farther from the building. No precious packages chilling out there.

I pulled back into the building and scanned the hall. There was another room between the door and the mailroom—a supply room I'd had to go into only once in search of a new pen. Most of the mailroom-specific supplies were kept right on hand.

Pulling open that door, I peered into the dim room. My fumbling hand found a light switch. There were shelves stacked with boxes of pens, pencils, and highlighters, reams of printer and photocopier paper, spare keyboards and computer mice... Oh, and there was a cardboard box that didn't look like it really belonged shoved under one of those shelving units with only a bit of the corner in view.

I knelt down and tugged it out. Yep, addressed to Casper Dodds, marked urgent. Someone had stashed it in here, probably to drop it off in the mailroom later as if it'd been there all along, trying to make *me* feel insane.

So much for that, suckers, I thought at my unknown opponents, and pictured waving the package in Nolan Gauntt's face for good measure. Then I dashed off to deliver it to its intended recipient like it was a box of dicks I couldn't wait to get off my hands.

I'd gotten through this attempt at ousting me, but it didn't seem likely that it'd be the last. How far would they go next time?

eighteen

Lily

I'd told the guys that I didn't want them experimenting with their superpowers in my apartment, especially now that I'd need to be claiming that damage deposit tout suite. But their supernatural gifts involved frying things, and mine only brought all the frogs in the yard—or got things kind of wet. So I cut myself a little slack when it came to practicing.

And if I did it while they were out doing their gangster things, they couldn't even hassle me about any apparent hypocrisy.

Because I didn't want to explode the pipes in the apartment, and working on subtle effects was better for my control anyway, I'd set up a few water bottles on the table as well as some empty cups. My goal was to practice compelling the water out of the bottles into the cups with minimal spillage. And also to get it jumping between bottles or work my powers on more than one at a time, if I felt ready to get that ambitious.

If I ended up having to go head-to-head with the Gauntts, I'd better be able to wield my marshy magic with all possible skill. I didn't want there to be any chance of screwing up. And the clearer it was that *I* was a conscious force to be reckoned with rather than the pipes just happening to burst at the wrong moment, the better.

The hard part, like when I'd been down at the marsh, was getting myself keyed up enough to provoke the hum of power inside me. I still couldn't accomplish anything just by glowering at the table. I dragged in a breath and thought back to the prick who'd barged into the mailroom to berate me—and the Gauntts setting me up so I'd look totally incompetent.

My hands curled into fists at my sides. My jaw tightened. And anger resonated through my chest at just the right harmony.

"No fucking way," I informed the bottle I decided represented Nolan Gauntt, because it looked a little more puffed up than the others. Pretentious prick. "You aren't knocking me down that easily."

I concentrated on the liquid contents, silently calling them to me. But not in a sudden splash—slowly, deliberately.

A wavering stream of water rose up from the mouth

of the bottle. A few splatters dropped to dapple the tabletop with tiny puddles. A sudden thin jet shot out and smacked me in the face.

I sputtered, and the rest of the water splashed onto the table, some of it dripping off the sides.

Cursing Nolan—both the real one and his bottle equivalent—and all things aquatic, I sopped up the mess with a dishtowel and squared my shoulders to try again. At least this time I had plenty of irritation coursing through me before I even thought about the jerks I was up against.

After several attempts and a few more watery facials, I finally managed to get all the remaining liquid from one bottle into one of the cups. Then I emptied two simultaneously, switching my focus back and forth as one or the other stream got shaky.

I was about halfway through when a knock thumped on the apartment door.

I flinched, and water spewed everywhere. And I do mean everywhere. It sprayed droplets across the kitchen cabinets, counter, and fridge, rained over the floor, and spurted all over my chest as if several aquatic gods had gotten very enthusiastic with their money shots all at once.

"Lily?" Marisol's voice carried through the door. "Are you home?"

My pulse hiccupped. I grabbed the dish towel, which was unfortunately only slightly less wet than I was, and dabbed at the sopping spots on my shirt as I hustled over to the door. "I'm here. Is everything okay?"

I opened the door maybe a little more frantically than was totally necessary. My little sister peered in at me, her backpack slung casually over one shoulder, and gave me a perfect expression of teenage bemusement. I realized that drips were trickling down my arms from my hair. I basically looked like I'd stepped out of a shower I'd been taking fully clothed.

"Are *you* okay?" Marisol asked.

"Yes, yes," I said, fumbling for an explanation. "I was just… washing dishes, dropped a pot into the sink too fast and splashed myself. No big deal. It'll dry."

Marisol nodded slowly. "Okay. I just—I got your address from some paper at the house. I think the hospital sent it to Mom when you were moving back. I thought since we're going to be living together soon anyway, hopefully it'd be all right if I hung out here for a little while? I can't get away with browsing the bookstore all weekend, and being at home…" She made a face.

A pang of mourning for all the things my sister should have had resonated through me. I motioned her into the apartment past me. "Of course. I—" I followed her path with my gaze, and took in exactly what I was welcoming her into for the first time.

Not that I hadn't known how crappy this apartment was or how chaotic it'd become since the guys had essentially moved in. But I hadn't really *looked* at it, not from the perspective of someone who didn't already have all the backstory, in a while.

A puddle of water was still spreading across the table

and dripping into another puddle on the floor. Bottles and glasses stood in its midst like transparent islands. In the living room area, the guys had been cleaning up after their constant snacking, but a couple of chip bags and a few wrappers had been missed, peeking around the shabby furniture. The uninflated mattresses and sleeping bags had been tossed into a haphazard heap like a fabric mountain looming over the back of the futon.

The futon itself was stacked with Kai's latest haul of library news magazines, while the crates that served as end tables had become display stands for Jett's favorite artistic compositions. One of those involved my salt and pepper shakers standing upside down with a tissue box balanced on top of them and an empty Chinese takeout container on top of that. The other was a painted piece of paper folded to stand upright, which wouldn't have been all that concerning if I wasn't abruptly sure that several of the deeper reddish-brown streaks were blood, not paint.

And the place smelled. Not in a horribly offensive way I didn't think, but in a leathery, boozy, vaguely musky way it definitely hadn't before four former gangsters had moved in.

Marisol stopped in her tracks a few steps inside, taking the whole scene in. Her nose wrinkled for a second, and her posture tensed. I got the impression she was considering backing right out again.

"It's been a crazy few weeks," I said quickly. *And I mean that literally.* "I had some unexpected guests come by. But the new apartment I've lined up in Mayfield is way bigger and nicer than this. You'll love it! And we'll get better furniture and stuff as soon as we can." The guys would probably volunteer to fund an entire Pinterest makeover, but I was trying to rely on their generosity—and the questionable methods that funded that generosity—as little as possible.

"Okay," Marisol said again, but she definitely sounded more hesitant now. My chest constricted. She glanced around, her hand tightening around the strap of her backpack. "Can I sit down?"

It was a reasonable question, because the chairs by the kitchen table all held puddles of their own, and Kai's magazines had the prime spots on the futon. I rushed over and hefted them onto the floor, which wouldn't score me points for neatness but at least opened up a seat.

"There you go," I said. "Do you want anything to drink? Or a snack? I'm sure I've got something around." Please, dear Lord, let the guys not have completely cleared out the fridge before they left.

Please let them not come bursting back in here while Marisol was around. I still had to prepare her for meeting *that* craziness up close and personal.

"No, I'm fine," Marisol said in a tone that didn't sound fine at all. She was probably terrified to eat anything that'd been stored in this place.

I groped for the right thing to say to make this better. It wasn't like I could tell her I'd been experimenting with supernatural abilities or that I'd unexpectedly had some childhood friends I'd thought were imaginary show up as houseguests with a kind of skewed sense of propriety. Although maybe she already knew something about my abilities? I wasn't sure how much she'd seen when I'd freaked out all those years ago.

There were still too many things locked away in that blank gap in my memory.

The spot with the birthmark under my arm started to itch. I let myself scratch at it as I sat down on the other side of the futon.

Marisol had started studying Jett's painting. I guessed that wasn't surprising considering her own visual art interests, but I didn't really like her looking at it so close up. Much more chance she'd notice the odd hue to those particular streaks. And had he incorporated some smears of juice from one of Ruin's lemons too?

"This is kind of cool," Marisol said. "Did you make it?"

I couldn't blame her for the skepticism in her voice. When I'd doodled alongside her when we were younger, my attempts at drawing the same sorts of mythical creatures she did had generally resulted in them looking like centaurs or nymphs that'd been run over by a tank. And then pecked at by vultures for good measure.

"Ah, no," I said. "One of my guests. He's quite an artist. You'd probably like him." I hoped that was true. At least she had something in common with one of the guys.

Marisol's gaze flicked to me, and I realized my mistake a moment too late. "*He?*" she repeated, arching her eyebrows. "Was he one of those guys who honked at us the other day at the house? Is this a *boy*friend?"

The funny thing was, out of all four of the guys, Jett was the one who'd been least enthusiastic about anything resembling a dating relationship. But I wasn't going to open that can of worms with my little sister. Instead, I fixed her with my best big sister glower. "Should I start asking you about your love life? All the boys you've been crushing on at school?"

The blush that spread across her cheeks told me I'd won the standoff. She stuck her tongue out at me and then paused as if formulating another question. I wasn't sure whether to be relieved or have another panic attack when a text alert chimed on my phone.

It was from Nox. *We're heading back soon. Figured we'd bring lunch. What do you want? Ruin promises that he'll keep his extreme spice to himself.*

My lips twitched with a smile, and Marisol's eyebrows lifted even higher. Panic attack—panic attack was definitely the correct option here.

No need to bring me anything, I typed hurriedly, and then inspiration struck. *I'm going out to lunch with my sister.*

Perfect! It got Marisol out of the apartment and away from the guys' arrival all in one go, without making her feel unwelcome.

"Hey," I said to her, getting up. "Why don't we get out of this place and grab something to eat? It'll be on me, of course. Do you still like that burger joint over on Washington Avenue?"

"Well…" Marisol said as she stood up too.

I nudged her with my elbow. "It's okay if your tastes have changed since you were nine. I realize you're a sophisticated sixteen-year-old now."

Marisol grinned. "I'd love to go to the Greek place that opened up on Main Street. I had no idea souvlaki was so good! But Wade doesn't like it, so we only went the one time." A shadow crossed her face.

I'd have cracked open my own ribs to stop her from ever having to look like that again. At least I could give her a temporary reprieve. Soon—soon she'd be away from him forever.

"Sounds perfect to me," I said, tugging her along. "And you can tell me all about what kind of school you want me to find for you in Mayfield. I'm sure they've got more choice than we have out here."

My sister's smile came back, just as bright as before, and that felt like a victory—even when I had to stop at the door and rush back to change into a dry shirt, because I'd forgotten my earlier watery accident.

I managed to feel confident through the lunch and after I waved goodbye to Marisol and returned to the apartment to hear about the guys' adventures trying to arrange a confrontation with this Skeleton Corps gang, all the way until I was crawling into bed that night.

But the doubts must have been lingering underneath. It felt like the second I closed my eyes, I was drowning again. The weeds were clutching my ankles and the marsh-water closing over my head. The darkness was choking out the light and suffocating me.

Twisting currents turned my skin clammy; chilly liquid flooded my lungs. I kicked and kicked but I just kept sinking down—

I woke up with a jolt and found myself drenched in a cold sweat. Swallowing hard, I swiped my hand across my damp forehead. The darkness of the cramped room around me felt almost as suffocating as my nightmare had.

I'd lost something. Something that was buried way down in the murky depths of my mind, beyond my reach.

For all I knew, it was lurking there ready to pull me under at the moment I least expected it. And if Marisol was with me when that happened, it might drag her down too.

nineteen

Nox

"They're obviously *really* scared of us," Ruin said in his usual breezy way as we got off our bikes outside our new base of Skullbreaker operations. "Why else would the Skeleton Corps be avoiding us so much? They know we'll crush them as soon as we get the chance."

Kai raised his eyebrows at our eternal optimist. "Or they don't think we're worth bothering with. They don't know who we are. We haven't established anything yet. The fact that we're bothering them about murders from more than twenty years ago probably makes them think we've got a screw loose."

"Or they know they're guilty and so they're laying low," Ruin insisted.

"We'll dig them out eventually," I said, stopping at the former restaurant's door to pull out my keys. "And then they'll find out just how many screws got loosened in the last twenty years."

Before I could put the keys to use, a figure got out of a car a little way down the street and ambled over to us with a casual but purposeful air. It was obvious he was aiming for us. I paused, tossing the keys in my hand and studying him.

He looked the equivalent of five in gangster terms, like a kid who's gotten confident on his feet but has no idea how much he doesn't know yet. In actual years, he wasn't much more than a kid either. With that babyface, I didn't figure he'd hit twenty yet. I'd wreaked plenty of havoc before I'd reached official adulthood myself, but he obviously wasn't any sort of high authority figure.

"Gentlemen," he said with a sarcastic lilt to his tone as he came to a stop in front of us. I immediately bristled at the aura of condescension radiating off him, as if he found it *amusing* that he was stooping to speak to us at all. "I heard you've been trying to arrange a meeting with the Skeleton Corps."

At those last two words, I perked up despite my annoyance. Maybe all the busting heads we'd been doing for the past few days had gotten some results.

"We have," I said, stepping in front of the others with a flex of my muscles, which through the magic of ghostly possession and all the workouts I'd been getting while busting those heads were now back to nearly their previous substantial brawn. "Are they ready to talk to us?"

"*I'm* here to talk to you," the kid said, like we should be honored he'd bothered to grace us with his presence. "If you've got anything to say worth passing on, I'll bring it to the rest of them."

I cocked my head, looking him up and down and not finding anything that made me happier in my assessment. The guy clearly hadn't even been born yet when our first lives had ended. He'd know fuck-all about our murders.

I jerked my chin toward him. "We need to speak to someone higher up, someone who's been part of the crew for a while."

"The Skeleton Corps doesn't show up at anyone's beck and call," the kid retorted. "And nothing we've heard has made us think you've got anything to say worth bringing in people who have much better things to spend their time on."

My hands clenched at my sides, and Jett let out a peeved grunt behind me. We'd show them what we were worth, that was for sure.

"We need information about a hostile takedown in Lovell Rise twenty-one years ago," I said. "We were told your boys are the ones most likely to know who involved. Or maybe your boys are the ones who carried it out."

The kid shrugged. "And why should we dredge up ancient history for a bunch of nobodies who've been going around making a nuisance of themselves?"

Ruin gave a low growl. I suspected we were all quickly getting to the same page that there needed to be a little more head-busting before the day was over.

I moved closer, drawing myself up as straight as I could so I loomed a good six inches over the kid. "Why should we have to explain ourselves to you? There are things you don't know, pipsqueak. Things that are important that you haven't got a clue about. You can get your head out of your ass and arrange a real meet-up, or maybe we'll insert a few more things into that hole for proper motivation."

The guy shook his head with an air like he was five seconds away from tsking his fucking tongue at us. "I'll go with neither. Have a nice life!"

He turned on his heel like he thought we were going to let him just walk away with that send-off. Time to show these pretentious pricks exactly who they were dealing with—and that we wouldn't be ignored.

I made a quick gesture with my hand as I lunged at the guy. My friends followed without a second's hesitation.

He wasn't a total idiot, I'd give him that. He dodged my first punch even though it came from behind and swung around, jerking a gun from the waist of his jeans. But I didn't even give him time to aim it. I was already smashing my elbow into his wrist.

The pistol skittered under a car. The kid sprang backward, and then Ruin and Jett were on him.

Ruin plowed right into the guy, flipping him off his feet. Jett caught him in mid tumble and slammed him downward so his skull smacked against the concrete. As the kid let out a pained grunt, Kai swept in with a few quick strikes that sent him spinning on his head.

Jett chuckled darkly as he whipped the guy around even faster, turning him into a human dreidel. The kid swung out an arm and managed to grab Jett's leg, but Jett simply released him right as I landed a kick to his side that sent him sprawling on his stomach instead.

Before he could scramble upright, I planted one foot between his shoulder blades with just enough weight to strain but not fracture his spine.

"You delivered the Skeleton Corps' message," I said, ignoring the curses he was spitting at us. "Here's one from us: We don't fuck around. It's up to you whether more of you end up bruised and bleeding, but we're getting our answers either way. You know where to find us when you're ready to talk real business."

I finished off with a boot to his butt. He threw himself to his feet and whirled around, but looking at the four of us while he stood unarmed and battered, he made one smart choice. Instead of taking another jab at us, he staggered to his car and dove into the driver's seat.

It only took him a matter of seconds to start the ignition and roar off down the street like a bat out of hell. Or maybe into hell, from the way things were going.

Ruin whooped and pumped his hand in the air. I couldn't share the same exuberance.

"We have to be even more on guard from now on," I told my men. "They might take this as a sign that we deserve serious consideration—but that serious consideration might mean attempting to wipe us off the map all over again. Stay alert, especially around the new headquarters."

I wanted to feel satisfied, but we hadn't gotten any answers at all, only confirmation that these Skeleton Corps assholes knew we existed. If that got us slaughtered all over again because I hadn't made a clear enough impact, I'd come back just to kill *myself* for being such a disaster.

We headed into the former restaurant, but even sitting on the fake throne didn't give me the boost of certainty I wanted. Also, it made me think of Lily and all the fun we'd had there the other night, which I couldn't have without her here. I gave Jett a little while longer to finish rearranging the tables to his indecipherable standards and then announced that we were heading back to her apartment.

Apparently it was a day of interruptions, though. We'd only just come out to our bikes when a white van pulled up on the other side of the street. I wouldn't have thought much of it if three hulking dudes hadn't jumped out of the back, charged straight at Kai, snatched him up, and hauled him away.

"What the fuck!" I shouted, charging after them. But the element of surprise had bought them just enough time that the doors were slamming shut as I reached them. The van roared off down the street so abruptly it nearly tore off my fingers where I'd been grabbing at the handles.

I hurtled back to the bikes and threw myself onto my own. "After them!" I hollered, and the three of us careened after the fleeing vehicle.

Jumbled thoughts whirled through my head as we sped after the van. Had the Skeleton Corps retaliated already? We'd only sent off their kid about a half hour ago. And why would they have wanted specifically Kai? He'd done the least amount of fighting. If they were going to target anyone, it should have been me.

The men who'd grabbed Kai hadn't given me a gangster vibe, now that I looked back on the moment. They'd charged in there so quickly I hadn't had much time to reflect on the details, but they'd been wearing plain tees and slacks, and I didn't remember any tattoos. Tough but more clean-cut than you'd typically get from guys working the street, especially the muscle.

It didn't matter. Whoever they were, they were going to pay. Nobody messed with my men and survived.

The van swerved around a corner up ahead. I motioned to Jett and Ruin and shouted my instructions over the rumble of the engines. "Stay on their tail, as close as you can get. I'm going to try to cut them off."

They both nodded. I shot down the nearest parallel side-street, gunning my engine to even greater speeds. I was probably leaving rubber behind on the asphalt, but that was a small sacrifice to make to the gods of the road.

I wove in between the other vehicles on the street, ignoring the protests and insults yelled after me. The van wouldn't have the same advantage. I needed to get ahead of them. And if there was a space I could squeeze through, who the hell was anyone to tell me I shouldn't take that opening?

After five blocks, I estimated I had enough of a lead. I veered down one of the cross-streets and slowed as I reached the next intersection.

The van was just a block away, rushing toward me. I pulled out my gun and got into position. As I shot at its tires to blow them out, I pulled my bike partly in front of them.

Two of my bullets hit their marks. The van swerved and shuddered as the tires went flat. Jett and Ruin zoomed up on either side.

The guy staring at me through the windshield was about half the size of the hulks who'd kidnapped Kai and looked totally terrified. I shot him through the glass and tore around to the back of the van, not caring about the shrieks that were starting to rise up from bystanders along the street or the traffic we'd stalled. We'd be out of here long before the police could show up.

The back doors flew open as the three of us converged on them. Jett and Ruin had taken out their guns too. In near-perfect unison, we blasted away the three beefy dudes who were making to spring out at us.

They crumpled in a pile by the back tires. It'd been almost too easy. I squinted into the dimness of the van's interior to see what the hell they'd been doing to our guy... and found him tied up and gagged with four dorks who looked like they'd stepped out of a suburban soap opera poised around him.

The middle-aged woman had a fluffy pixie cut and a cardigan tied around her shoulders. The man next to her had slicked his hair back like a business exec and stuffed his broad chest into a polo shirt. They were staring at me with panicked expressions, all the color drained from their faces. The older man and the twenty-something woman with them looked like they were ready to puke.

These were definitely not gangsters.

"Who the hell are you?" I demanded, leaping into the back of the van with my gun still ready. "Get away from him."

"He's our son," the middle-aged woman wailed even as the man I figured was her husband wrapped her arms around her defensively. "I don't know what you've done to our Zach, but he belongs with us."

Oh, fuck. It was Kai's host's family. Unlike Jett's, these folks hadn't been satisfied with phone calls.

Ruin had dashed over to free Kai. As soon as the gag was out of his mouth, our smart-aleck sneered at the suburbanites. "I'm not your son anymore. I don't need any fucking intervention."

"But—" the woman started.

Kai got up as soon as Ruin had untied his legs and glowered down at her. "I'm an adult. That makes this kidnapping, you idiots. Which is illegal, in case you didn't know."

We weren't really in a position to be lecturing them

about criminal activities, but his supposed parents cowered a little.

"We're looking after 'Zach' now," I said, folding my arms over my chest. "He's got better things to do than spend time with you all. If you hire any other thugs to arrange some stupid 'intervention,' next time you'll be lying on the pavement with them. Got it?"

At my last words, all four of the family members flinched. No one argued. I nodded to Kai, and we tramped out of the van to return to our bikes, leaving the dimwits inside to figure out where they went from here with a busted van and four murder victims.

Kai tipped his head to me as he got onto Jett's bike behind him. "Thanks. They were babbling all kinds of new age feelings woo woo to try to un-brainwash me or something. And people think *we're* crazy."

The sense of accomplishment I'd been missing earlier trickled up through my torso. I'd done my job as the leader of the Skullbreakers—I'd protected my own. I gave him a grim but genuine smile. "We've got your back, like always."

If only we could have hoped that the Skeleton bozos would be half as easy to terrorize.

twenty

Lily

I'd been in worse ladies' rooms, but the restroom on the fourteenth floor of the Thrivewell Enterprises building wasn't exactly a pleasant place to while away the hours. For one, I had to stay in the stall perched on the toilet's tank with my feet on the seat so that anyone who poked their head into the room wouldn't spot my shoes. For another, the sickly-sweet smell of the cleaner they used to make sure the room didn't smell like urine was almost as bad as urine itself.

And then, an hour after my shift ended, the lights went off. Wonderful.

I distracted myself by fiddling around with my phone and hoping that Kai was having at least as bad a time in the men's washroom, since this strategy had been his idea, after all. We'd slipped away right at the time when our shifts usually ended and were now waiting out the last few stragglers in the office. Kai had determined that the security guard did one sweep of all the floors and then settled in on the ground level to watch over the entrance. As soon as he was gone, we could roam freely.

And that meant we should be able to roam right up to Nolan Gauntt's office. *He* definitely wouldn't be working late, because he and Marie had that benefit dinner tonight. Kai had managed to pick up the code to unlock the private upper-floor elevator from surreptitiously watching the secretary. How he planned to get into Nolan's office itself, I didn't know, but he rarely seemed to act without a strategy in place.

I'd been sitting there another half hour in the dark when the text from Kai finally arrived, with a faint vibration of my phone since I'd turned all the sounds off for this mission. *All clear. Meet me at the stairs.*

On my way, I wrote back, and scrambled out of the stall as fast as my feet could take me.

It was dark in the vast room of cubicles too, only a thin light emanating from the emergency exit sign over the stairwell. The glow gleamed off Kai's glasses as he waited for me to reach him. He motioned for me to follow him into the stairwell.

"I heard the security guy go by twenty minutes ago," he said in a low voice as we headed up to the highest floor we could access by stairs. "Based on his typical schedule, he should have taken the elevator down to the lobby about ten minutes ago. As long as we don't make a racket loud enough to reach down there—and we're careful going out the back way—we should be fine."

I worried at my lower lip. "Are you sure there aren't any security cameras in Nolan's office?"

"There could be," Kai said with no apparent concern. "But it'd only be something he could check on his own after we're long gone. The head honcho wouldn't want any lowly grunt workers getting a glimpse inside his private sanctum." He patted the leather shoulder bag he was carrying. "We'll put on ski masks before we go up that far so that if any of the top brass checks the footage later, if they bother to, they won't be able to tell who we were."

"Okay." I suspected Nolan would be able to guess, but what really mattered was whether he'd have any proof he could give to the police. I suspected I was still on kind of shaky ground with the local law enforcement after the whole being accused of spray-painting dicks on the grocery store incident.

Kai moved with an eager, purposeful energy I didn't often see in him. It reminded me of when we'd gone to interview for these jobs in the first place. Seeing that assured intensity in him again sent a tingle over my skin that I really couldn't indulge right now.

On the fifteenth floor, there was a door to the next level of the stairwell, which was naturally locked. The bigwigs needed an escape route, but they didn't want us plebs having access to them through it. We slipped out into the room where Kai usually worked instead.

He took my hand, the skin-to-skin contact sending a ripple of heat up my arm, and guided me through the dim space toward the exclusive elevator. We'd almost reached that end of the room when the regular elevator, behind us, pinged to signal that the car was about to arrive.

"Shit," Kai hissed, and hauled me through a doorway just ahead of us.

The door clicked shut in our wake. My hip banged into some large rectangular object just inside. Kai steadied me and tugged me farther inside, past the thing.

"Photocopy room," he muttered under his breath. "Security officer must have forgotten something. No reason for him to come in here."

This room was pitch black. I reached out and found the hulking photocopier just inches from where I was standing. My elbow brushed a cabinet on the other side. The space wasn't much bigger than a closet.

We stood there, no sound but the faint rasp of our breaths and the thumping of my heart—until the thud of heavy footsteps reached my ears. It sounded like the security guard was heading right this way.

I froze, knowing we had nowhere to run. Kai's grip on my hand tightened. He held in place for the space of a few more heartbeats and then, when the footsteps came even closer, yanked me deeper into the room.

We stumbled into the gap between the back wall and the cabinet, so narrow I had to round my shoulders so they'd fit. When the door handle squeaked, Kai pushed closer against me to stay completely hidden by the cabinet.

Our bodies aligned from chest to feet. His compact frame was hotter than I'd expected, almost blazing, and it set my own alight as his breath tickled over my face. The scent of his skin filled my nose, a citrusy tang mingled with musky leather. And despite the precarious situation we were in—or maybe partly because of it—a different sort of adrenaline raced through me alongside my fear.

I had the sudden, wild urge to pull him as tight against me as I could, to soak in all his heat and the solid planes of footballer muscle that had gotten leaner but not disappeared since he'd taken over Zach's body. To run my hands down his chest and up into his hair. To find out what noises I could provoke from this intently analytical man's mouth.

He'd said before that he'd noticed my "appeal." That he wasn't going to pursue it only because it'd be a distraction. Of course, what else could it be right now when we were literally in the middle of the riskiest gambit we'd attempted since setting our sights on Nolan Gauntt?

The door swung open. My pulse raced even faster. The beam of a flashlight bounced around the room behind us, and there was a faint tap of something being lifted off a hard surface.

"There you are," the security guard said with a self-deprecating chuckle, and left again with a thump of the door.

Neither Kai nor I moved. There was no way of knowing how close the guard still was, whether he might hear us. Then, slower than before, the heavy footsteps thudded away. The faint chime of the elevator admitting him filtered through the door.

I sagged against the wall. Kai bowed his head over mine, his hands braced by my shoulders. Ever so slowly, he lifted one to trace his fingers along my jaw. It was a whisper of a touch, but it sent a giddy shiver over my skin.

"You smell so fucking good," he muttered.

I held in the giggle that bubbled in my chest. Longing swelled around it, spreading through my limbs and up into my throat. "So do you."

Kai's breath hitched slightly. He shifted his stance, and for one wrenching moment I thought he was going to pull away even though every particle of my body was screaming for… something.

"Fuck," he muttered, with an almost desperate edge to his voice that I'd never heard before. Then his head jerked down, and his mouth crashed into mine.

This. *This* was what my entire being had been screaming for. I kissed him back with everything I had in me.

Kai wrenched off his glasses and shoved them into a pocket before tilting his face at an even more delicious angle. He pressed against me like he had when the security guard had opened the door, but with a very different sense of urgency.

I ran my fingers into his floppy hair like I'd

imagined, rumpling it from its previous neatly gelled, business-appropriate state, and couldn't resist tugging on it. A groan reverberated from Kai's throat, even more intoxicating than I'd hoped for.

"Fucking hell," he murmured against my lips. "Fuck it. He's gone now. We have time. We'd fucking well better have time."

With those last words, he caught me by the waist and spun me around, with every appearance on making good on those f-bombs. My ass bumped the photocopier. He shoved the top section back and set me on the edge of the flat, glossy surface underneath. Then he tugged my face down to meet his so he could claim my lips again.

It was a little strange, perched in a spot that made me a few inches taller than him. A weird sense of power washed over me with a thrill I couldn't deny.

I kissed Kai back hard, absorbing the unexpected softness of his lips, the flavor of sugared coffee that slipped from his tongue over mine, the determined sweep of his fingers down the sides of my body to my thighs.

He yanked my skirt all the way to my waist in one swift motion and peeled my panties off an instant later, leaving them to hang from one ankle. The smooth surface of the photocopier pressed into my naked ass. I only had a few seconds to register that before one of our legs jostled a control, and suddenly the machine was humming underneath me.

The vibration rippled through my sex, making me

gasp. Light flashed over us. Kai blinked and fished a paper from the output tray, a lewd grin curving his mouth. He waved it in the thin glow of the machine's running lights, showing off the photocopied globes of my butt cheeks. "Now that's fucking art."

A blush burned my other cheeks even as I laughed. Kai folded the paper into a few squares and tucked it into his pocket. His hands returned to my thighs, stroking up and down them as he eased closer between them. His eyes smoldered as he held my gaze.

"I think we're going to need to have a little more fun with that. But first…"

He jerked me forward so I was balanced even more precariously on the edge of the machine. Our mouths collided, my weight leaning into him. He held me firmly, dipping his hands beneath me to squeeze my ass in time with the rhythmic motions of his lips and tongue. I shivered with delight, aching for more.

Still holding on to him for balance, I let my other hand drift down over his chest between us, all the way to the waist of his slacks. When my fingers traced the bulge of his erection, he groaned and ground into me. The tantalizing friction shocked a whimper out of me.

"Naughty girl," Kai said in a voice that sounded just as pleased as Nox's when he called me a "good girl." "You're not a minnow or a siren, I think. You're an absolute barracuda."

Without warning, he tugged me right off the photocopier and whirled me around in front of him so my ass pressed into his groin.

I found myself braced against the machine, bowed at the waist with my elbows leaning against the glass surface. Kai slid up my sweater and scooped my breasts free from my bra. He branded kisses to my spine as he tipped me even farther over so my nipples pebbled against the hard surface. Then he hit the copy button again.

I let out a faint sound of protest as the machine spat out another image of my naked body. Kai chuckled and tucked his hands around me. His fingers swept over the sensitive flesh, fondling the curves and flicking over my nipples. He hummed in approval at their already stiffened state.

"I don't just want a record of you," he said in a scorching whisper. "I want a record of how you were *mine*."

He hit the button with his knee, holding my breasts so the next printout would show his hands cupped around them, marking them as his. The vibration sent a fresh thrill through my chest. So much arousal had pooled between my legs that an embarrassing trickle trailed down my inner thigh.

Kai's breath had roughened, his own need intensifying alongside mine. He didn't leave me hanging for long. He dipped his hand between my legs, stroking my slickness from my clit and along my opening. I let out a needy whine and pushed back against him.

"So impatient," he chided, but the hitch in his voice gave away how close to losing control he was. He kept that hand working over me, curling one finger and then two right inside me, as he fumbled with his fly with the other. "Are you my woman too, Lily? Not just Nox's and Ruin's? Do you want everything I can give you?"

At the pulsing of his fingers, a moan tumbled out of me that was probably an answer all on its own. But I made myself say, in a ragged voice that was the best I could produce, "Yes. Everything. I want all of you."

He kissed my shoulder blade as if in reward and removed his hand for just long enough for the sound of tearing foil to reach my ears. "Good thing I didn't trust my self-control so much I skipped on necessary precautions," he said with a breathless laugh. Then the head of his cock pressed against my slit.

I spread my legs wider instinctively. Kai swiveled his fingers over my clit a few more times, drawing another gasp from my throat, and plunged into me so fast I saw stars.

"Oh, hell, yes," Kai muttered, easing back and ramming into me again. He set a steady, forceful pace, not rushing things but filling me to the brim with every thrust. After just a few, my body was reverberating with pleasure, like I was a fucking gong he was ringing each time he bucked against me.

He didn't neglect the rest of me. His hands traveled all over my body, pinching my nipples, tweaking my clit, finally spreading a little of my slickness into the crack of my ass to tease over my other opening. The unexpected jolt of bliss that came with that touch had me moaning all over again.

"Not too loud," he reminded me, even as he

pounded into me with a rhythm that was sending me spiraling more and more out of control with every beat. "I'll have to give you an ink cartridge to bite down on, and that could get messy."

As I sputtered a laugh that turned into a whimper halfway through, he circled my asshole again, lighting up all the nerve-endings there. "So very naughty," he said. "We'll play with this in other ways later, when we have more room to explore. For now, I'll stick to…"

He eased his thumb inside me just as he thrust into me again, and the heady sensations exploded through my body. My sex clenched around his pounding cock, and my head dropped down so my forehead smacked the photocopier, but I barely noticed the momentary prickle of pain with all the ecstasy sweeping through me.

Kai growled low in his throat and bucked into me faster. He pulled me against him as if he could bury himself even deeper than he already had. Then he was letting out a strangled sound of release as he reached his own peak.

A brief worry flashed through me that the normally detached guy would get awkward in the aftermath of our feral fuck. But Kai stayed in a slyly affectionate mood, planting a teasing kiss at the crook of my neck as he sorted out my bra and sweater, shaking his head at himself as he peeled off the condom with its load. "I wonder which of my wonderful coworkers should have this left on their desk."

I paused in the middle of yanking up my panties. "You wouldn't."

He smirked at me. "No, probably not, but only because I don't figure it'd be wise to leave my DNA lying around in hostile territory. Not because they don't deserve the horrified shock."

He swiped the other two photocopies from the tray. "Can't forget these treasures." He folded them to fit his pocket like the first and retrieved his glasses, and just like that, he was his typical pulled-together self, other than his mussed hair. If his face was still a bit flushed like mine, I couldn't tell in the dimness.

But that was Kai for you—straightforward and to-the-point. His even-keel-ness steadied me too. We did still have a job to do here, as diverted as we'd gotten from it.

I inhaled and exhaled slowly, the afterglow of the sex warming me but easing enough that I could concentrate. A renewed flicker of confidence had sparked inside me. "Up to the penthouse?" I suggested.

Kai took my hand like he had before. "No time like the present."

At the exclusive elevator, we tugged on the ski masks and gloves he'd brought along. Then he punched in the code. The door opened before I had a chance to even wonder if he could have made a mistake. We soared up to the building's top floor, Kai's hand lingering on my side with a new possessiveness I couldn't say I minded, and stepped out into that posh executive space.

There was an electronic lock on the door to Nolan's

office. I knew Kai wasn't as quick with technology as he was with people, but he fished a device out of his satchel and attached it to the lock.

"I've been making some new contacts while we get settled in here in the city," he explained as the lock started blinking with flickers of codes. "One of them helpfully supplied this ingenious device. Humanity has come up with a few useful inventions in the last two decades."

"Yes," I said dryly, "I'm sure the greatest recent achievement of humankind is the ability to more easily break and enter."

Kai snorted and then inhaled sharply as the device beeped. There was a pause, and then a *thunk* as the lock mechanism slid over.

We nudged open the door and crept into Nolan's office. I stopped breathing for a second, half expecting to find the man in charge standing by his desk as if he hadn't moved since I'd been in here last. But the vast space was empty. The glow of city lights seeped through the huge windows along the far wall.

"Okay," Kai said. "Let's see what the big boss has been keeping hidden away in here."

We peered at Nolan's bookshelves and pawed through his desk drawers, careful to leave everything in the same place we'd found it. It all looked like typical, above-board business stuff to me at first, other than a toy soldier tucked in the corner of one drawer. I studied it in my gloved hand, frowning at the antique styling and faded paint. "I wonder why he keeps this around." It looked older than Nolan was.

Kai shrugged. "Family keepsake? Oh, look at this. I wonder if he's been thinking he needs better security."

He showed me a business card he'd fished out of the back of the drawer—white with dark lettering and a red logo. *Ironguard Security*, the company name said. On the back, Nolan had jotted down a few phone numbers.

"Do you think that's important?" I asked.

"Not for our purposes, but it'd be good to know if he's adding new systems to this building or his home." Kai snapped a picture of both sides, tucked it away where he'd found it, and we both kept digging.

I'd reached the bottom drawer on my side when I lifted a paper and saw something that made me stiffen in place. Kai's head jerked around at my reaction. "What?"

I motioned to the document I'd uncovered, my throat too tight for me to speak.

It was a resume with my name at the top. My address in Lovell Rise was circled.

Nolan Gauntt had been keeping a close eye on me from the moment I'd applied at Thrivewell... and he'd paid particular attention to where I went after work hours, if he wanted to find me.

twenty-one

Lily

I knew the guys were worried when they all insisted on piling into Fred 2.0 to escort me to work instead of riding alongside me on their motorcycles.

"We have to keep a low profile," Kai had said before he'd set off in his own car, since we didn't want to be seen arriving together.

"Right!" Ruin had nodded and cracked his knuckles with an eager grin. "Better if that psycho doesn't know you have protection. We can take him by surprise for his beat-down."

I might have pointed out that the four of them weren't really in any position to be accusing other people of being psychos, but, well, the knowledge that

Nolan Gauntt had been making particular note of my home address... that he might be making plans to launch some attempt at screwing me over outside of work as well as on the job...

Well, let's just say it didn't have me farting rainbows of joy.

Maybe I should have taken comfort in the fact that he hadn't done anything yet, even though he'd had my resume available to him for almost three weeks already. Still, my discovery definitely cast a gloom over my return to work, knowing the guy would be skulking in his office twenty floors over my head.

As the car—which I had to admit ran much more smoothly than the original Fred, bless his vehicular soul —came up on the Thrivewell Enterprises building, I dragged in a breath. "I must have some leverage," I said, as much to reassure myself as the three guys around me. "He's trying to get me out, but he's going out of his way to make it look like a legit firing. He'd only be doing that if he thinks I could get him in trouble if he doesn't have all his bases covered."

"That doesn't mean he won't change his tune." Nox aimed a death glare at the building as I cruised past it and then glanced over at me. "We'll be staked out nearby the whole day. You get any shit at all from him, you text us *immediately*."

Imagining the havoc the former Skullbreakers could wreak on Thrivewell's orderly offices amused and horrified me simultaneously. It'd certainly be quite a show.

"I don't think it's going to come to that," I said as I parked a few blocks away, where no one was likely to notice the company I'd brought with me. At Nox's pointed look, I added, "But yes, if he comes raging at me, I'll give you a heads up before I'm torn limb from limb."

"We'll tear *him* limb from limb," Ruin announced with a pump of his fist.

Jett just eyed the two of them as we all got out and gave a skeptical grunt. "I get to pick where we're hanging out," he said.

Nox clapped him on the shoulders. "Right. We wouldn't want your sensitive artistic sensibilities to be offended."

He was jovial enough about the teasing that Jett's lips twitched with a hint of a smile before he forced his mouth into a grimace. "No, we wouldn't," he replied, and paused. His gaze slid to me. "But what's most important is that we're in easy reach if you need us, of course."

From the guy who rarely said much of anything, let alone anything affectionate, that was practically a declaration of undying loyalty. Not that I had much doubt about his loyalties considering how enthusiastically he'd punished my bullies in the past.

I shot him a smile. "Since it may be a long wait, I'd rather you got to enjoy the scenery in the meantime too."

"I've already gotten to see *my* favorite scenery," Nox said with a smirk, and tugged me to him to kiss my neck so he didn't mess up my lipstick. Ruin took that as his cue to do the same on the other side, and I was lucky I walked away only with giddy heat racing through me and not a pair of matching hickeys.

I headed over to the office building alone and started the new process of my workday. Before I even went into the mailroom, I checked the hall to the back delivery area and the storage room in it. Like the past couple of days, I found a couple of urgent parcels tucked away behind the other supplies. Whoever was trying to screw me over this way hadn't picked up on the fact that I was on to them—or they didn't care.

Maybe they liked knowing that *I* knew someone wanted me gone.

I checked the storage room again on my morning break and during lunch, and found one more envelope the second time. Otherwise, no trouble came my way other than Rupert's chorus of huffs and narrow sideways glances. I still wasn't sure *he* wasn't responsible for the waylaid deliveries.

But nothing required the assistance of my ghostly gangsters. Nothing went really wrong at all... until I returned from a quick pop into the restroom to a bitter smell in the air that hadn't been there before.

Rupert had gone off somewhere or other. I eased warily into the room, taking sniff after sniff, until I stopped at the mail cart I'd been almost finished loading before my bladder had demanded my attention. Then I halted in my tracks and stared.

Dark splotches were splattered across almost every

envelope and package in the cart. Dark splotches that still had a faintly wet sheen and that were giving off the bitter scent of black coffee.

It looked like someone had poured an entire freaking pot over the heap.

Oh, fuck. The wheels spun in my head for several seconds before I was capable of conscious thought again. My entire body had gone rigid, my stomach knotted into a solid lump.

No doubt they had a way of blaming this on me. Careless with my morning beverage, ruining a multitude of important documents. The second Rupert walked back in here and saw this—

The memory flashed through my mind of making a spurt of his coffee leap on to his shirt the other day. I paused, inhaling and exhaling slowly as I willed down my panic so I could think clearly.

Coffee was mostly water. I'd manipulated it before. Was it possible I could simply un-drench the cart and pretend this had never happened?

I had no idea, but the thought came with so much vengeful satisfaction that the hum was already resonating in my chest.

I stared at the parcels and envelopes, at the dark liquid staining them, and focused on my frustration with the job. On how pissed off I was with the people who were trying to kick me out and their underhanded methods. On Nolan Gauntt sitting up there in his huge, fancy office probably laughing manically to himself about how he'd gotten the better of me.

No. Fucking. Way.

The hum spread up into my skull and out to the tips of my fingers. I glanced around and grabbed an empty plastic crate so I had somewhere to send the offending liquid to. Then I focused all my searing energy on the cart.

Out. Out. I urged the splatters of coffee with my mind and beckoned to them with my hands. Flickers of warmth washed over my skin as if emanating from the hot beverage. The brown liquid began to rise off the heap of mail in drips and thin rivulets.

I directed them all over to the plastic crate and let them fall there in a dingy rainfall of coffee. Thin liquid snakes wove through the air and fell into the container. I pulled and directed it all, a marshy flavor creeping through my mouth. My body was outright tingling now with the energy flowing through me as I carried out this precise maneuver.

Finally, a faint ache started to creep through my muscles alongside the hum. The rivulets thinned until they were barely visible. I tugged with my powers more and more, determined to pull every driblet I could out of the stack of mail. Then, when nothing more came and it felt like I was yanking at nothing, I let my hands drop to my sides. My breath rushed out of me with a sag of my shoulders.

The bottom of the plastic crate was full of coffee. The packages and envelopes in the cart looked good as new. Maybe there was a slightly darker tint to the paper here and there, but nothing anyone could say was a definite stain. Nothing that could be pinned on me.

Despite the fatigue prickling through me, a smile stretched my mouth. I'd done it. They'd thought they could tear me down, and I'd beat them at their own game.

That sense of triumph faded quickly, though. I carried the crate into the restroom to pour out the coffee and rinse it, since it'd be hard to explain what'd gone on there if anyone else saw it, and by the time I returned, my spirits had dampened.

I'd beaten my enemies *this* time. What were they going to throw at me next? It'd only been luck that their current gambit had involved something I could use my powers on. Next time they might smear packages with cocaine dust or marmalade fingerprints, and there'd be shit-all I could do about that. The longer I waited, the more chance I'd get banned from the building and lose whatever access I had now.

My gaze lifted to the ceiling with the thought of the head honcho in his high office, scheming his schemes. A surge of defiant resolution filled me.

He was trying to push me around, to push me *out*, because he thought he could get away with it. I wasn't sure I could find out much more working here anyway. We'd taken everything we could from his office, which hadn't been a whole lot and nothing we could use to get the upper hand. But I had my own ways of intimidating people.

I could get my full revenge for whatever he'd put

Marisol through later. For now, I just needed him to stay the fuck away from me and her. Nolan Gauntt might be full of pompous business authority, but he'd never had to deal with anyone like me. I had to terrorize him enough that he'd decide it was better to steer clear rather than keep coming at me.

My decision solidified in my head as I brought around the cart of newly cleaned mail. The guys wouldn't have liked this plan. They'd have wanted me to call them in so they could carry out the terrorizing. But they'd already stood up for me so much, and all I'd done in return was get them into more danger. I could handle this myself, like I had with Peyton and Wade.

It was my problem, and I was strong enough to fix it on my own.

Well, mostly on my own. There was still an exclusive executive elevator standing between me and the big boss, and I couldn't waltz right over to it and step on even though I knew the code from watching Kai yesterday. So after I'd dropped off the empty cart in the mailroom, I texted my coworker accomplice a quick message.

I'm coming up to your floor. Need to get on the special elevator. When you see me, can you divert the secretaries' secretary?

The answer came in less than a minute. *Of course. What are you up to? I can join in.*

I'm taking care of this one by myself, I said. *Just get me in.*

Kai didn't argue. When I reached the fifteenth floor,

my nerves were already thrumming with a mix of apprehension, anticipation, and righteous anger.

I strode over to the executive elevator as if I did this every day. From the corner of my vision, I saw Kai saunter over to the secretary's desk. He started talking in low, urgent tones that had her springing from her desk and dashing to another part of the room with him.

I didn't glance over to see where they'd gone. I simply drew up in front of the elevator, tapped in the code as quickly as I could, and launched myself through the doors as soon as they opened.

"Hey!" someone said from behind me—maybe not even to me, but I wasn't taking any chances. I jabbed the button for the top floor and didn't breathe again until the doors had closed and the car was gliding upwards.

Naturally, when I reached the top floor, I had another problem that I hadn't fully considered in my sudden rush of determination. Nolan's admin assistant was at his desk, guarding the boss's office door.

Since I didn't have any clever tricks up my sleeve, I decided to see how far bravado would get me. I marched up to him with as commanding an air as I could produce. "I need to see Mr. Gauntt. *Now.*"

The assistant blinked at me, eyeing me as if I had two heads—and both of them were smeared with dog shit. "Who are you, exactly?" he said in a disdainful tone. "*If* you have some business that would concern Mr. Gauntt, his schedule does require a significant amount of advance notice. And I'm afraid—"

I didn't get to find out what patronizing comment he'd make next, because right then, the office door swung open.

I didn't think, just reacted. On a jolt of adrenaline, I sprang past the woman who was just leaving the office and hurtled inside—right past Nolan, who was standing on the other side of the doorway to see his guest out. I spun around to face him, my chin high and my voice firm. "We need to talk."

"I'm so sorry, Mr. Gauntt," the assistant's voice carried from outside as he scrambled to pursue me.

Nolan gave me a measured look, something in his posture making him feel about ten feet taller than me even though it was more like eight inches, and stepped into the doorway. "It's all right," he told his assistant. "I'm sure Miss Strom is only here to follow up on a discussion we had last week. It won't take long."

Oh, he was so sure about that, wasn't he?

His confident air as he shut the door and turned toward me both unnerved me and infuriated me. I held on tightly to the fury, fanning the flames inside me so the hum of supernatural energy rose into a roar.

"This *will* be quick," I said before he could say anything else. "I'm just here to tell you that from now on, you'd better leave me and my sister alone. You don't keep tabs on me or her, and you and anyone working for you had better stay the hell away from my home." Hopefully he couldn't track me to our new apartment, but I wouldn't put it past him.

Nolan continued studying me for a moment

without any hint of concern and then ambled deeper into his office. "What makes you think I'd want anything at all to do with you and your sister?"

I stalked after him. "You sure seemed interested in her seven years ago. There won't be any repeats of that."

He rotated on his heel again to fix that penetrating gaze on me. "And what exactly did I do back then? You don't know that I did anything at all, do you? Other than having a simple conversation, and there's no crime in that."

"It was more than a fucking conversation," I snapped, and then reined in my temper. He obviously knew I didn't remember—whether from his observations recently or getting access to my doctors' notes or who knew what. And now he was going to play innocent?

Nolan shrugged like the total douche-canoe he was. His hand twitched where it hung loosely at his side. "That sounds awfully vague to me. Throwing around baseless accusations can get you in a lot of trouble, you know."

Oh, now he was threatening me? My teeth gritted, and I decided we'd done enough talking. He was never going to admit to anything. That wasn't why I'd come up here anyway. I needed to show him how much trouble *he'd* be in if he kept messing with me and mine.

My senses were singing with the awareness of the water running through the building around me. There was a pipe running through the floor and into the wall —a private bathroom just off Nolan's office. I focused on it, on willing a torrent of water to rush up through the pipes. My skin quivered.

"I don't care what excuses you make," I said, low and fierce. "You'll leave us alone from now on, or you'll regret it."

As I said those last three words, I unleashed the pressure I'd forced into the bathroom fixtures. Water exploded from the sink faucet, the shower head, and the toilet tank and slammed into the door so hard it burst open.

The wave crashed into Nolan, tossing him off his feet. He landed on his ass just as a second wave surged out to batter him again. I held off on another, keeping the water at the ready with a heady rhythm flowing through my veins, waiting for his reaction.

Nolan wiped off his face and looked at the carpet around him, which was soaked and covered in puddles where the water hadn't quite absorbed yet. His eyes had widened, and his lips had parted with surprise. Another twitch shook his hand, this one rippling up his arm. But as I watched, his mouth curved into a shape that looked almost… amused?

With a rough chuckle, he pushed himself to his feet, barely seeming to mind the way his drenched suit clung to his broad body. He slicked his hair back from his face again and met my eyes, still with that sharp smile.

"Well," he said, "that *is* interesting. There must be quite a story there. I assume that's why your stepfather was so overwrought. I thought he was just a hysterical personality. It worked in my favor regardless. No one wondered why you were kept shut away under medical supervision for so long without any clear symptoms."

The bottom of my stomach dropped out. Nolan didn't seem scared or intimidated at all. How could he be so blasé about me hurling water around with the power of my mind? And—

My voice came out taut. "Are you saying that *you* made them keep me in the hospital for all that time?" I'd wondered now and then why my extended stay had been necessary, but the staff had always been quick to assure me they only had my best interests and a smooth recovery in mind…

Had he been paying them off to keep me out of the way?

"I'm not saying anything at all," Nolan said drolly, and squeezed a little water out of his tie. "Did you think that silly stunt would frighten me? I've faced much more difficult issues than getting a little *wet*, you ridiculous girl. Now I'll give you ten seconds to get out of my office and another minute to vacate this building forever, or you can be sure the next time the police haul you away, you won't be coming back."

I didn't know whether he could follow through on that threat or if he was bluffing, but he didn't look the slightest bit worried. And I had no other cards I could play. My thoughts had scattered in bewilderment, my nerves jangling with panic.

If he meant it, if he had that many authorities in his pocket, I'd completely lose any chance I had of helping Marisol. Nothing was worth that risk.

So I fled. I spun and ran for the door, jammed my thumb against the elevator button, and heard nothing but the racing of my pulse as it carried me down to the fifteenth floor. I didn't dare stop to catch Kai's attention. I just kept walking, to the other elevator, pacing back and forth in that car as it carried me to the ground level, and then out onto the sidewalk. There, I exhaled in one long, ragged rush and pressed my hands to my face.

I'd lost. I'd faced the dragon with what I'd thought was an unbeatable enchanted sword, and he'd chomped it in half and sent me scrambling away with my ass on fire.

And now Nolan knew without a doubt why I'd come to Thrivewell. He knew how far I was willing to go. How long would it be before he decided firing me wasn't enough?

twenty-two

Lily

"You shouldn't have gone in there alone," Nox said for approximately the thousandth time as his hands clenched the steering wheel. He'd insisted on driving Fred 2.0 after the guys had seen how shaken I was by my confrontation with Nolan.

"Right," I said. "Because three gangsters storming into the building totally wouldn't have drawn any attention and gotten a heap of security called. You might not even have made it past the first floor."

"We could have tried," Jett grumbled from behind me.

"We'd have shown that asshole a thing or two," Ruin agreed, swinging punches at the back of Nox's seat.

"I don't know." I sank deeper into my own seat, worrying at my lower lip. Would Nolan Gauntt have been afraid even if my guys had come at him with their electrical attacks? I guessed those would have been more painful than the punch of water I'd thrown him. But I could way too easily imagine him sprawled on the floor with his skin singed and his hair smoking while still smiling that same unaffected smirk.

A shiver ran down my spine. "I'm done there now," I said. "I'll have to find *another* new job. At least there are more of those here in the city." I rubbed my hand over my face. "Kai's still at Thrivewell. It's possible the Gauntts will back off now that I'm not nosing around, but if they don't, he'll still have an inside edge."

What exactly we could do with that edge, I wasn't sure. It seemed pretty risky to go in aiming to beat the man to a pulp if we weren't sure that would cow him. A tactic like that could just as easily backfire and end with all of the guys—and maybe me too—behind bars.

Nolan had been too calm about all of it. What could have been going through his head? He obviously hadn't been at my house when I'd unleashed my powers before, because he'd definitely been surprised, just not shocked into a horrified stupor like Wade had been.

But then, maybe it'd been ridiculous of me to think the head of Thrivewell Enterprises would be intimidated as easily as my bully of a stepdad had been.

"That's right," Ruin said, ever chipper. "And we'll use that edge to cut him into little pieces."

Could it be as simple as that? Just eliminate the

guy completely? I wasn't exactly an advocate for murder—I'd *stopped* the guys from murdering people on various occasions—but if Nolan was a total menace to society, or at least to Marisol… wouldn't it be better to remove him from the game board?

I just couldn't quite believe it'd be that simple. He'd be even more on guard now than he'd been before. He'd already been looking into that security company. And who knew how many other people in his family or the company were mixed up in the whole thing, who'd come after us even if we succeeded in eliminating Nolan?

I shook myself, closing my eyes. My head was spinning again, my thoughts colliding and fracturing without getting me any answers. I needed to step back and take a breather, and then maybe I could find the right way to come at this problem.

The last of Mayfield's buildings fell away as we passed into the short stretch of countryside between the city and Lovell Rise. Ruin reached over and squeezed my shoulder. As I turned to smile at him, grateful even if the affectionate gesture didn't fix anything, my phone rang.

My heart lurched, though I had no reason to assume the call was about anything bad. I pulled out my phone and raised it to my ear. "Hello?"

"Hello, Miss Strom?" a woman said. It took me a second to place her clipped voice in combination with the company name that'd turned up on my call display.

It was the rental agent who'd shown us the new apartment.

"Yes?" I said cautiously. Did she need more paperwork signed? Oh, God, she hadn't already found out that I'd lost my job, had she?

The ripple of tension that carried through the woman's words put me even more on the alert. "There's been an… issue with the apartment on Kastle Street. We're hoping you might be able to shed some light on the situation. Can you come by the building later this afternoon?"

"I can come right now," I said, motioning to Nox so wildly that he gave me a puzzled look. I didn't know how to convey my directions in sign language. "What kind of issue?" My heart was already sinking. Nolan Gauntt must have been pissed off at me for challenging him, even if he hadn't shown it. He'd found out about the apartment somehow—he'd screwed me over in some other way…

"I think you really need to see it," the agent said, which wasn't ominous at all. "How soon can you get here?"

"Um, about twenty minutes? I'll hurry."

I hung up and flailed my arm at Nox again. "We've got to go back to the city. To the new apartment. Something's gone wrong."

"What?" The question came out in a growl. Baring his teeth, the Skullbreakers' leader yanked the car around in a U-turn so abrupt the tires screeched and several honks followed in our wake. But it did get us racing back toward the city in no time flat.

"I have no idea what happened," I said as the engine rumbled with the jam of his foot against the gas pedal. "The rental agent said she wanted me to see it. Let's not get pulled over for speeding before we even make it to the building."

"The cops can eat my exhaust," Nox muttered, but he did slow down enough that my heart stopped trying to jump out of my throat.

I texted Kai, who was still at the office, to let him know about our unexpected detour. I'd only meant to keep him in the loop, but he replied an instant later saying he'd claim he was sick and be right over.

You really don't have to, I wrote back quickly, but he was apparently so busy putting on his show of illness that he didn't even read that message.

As we swerved onto the street the apartment building was on, I didn't expect to see anything all that shocking yet. I assumed it was something to do with only my specific apartment. But when the brick walls came into sight, my gut twisted in on itself. "Oh, fuck."

The windows all along the first floor had been smashed—and they were barred, so someone had gone to a lot of trouble to work around the wrought-iron protections. A few shards of glass still glinted on the sidewalk. The front door had been bashed right off its hinges and now was propped next to the doorway, the steel surface dented like a battering ram had gone at it.

Jett let out a low whistle that was almost as impressed as it was horrified.

"I guess... if they were broken that easily... it's a good thing they'll need to be replaced?" Ruin said, for once in his life struggling to find a cheery way of spinning this particular situation. "Who the hell did this?"

It didn't feel like Gauntt-style work, I had to say. We parked a couple of car-lengths away from the building and got out cautiously.

The rental agent emerged from the entry hall as soon as I'd closed the car door behind me. She glanced from me to the three guys flanking me, and her lips pursed in a way that made my hackles automatically rise.

"What the heck happened here?" I asked, sweeping my arm to encompass the stretch of wreckage.

Somehow, the woman's lips pursed even tighter. She might have been able to turn coal into diamonds with them at this point.

"The building was vandalized and defaced a few hours ago," she said stiffly. "And seeing as the only individual apartment specifically targeted was the one you're due to move into shortly, I have to assume it has something to do with your... associations."

Her gaze flicked to the guys again. They had started looking increasingly gangster-y since they'd taken possession of their bodies, what with the extreme hair colors and their tendency toward hoodies and jeans loose enough to wedge a pistol in them. She'd seen Jett's motorcycle when he'd come with me to check out the apartment the other day. If that was even what she meant.

She didn't think *my* guys had done this, did she? How would that even make sense?

But it couldn't have had anything to do with my conversation with Nolan Gauntt, I realized with a wash of cold. She'd said it'd happened a few hours ago, and it'd been only about one since I'd left his office. He might be an uber-powerful corporate magnate, but I didn't think even he could travel back in time to fuck with my living space.

So who had done this, then? And why would they have gone after my apartment?

It wasn't really mine yet, of course.

"I don't know who could have done this kind of damage," I said, gathering my confidence. "I'm not even living here yet. It probably has something to do with the previous tenants."

The rental agent gave me a withering look. "The previous tenant was a ninety-year-old woman who never left the apartment except to play bingo on Tuesdays."

"You never know," Nox said. "Those bingo halls can get pretty intense."

As the agent glowered at him, I sucked my lower lip under my teeth. As I groped for another alternative suggestion, she motioned for me to follow her into the building. "Why don't you take a look at the message they left behind?"

Message? I stepped into the hallway, my skin

creeping with apprehension. Despite the destruction on the outside of the building, it was true that nothing inside appeared to have been touched. Well, not until we got to the third floor, where the chemical smell of spray paint still hung in the air.

It was obvious why before we even went into the corner apartment that was meant to be mine. Someone had sprayed black paint in it in the shape of two bones forming an X, like the bottom of a pirate flag logo. Which I guessed was better than the boner that'd been painted on the grocery store, but not by a large margin.

"Not the same guys," Jett muttered, possibly thinking of the same previous incident that I was. With his artist's eye, he should know. The bones definitely looked more deftly sketched than the crude images before.

The rental agent shot him a sharp look as if he'd admitted guilt. Then she pushed the door open. The lock was broken, and the hinges creaked as if they were a thread from giving way.

The same crossed-bones graphic marked the walls all through the apartment, stark against the white paint and the windowpanes. It'd even been sprayed on the floor—along with puddles that gave off a rank smell that had my stomach turning in an instant.

They'd pissed in here.

In the bathroom, the intruders had marked up the bathtub too. They'd smashed the sink, which now lay in several pieces on the tiles.

My lungs had already constricted when I reached

the master bedroom. There was more piss on the floor and bones dancing across the walls… and letters marked in red paint in between the partial pirate graphic.

This was what the rental agent had meant about a message.

Corps crushed the Skullbreakers. We'll crush you too.

For a second, I was confused, thinking the vandals had misspelled "corpse." Nox came up beside me and let out a string of violent curses that made the rental agent cringe. Then understanding clicked into place in my head.

The X of bones—that must be the Skeleton Corps' tag. They'd noticed the guys coming by here with me, or maybe they figured I was part of the gang, which wasn't totally wrong. So they'd decided to send a message.

And now we knew for sure who'd been responsible for the Skullbreakers' first deaths. It didn't feel like good news.

It took a moment for me to realize the rental agent was talking. Her voice came out even brisker than before, almost frantic. "As you can see, it appears you've drawn the attention of some… unsavory characters to our property. There are standards that have to be maintained, and there's the security of the rest of the tenants to consider. I can return your deposit check to you and—"

Panic hit me in an icy splash. I'd lost my job, and now she was trying to take my new home—Marisol's new home—away from us.

"No," I burst out, and fumbled for my composure. "No, I—this won't happen again."

Kai's even voice rang out from the living room. "You and Lily have been the victims of a crime," he said, walking over to where the rental agent was standing. "It seems a little backward to blame her instead of attempting to prosecute the actual perpetrators."

The agent startled, probably wondering where he'd come from. He'd made it here fast. I wondered if he had any treads left on his tires.

In her hesitation, Nox jumped in with a crack of his knuckles. "We'll handle getting this place cleaned and fixed up," he said firmly. "The apartment, and the windows and door downstairs too. You and the management company won't have to lift a finger. As long as you let Lily keep her lease."

Kai nodded. "Let us take care of it. If you approve of the fixes before it's time for Lily to move in, you let her keep the place. That's a fair deal, isn't it? And, I mean, it'll be even harder to rent it to anyone else if word gets out that the building's become a target."

"The people who targeted it won't make that mistake again," Jett said darkly.

Ruin nodded with an eager jerk of his head. "We can take care of that too. Hell, yes."

The rental agent's gaze slid from one of them to the other, somehow hopeful and terrified at the same time. When her eyes reached me, I managed a pained smile. "Please? Give me—give us—a chance."

She let out her breath in a rush. "I—I'll have to

check with the office, but I think I can give you a few days to prove you can get things in order—and that there won't be another incident like this. If we have any more issues—"

I held up my hands. "Of course. I totally understand."

With another sigh, she ushered us out of the apartment. Despite her tentative agreement to the deal, my stomach still felt as heavy as if I'd swallowed one of those chunks of sink.

I suspected the only reason she'd agreed was Kai's point about how difficult it'd be to find a new tenant. But that only mattered if my presence wasn't running off the tenants they already had. Could we really clean all this up in just a few days?

And could the guys take down the Skeleton Corps before they came back to make good on their promise?

twenty-three

Jett

Of all the things I'd never wanted to need to know, how to remove piss from hardwood was definitely up there at the top of the list. I wrinkled my nose as I gave the last rag one final scrub over the boards before studying them.

It was lucky they'd already been pretty marked up before the Skeleton Corps had come through here. I couldn't really tell that this spot was any more battered than the rest of the floor. And it didn't stink anymore.

The rag, on the other hand…

I chucked that into the garbage bag sitting open in the middle of the living room and glanced around. Nox was just finishing reinforcing the hinges on the new door he'd picked up for the apartment. From the looks of the thing, it was meant for a maximum-security military base rather than a low-rent apartment building, but I wasn't going to complain if it made it that much harder for the pricks to break in here again.

I'd managed to use my color changing power to erase the gang graffiti in the living room and one of the bedrooms, but then my ghostly juice had run out there. Ruin was swiping a layer of white paint onto the walls in the second bedroom, whistling a happy tune as he did like he was in a fucking Disney movie. I could see Lily doing her own painting, with somewhat less enthusiasm, through the third bedroom's doorway. Kai had gone downstairs to oversee the replacement of the broken first-floor windows.

We'd managed to get through a hell of a lot so far today, but we were hardly done. Even with the windows open, letting a chilly evening breeze wash over us, we wouldn't be able to put down a second layer of paint to cover the last traces of the spray paint until tomorrow. The bathroom sink was still in several pieces. And Kai was working out the best solution for a secure door to the entire building, which also required getting new keys to all the tenants.

But really, the rental company should have been *thanking* us for the renovations we'd had to do on their behalf.

The window replacement people must have finished up, because Kai came striding into the apartment. He scanned the space through his glasses like he was searching it for murder clues.

"As soon as you're done, we should head out," he said to the room at large, nodding at the thickening darkness beyond the windows. "We need to gather all the reinforcements we can as quickly as possible for when we go head-to-head with the Skeleton Corps. And we want to focus their attention on our new headquarters so if they're going to come at us, they do it there, not here."

"Agreed on both." Nox stepped back from the door and wiped his hands together with a satisfied air. Then he glanced toward Lily, who'd just emerged from her room, finished with her painting. "Someone needs to stay with Lily. We can't leave her on her own while they're pulling shit like this."

"They don't seem to know about my apartment in Lovell Rise," Lily said. Nox had ridden out there to confirm it hadn't met the same fate as the new apartment earlier today. "I should be fine there."

Nox let out a dismissive huff. "They tracked us all the way out there in our first lives. If they could connect us to this place, we can't count on them not knowing about where we've been crashing for weeks. And that place has just one crappy door between you and the street." He patted the new one he'd installed. "I think you should stay here with one of us."

It was some kind of crazy world when a place that'd just been broken into and defaced was our safest option, but I had to agree with him. I looked at Ruin, who was just setting aside his paintbrush, expecting him to volunteer for protective duty, but Kai spoke first. "Jett should stay."

My head jerked around. "What? Why?"

The know-it-all glowered at me as if offended that I'd questioned his declaration. "Nox and Ruin have supernatural talents that'll help us show who the new bosses in town are with the other gangs. I don't think giving them a makeover is going to have the same impact."

"*You* haven't figured out what your superpower is at all," I had to point out.

Nox snorted. "Kai knows how to talk people into just about anything and how to get a read on the ones he can't convince. Can't beat that for this job, even with superpowers."

I opened my mouth and closed it again. Lily was watching me, her expression solemn. Maybe she was wondering why I was protesting so much.

To some extent, it was a matter of honor. But also—spending the night with her, alone—there were too many things I wanted that were nagging at the edges of my mind even without me letting myself think about them.

"There's nothing in this place," I said finally. "All our stuff is back at the other apartment."

Nox jabbed his thumb toward the tiny kitchen. "There's the food we picked up. You won't starve. And the one bedroom has that Murphy bed. I'm sure you'll manage." He smirked at me as if *he* knew exactly what urges I was trying to shove way down deep in the basement of my mind.

"I have an emergency blanket in the trunk of my car that I can bring up," Lily said quietly. "For one night— we could make do."

I could tell from her voice that she was already exhausted. And why wouldn't she be? She'd thrown everything she had at that creep Nolan Gauntt and had him laugh in her face, and then spent the rest of the day mopping up piss and painting over deathly graffiti in a panic over losing her new home.

The last thing I wanted was to make this situation any harder for her than it already was.

I shrugged. "Okay. I'm the weakest link. Whatever."

Ruin chuckled and prodded me in the shoulder. "You're not weak. You'll kick the asses of anyone who comes at Lily. And hey, slumber party!" He wagged a finger at Kai. "Next time, it's my turn."

"We'll see how helpful it is to have you literally putting the fear into the bozos around here," Nox said. "Okay, let's move out. I bet the Skeleton Corps aren't sitting around on their asses."

We all headed downstairs, the other guys going to their bikes to take off and me escorting Lily to her car. I peered through the dusk, my nerves jumping at the sight of a figure that turned out to be just a skinny teenager practicing his dance moves to the beat that blared from his headphones. He looked like a scarecrow getting electrocuted, but I decided against offering that critique.

Lily and I didn't talk much as we ate a dinner that consisted of an odd mix of junk food and fresh fruit, which Ruin seemed to think were the only acceptable meal items when there wasn't any microwave for heating things up. Lily just looked tired, and I didn't know what to say to her. My strength was in expressing myself with images, not words.

So maybe Nox and Kai had a fair point about my usefulness in the recruitment campaign.

We were just cleaning up, no interruptions from murderous gangsters so far and a deep weariness sinking into my bones, when Lily spoke up.

"Do you really think it'll be okay? You guys will be able to make sure the Skeleton Corps don't vandalize the apartment building again—you'll be able to make sure they don't *hurt* you?"

I shot her my best confident smile. It felt stiff on my mouth. I didn't do a whole lot of smiling in general, and tonight it felt like an epic task.

"We've beat down everyone who came at us so far, haven't we?" I said.

"I know. But these guys seem a lot more organized than the jerks at the college. And there must be a lot of them." She paused, and a yawn stretched her jaw. "I'm just tired. You all know what you're doing with this gangster stuff way better than I do. Let's get the bed down."

The hinges squeaked as we lowered the Murphy bed. The mattress looked a bit lumpy, but at this point I didn't figure Lily cared. Her eyelids were drooping. As she spread out the wool blanket on it, I turned to leave the bedroom.

"Where are you going?" she asked, stopping me in my tracks. "You need to sleep too, don't you?"

The truth was that I'd assumed I'd hunker down on the floor somewhere and make the best of it. We'd closed up the windows now that the paint smell had mostly aired out. But it was still cold enough to freeze a guy's nuts off in here, and the leather jacket I'd been wearing for warmth—and image—while cruising on my bike only took some of the edge off the chill.

It wasn't going to be a *fun* night, that was for sure.

"I'll be fine," I said brusquely, not wanting to give any impression that I was fishing for an invitation. "I spent twenty-one years lying in the bottom of the marsh. This is luxury."

Lily made a scoffing sound. "Don't be silly. I'm not going to make you sleep on the *floor*. It's a double bed—that means it's meant for two. And the blanket's big. We can share it without having to get at all close to each other, if that's what you're worried about."

It kind of was, but when she'd put it that way, I didn't want to admit it. I looked at the bed and the blanket, focusing on them rather than the woman my gaze wanted to travel to as I weighed my options.

At my hesitation, something in Lily's face fell. My heart plummeted seeing it, and suddenly words were tumbling out of my mouth without consulting my brain. "Yeah. Sure. That'll be better."

Once I'd said it, I couldn't really take my

agreement back without making her feel even more rejected. She lay down on one side of the mattress, folding her arm under her head as a sort-of pillow and leaving plenty of blanket on the other side for me. I eased onto the springy surface gingerly, staying as close to the edge as I possibly could, and tucked a bit of the blanket over me.

I kept my back to her, but I was sharply aware of her presence on the other side of the mattress. It trembled when she adjusted her position.

There were three feet between us. I'd stood closer to her than that in the past few days. I could handle sleeping that close without losing my head.

Even if the impulse to roll over and tug her to me was starting to spread through my limbs.

Lily was so quiet for several minutes that I thought she'd fallen asleep. I was still arguing silently with my dick, which had gone half-hard in defiance of my intentions, when her drowsy voice reached my ears.

"It's okay, you know. That you're not into me that way. I'm not—I'm not some nympho who's going to throw herself at any guy in a hundred-foot radius or get all offended that I can't bag every man I meet. I never expected *any* of this to happen this way. You don't have to worry that I'd force anything just because we're alone or whatever."

"I know you wouldn't," I said quickly, my pulse stuttering at the realization that she thought I was worried about *her* self-control. Christ. But how could I tell her she was wrong without opening up a whole can of worms that'd spring free all over the place… or dicks. Yeah, it was more like a can of dicks.

How could I explain how I felt about her? I wanted to paint her, and I wanted to paint my fingers all over her body. But every time I imagined that, I couldn't help picturing the other guys' hands touching every part of her…

It wouldn't be something special to just the two of us. I'd only be one more Skullbreaker looking to get off.

Every part of me balked at that idea. Whatever happened between Lily and me, whatever she became to me, it should be better than that. If I gave in to my baser urges, I might sour everything else amazing between us.

And here she was trying to look out for *me* while I grappled with those urges. She'd always been like that, even when she'd been tough and defiant as well—so soft and gentle when she'd felt someone she cared about needed it.

An unexpected warmth spread through my chest to have that kindness directed at me. *She* was goddamned special, and she deserved to be treated like it.

I wasn't totally sure how to be gentle in return, but I gave it my best shot. "You've never made me feel at all uncomfortable," I added to my initial remark. "I'm always happy having you around. I didn't want to impose on *you*."

"Okay. Well, good. And you didn't."

She gave another yawn and tugged the blanket

tighter over her shoulder, and then her breath evened out into the rhythm of sleep.

It took a long time before I drifted off too. I wasn't even aware I had until I jolted awake again to a yank of the blanket and a panicked gasp.

As I sat up, I whirled toward Lily. I found her facing away from me, clutching the blanket with her eyes still shut and her expression taut with tension. Another strained sound escaped her, like she was trying to gulp for air. Her arms twitched, her hands jerking at the blanket.

"Lily?" I said. "Lily!"

My voice didn't wake her. Her head whipped from side to side, and her legs shifted under the covers. A low, anguished moan escaped her lips.

It killed me seeing her like that. I'd stayed here to protect her, and now her own mind was beating up on her.

I didn't let myself debate any longer. I scooted across the mattress and wrapped my arms around her, hugging her to me.

"Lily," I said by her ear. "It's okay. You're all right. Everything's fine, and I'm here with you."

I gave her a little shake, and her muscles jumped. Her eyes popped open. I might have released her right then, but a second later, a shiver ran through her body.

She was cold, I realized. The side of her arm, her hair where my face rested against it…

She'd left herself partly uncovered by the blanket so

that I could have more, all the way on the other side of the bed.

Horror and guilt wrenched through me, and I quickly heaved the blanket farther over her so it fully covered both of us. Then I nestled her closer against me. Her body started to relax next to mine.

"I'm sorry," she said. "I—I've been having that dream a lot lately. I don't know why."

I frowned. "What dream?"

"I'm back in the marsh. Drowning. Only this time I can't seem to fight my way back to the surface, no matter what I do."

She shifted her weight, and her ass brushed my groin. With a flare of sensation, I became abruptly aware that my dick was no longer settling for half-hard and had gone all the way to steel post status. Had she noticed? Damn it.

I tried to imperceptibly angle my hips so there was no chance of my erection pressing into her.

Lily swiped her hand over her face. "I'm sorry. I mean, it was just a dream. I shouldn't let it shake me up that much."

Why the hell did she think she had to apologize? "It's fine," I said. "A nightmare can shake anyone up."

"I just… I don't like getting weak."

A pang reverberated through my chest. I had to nudge my face closer to her, tucking my chin over her shoulder from behind. "You're not weak. You're the strongest woman I've ever known. You don't lose that just because things get to you every now and then."

The smell of her was flooding my lungs, sweet with an edge of wildness to it. Her body was so soft and now warming against mine. My cock throbbed, and I lost my grip on my resolve just for a second.

One taste, one tiny little taste couldn't be so bad, could it?

I brushed my lips against the corner of Lily's jaw. She exhaled with a soft little gasp of pleasure that took my desire from smoldering to blazing in an instant. I kissed her again, more firmly this time, letting my tongue flick out across her smooth skin to drink in that delicately delicious flavor.

Before I even knew what was happening, my hands were moving. One slid down to stroke over Lily's stomach. The other rose to caress her cheek and the other side of her jaw as I marked a scorching path down the side of her neck. Lily whimpered, arching back into me. Her ass rubbed against my dick, and a groan broke from my throat.

With a shaky inhalation, Lily flipped over to face me. All at once, her fingers were teasing into my hair and across my scalp, her breasts were pressed against my chest, and my mouth was colliding with hers.

Her lips tasted even better than her neck. I devoured them, grasping one of her legs and slinging it over my hip so our bodies aligned even better. Reveling in the needy noise that escaped her when I rocked my erection against her.

She gripped me tighter, her fingertips digging into my skin in a way I didn't mind at all. Our tongues tangled together, her other hand trailed down my chest, and she pulled just a little away with a stuttered breath—

And suddenly in the back of my head I was on the side of the road again. On the side of the road in the dark listening to the tune of a breath rattling out in perfect harmony with the splattering of blood, and thinking—thinking—

Not thinking at all, not really. Just like now.

A wave of cold washed over me, dousing my lust. I yanked myself away from Lily and stiffened my stance to try to hide how much I was shaking.

"Jett?" she said, her voice full of concern.

I should have been more concerned. I should have been thinking straight. Not—not getting caught up in my impulses and emotions, forgetting all reason…

The last time I'd done that, it hadn't been just me who'd paid the price but everyone around me too. The guys who'd counted on me to have their backs.

Lily was counting on me too. I couldn't fuck things up again by losing sight of what mattered.

I pushed myself off the bed. There wasn't anything I could say to make this better—I might only make it worse if I tried. I kept my voice as calm and even as I could manage.

"I got enough sleep. I'm going to go stand guard in the living room. We can't be too careful with those assholes going on rampages."

Then I left the bedroom without another word, guilt twisting through my gut sharper than ever before.

twenty-four

Lily

The odd assembly of characters the guys had pulled together roamed through the former medieval-themed restaurant like tourists taking in the sights. The Skullbreakers had gotten rid of all of the tables except the long one by the throne and a couple pushed off to the sides, but they'd left the throne in all its gleaming gold-painted glory, as well as the weapons and armor hanging on the walls. Watching from my spot off in the corner, I could tell the visuals had made an impact.

The newcomers looked as intimidated by the guys themselves as by their new clubhouse's décor. When Nox stood up in front of the throne and clapped his hands together for attention, a couple dozen heads swung toward him in an instant. Everyone fell silent.

"You've got your assignments," Nox said, casting his gaze over them with an air I had to admit was pretty regal in that moment. He'd even picked up one of the swords, which he waggled at his audience as he spoke, emphasizing his points with *its* point. "We're not going to let the Skeleton Corps bully us anymore, and the first step in that is making sure our properties stay secure. If you're on guard duty, get to it now! The rest of you, prepare to be called on and keep your ears to the ground in the meantime."

Several of the scruffy-looking gangsters who'd responded to the Skullbreakers' recruitment efforts glanced at the floor as if they thought he might mean that last instruction literally. But I noticed that many of them still paled and tensed up when he mentioned our nemesis by name. They shuffled out of the restaurant quickly, one of them taking up a post right outside the door.

Kai had ambled up beside me. He'd called in sick at Thrivewell so he could stick around to finish getting the new Skullbreaker allies organized.

"Are you sure they'll follow through on their orders?" I asked him. "Are they ready to go up against this gang that's been ruling the city for more than twenty years?"

Kai shrugged. "They're scared of the Skeleton Corps, but they're also scared of us working more of our supernatural voodoo on them. I think that'll work as an excellent motivating factor for most. And they don't *really* have to go up against anyone at this point. The only job we've given them is to keep watch around this place and your apartment building and notify us if they see the Corps coming around so we can intercept before much damage is done."

Nox had sauntered over while the other guy was talking. "Exactly. They'd better be able to handle that much, or they've got no business calling the sketchy organizations they were running 'gangs.' I have four guys scheduled to be around the apartment building at all times, switching off regularly, so even if one or two drop the ball, it's well covered."

My stomach twisted. "Do you really want to focus all your new manpower on defending the building? Don't you want to go after the Skeleton Corps guys for murdering you?"

Not that I particularly wanted him to say yes. I was kind of scared myself—that the men who'd supported me through so much might find themselves murdered all over again. But I had to ask.

Nox teased his fingers over my hair. The gesture and the fact that he still had that damned sword in his hand —it might even be the *same* sword he and Ruin had played with the other night—sparked a flare of heat over my skin. I mentally cracked a whip at my easily-distractable brain and then realized that a whip probably wasn't the best imagery to get my mind out of the gutter. I could picture Kai wielding one as he called me "naughty" way too easily.

Maybe I'd have to bring that imaginary element into reality too.

"We're going to keep you safe," Nox said. "That matters ahead of everything else. The Skullbreakers might as well be dead without you. And I'm including your sister in our mandate too. We have to be sure your home is fully protected before you move her in, and that you get to move her in without any pricks interfering. Once there's nothing left for you to be worried about, we'll get to work on bringing the bastards down."

"It's best that we gather as much intel and as many allies as we can first, anyway," Kai said. "We have our voodoo, but the Skeleton Corps clearly has numbers and influence. Rushing in won't do us any good."

"Kai always knows the smart approach," Ruin announced happily, coming up behind me and giving me one of his trademark bearhugs. "We're going to be so ready when we go after them, they're going to fall like dominos."

I wasn't sure there was any amount of preparation that would make the gang war go *that* smoothly, but who was I to dampen Ruin's enthusiasm?

My mind was still stuck on the other things Nox had said. Particularly the part about there being nothing left for me to worry about. A prickle ran over my skull, and I shivered automatically.

I tried to suppress it, but Kai caught on as quickly as he so often did. Just this once, he didn't figure out what my apprehension was about.

"I'll make sure these hotheads don't go charging into battle before we're sure of victory," he told me.

"It's not that," I said. "I—I don't know how we can be sure that nothing else is going to come up from *my* life that'll get us in trouble when I can't even remember the most important part of my past." I rubbed my forehead. "Even after meeting Nolan face to face, I have no idea what he actually did to Marisol, or what he said that day, or anything else... After the way he reacted when I tried to threaten him, I feel even more like there's something I'm missing."

"Maybe you're missing home," Ruin suggested, nuzzling my temple. "We could go out to the marsh again, walk by your old house—"

"No," I said quickly. A deeper shiver jittered through me at the thought of the marsh. It stirred up too many deep dark images from my nightmares.

I'd gotten a lot of power from the marsh, but my near death experience was haunting me now too. I didn't want to give my subconscious more fuel.

"It didn't work last time," I added. "I don't think just seeing things from back then is going to jog anything loose, or it'd have happened by now."

"I'm inclined to agree," Kai said.

Nox knuckled him. "So what would you suggest then, Mr. Know-it-all?"

Kai cocked his head. "Lily's been under a lot of stress ever since she got back in town. When you're tense, your body and mind go into defensive mode.

More might slip out from her unconscious if she was able to really relax."

Ruin straightened up with a wiggle of excitement. "We can make this Lily Day! Do all the things that she'd like, take care of everything for her. I already know where we should go. We just need to—"

"Hold on," Nox said with a laugh. "I don't think you should run the whole show, my very enthusiastic friend. It's a good idea, but if we're going to do that, we should make sure we each get a shot at pampering our woman." He grinned at me. "I've got a few ideas myself."

"We'll take turns then," Kai said in an unconcerned tone, as if he was confident that whatever scheme he came up with was sure to mellow me out enough that all the secrets of my mind would slip free.

My gaze slid to the fourth member of the Skullbreakers, who still hadn't come over to join us. Jett was standing by one of the weapons displays, meticulously rearranging the swords and pikes and other pointy objects into a composition he was more satisfied with. I couldn't have said exactly how he'd changed it, but somehow something about that spot did resonate with me better than the rest.

Since I'd gotten up this morning, Jett had barely spoken to me other than occasional grunts. I didn't know what to make of our hot but very brief collision last night before he'd fled the bedroom. Nothing about his mouth or his hands had *felt* uninterested in me.

But I wasn't sure how to bring it up, especially since he didn't go for talking much on the best of subjects.

"I'll tell Jett," Ruin said, bounding over to retrieve the artist. "But I think I should get first shot, since it was my idea."

"Technically it was mine," Kai muttered, but he was smiling at the same time.

"And technically I'm the boss," Nox reminded him, and shook his head. "We should let him get it over with, or he'll be going on about how great it's going to be through everything else."

"True."

And so it ended up that I found myself being escorted into a neon-colored store that said *Build a Big Bear* on the sign. That name obviously should have tipped me off. Ruin practically bounced off the walls getting everything he wanted from the guy who owned the place, who watched the bunch of us like he wasn't sure whether he should thank us for coming or call the cops, and the next thing I knew, I was shoving armfuls of foamy stuffing into a gigantic shell of faux fur.

"Ram it in there!" Ruin said with fierce enthusiasm. "Imagine you're pummeling around the guts of all the jerks who've hassled you. That's right!"

There was actually something tension-releasing about heaving that stuff around and punching it into place. When I was done, a teddy bear as tall as I was sat in front of me. Ruin laughed with delight.

"Now you put all that toughness into the bear. It's your protector. And you can lean on it for hugs if I don't happen to be around." He paused. "Although if you *really* need a hug, you should just call me."

"I'll keep that in mind," I said dryly.

The bear was kind of horrifying at the moment, because its face was totally blank. The store owner brought out a spread of features that we could choose from to attach. Ruin zoomed in to tweak, twist, and chop them up until he'd assembled an expression that was almost as terrifying as the blankness. The bear's eyes were narrowed, and its mouth pulled back from jagged teeth. It looked ready to chomp someone's head off.

"Ah," the store owner said. "That's not typically the vibe we'd go for—"

Ruin glowered at him. "She needs a bear that's going to defend her. It can be cuddly *and* vicious."

Possibly because he'd just witnessed Ruin switch between those two modes, the store owner swallowed whatever else he'd wanted to say and settled for ringing us up.

I hauled the bear out to the car and managed to squeeze it into the back seat. A little kid walking with his mom glanced over at the windows just as I was getting in and shrieked at the sight of the massive, fearsome teddy bear. Ruin grinned as if he couldn't have asked for a better response.

Nox and Jett had been riding their motorcycles while Ruin and Kai joined me in the car. The Skullbreakers' boss leaned over on his seat, catching my gaze. "Follow me. We can do better than stuffed animals."

He parked outside a bar that was pretty much empty—not surprising considering it was early in the afternoon still—and ushered me inside. In the back, he stopped at a pinball machine to rule all pinball machines.

It had multiple flashing lights. It played a jaunty tune if you hit the innards in just the right way. And there were about five hundred different shiny surfaces to fling the balls at. I'd swear it even had gold leaf on the fucking cabinet.

Nox rubbed his hands together, an eager gleam sparking in his dark blue eyes, but he nudged me in front of him in the player's spot. "There's nothing like getting in the zone," he said. "Nothing else matters when you find it. I'm going to teach you how to get there."

He stood right behind me, his body flush against mine, his fingers sliding over the backs of my hands to guide my grip. With encouraging words murmured in my ear, he had me whacking that ball all over the cabinet. This light flashed and that one did. All the different tunes played. The score on the digital display shot up.

After a little while, Nox withdrew his hands to rest them on my waist. He stayed close, his breath washing over the side of my face. The heat of his body wrapped around me as I played, and I wasn't sure how much I was absorbed in the game vs. absorbed in him.

I mustn't have been the only one having those kinds of thoughts, because it wasn't long before his hands started traveling again, this time to stroke over my belly just above the fly of my jeans. My core tingled, and an ache formed between my legs.

But at the same time, the bar door creaked open to admit a few more patrons. A prickle of self-consciousness ran through my chest.

"Not here," I murmured. "Not with strangers watching."

Nox let out a low growl. "I think *everyone* should see what a good girl you are."

His voice electrified me, but the jab of uneasiness remained. I looked over my shoulder at him. "I wouldn't find it very relaxing. Wasn't that the point of this?"

He grimaced at me, but he returned his hands to my waist.

Without him distracting me, I did get caught up in the flow of the game for a bit. But it was Nox's satisfied hum of approval when I hit my highest score yet that melted my frustrations the most.

Kai slid into the passenger seat next to me when we rejoined the giant teddy bear in Fred 2.0. "*I* know how to pick something that'll fit what matters to *you*, not what I'm interested in," he said, adjusting his glasses, and started giving me directions.

I didn't know if I'd ever gotten to watch Kai fully in action before. We stepped out of the car at what looked like a high school… and turned out to indeed *be* a high school… and he smoothly chatted up a woman in the front office until she was handing a key over to him while smiling at him like he was doing her a favor.

Which maybe he'd convinced her he was. From their conversation, which I couldn't totally follow, he'd already done some buttering up earlier.

He led us through the halls to what turned out to be a sound booth looking onto a large music room. An orchestra of teenagers was practicing on the other side.

"One way glass," he said, motioning to the window at the other end. "And soundproofed." He hit a button, and the song the orchestra was practicing filtered through a speaker mounted on the wall. "We can see and hear them, but they can't see or hear us. So you can do whatever you want with this."

I recognized the tune immediately as something Tchaikovsky. The dramatic strings and woodwinds lilted up and down, alternately urgent and playful. But it wasn't perfect. Here and there, a string twanged out of tune, or a horn didn't quite hit its mark, or a flute's rhythm fell briefly out of pace with the others.

Nox raised his eyebrows. "You brought her to see a crappy high school orchestra?"

"They're not 'crappy,'" Kai said, and glanced at me. "Are they?"

I shook my head, stepping closer to the glass. "No, they're really good. Especially for teenagers. This is a difficult piece."

Kai nodded. "But it hasn't become rote for them yet. They're still feeling their way into the song. It's raw and fresh for them. I think... there's got to be something vital about hearing the music that way rather than honed and polished."

He was right. I wasn't sure how he'd figured that out when he'd never seemed all that interested in music himself—any more than he was interested in any other collections of knowledge he stuffed into his brain—but there was something about hearing the not-quite-perfect rendition that called to me. My heart thumped alongside it. I started to sway with the melody, and words bubbled up my throat in a song of my own.

"New city, new start. So much lost and so much found. Can I hold on to my heart? Can I rise above the ground?"

As I let my voice spill softly out of me, Ruin beamed. "Okay, Kai's was the best. You should always be singing."

"Hey," Jett muttered. "You haven't seen mine yet."

The taciturn guy didn't say anything else until we'd finished watching the rehearsal and driven across the city following his bike. He stopped outside an old warehouse that didn't look like it was in operation on the outside but had at least a few random businesses operating out of it. He spoke to a woman who led us down a broad hallway to a small room and set out several cans of paint in different bright colors.

"Have at it," she said, and left.

Jett motioned to the paints and glanced at me. "You haven't remembered anything yet, have you?"

My mouth twisted with the answer. "No, I haven't."

I did feel lighter and looser than before, but nothing had tumbled free.

"Well, this is a way to let out tension and also see what you can create. Maybe when you're slapping paint around, you'll find that something from the back of your mind comes out that way. It works for me."

He was trying to give me a direct gateway to the parts of my past I'd lost. A pang shot through me, and I gave him a fond smile, wishing everything else between us didn't feel so messed up. "Thank you. It's perfect."

He allowed himself a small smile in return and gestured at the room around us, the walls of which were currently blank white. "We're allowed to put paint anywhere we want, as much as we want. It's all water soluble, so it doesn't matter how much of a mess we make—they just hose it down after. Let's get to it."

The woman had left paintbrushes too, but after swiping those around for a bit, I started dipping my hands right into the cans to use my fingers as my instruments the way Jett so often did. As I smeared paint across the vast canvas, the other guys joined in, taking over their own corners. I let my mood direct my motions, not questioning any impulse or letting myself really think about the choices I was making.

The lines and blotches we were creating started to wind together. Then Ruin accidentally brushed his fingers past my jaw while they were damp with paint.

He paused, his expression shifting from apologetic to mischievous in an instant. He reached out again and traced another paint-slick finger down my neck.

My pulse hiccupped, and a fresh heat woke up between my legs.

I swung toward Nox and teased my own colorful fingers across the bare semi-circle of chest above the collar of his tee. His eyes flared.

As he moved to lift my shirt just enough to trail streaks over my stomach, Kai stepped in to flick a finger along the underside of my chin. I grabbed Ruin and drew a sunny yellow smear across his forearm.

The heat in the room was rising—but not in Jett's corner. My eyes snagged on his gloomy form, his back to us, and my hands stilled.

I didn't want to do this in front of him, not when I doubted he'd join in. I had no idea what was going on in his head or his heart—or his pants—when it came to me, but whatever connection we had between us, it felt way too fragile to test it like that.

I pulled away from the other guys and looked down at myself. "I think someone's going to need to hose *me* down."

Ruin laughed. "I can see if they've got any hoses free."

He ran off out of the room, and I was too caught up in the exhilaration of the day to think that he probably shouldn't have been going off on his own in unfamiliar territory—until a gunshot reverberated through the walls.

twenty-five

Kai

Any doubts I might have had about whether the Skullbreakers were as unified as we'd ever been vanished the second the *boom* of the gun split the air. The four of us in the paint room all bolted for the door like one being.

But maybe I shouldn't have doubted it anyway. We'd come together for Lily today already. *She* united us, just as she'd held our souls in this world with her childhood games.

We burst into the wide hallway down the middle of the repurposed warehouse. Ruin was over near the front doors, grappling with a couple of men and splattered with enough paint that for a second I thought he was bleeding out. But unless he'd become radioactive, I didn't think his heart pumped anything in that vivid shade of scarlet.

As we raced over, the three of us pushing ahead of Lily like a shield, I read the situation as swiftly as I could zoom over a page of text. One of Ruin's attackers was holding a gun, presumably the one that'd gone off —yes, there was the entry mark in the ceiling just to the right of their tussle. Another pistol lay on the floor several feet away, like it'd been kicked there.

These guys weren't messing around. They'd been aiming to kill him this time, like maybe they had with the knife before—it wasn't just threats now.

Ruin was managing to angle the one man's hand away from him to stay out of range of the gun, but he was having to work too hard to deflect the blows of two attackers at once to land any solid strikes of his own. It didn't look as if he'd been able to inflict his weird emotional power on either of them so far.

But they were shit out of luck now.

Nox barreled into the guy with the gun, punching him with an electric sizzle and a fist that didn't even connect with flesh. That didn't matter—the man's head snapped to the side like he'd been pummeled in the jaw by a Mack truck. Jett sprang at the second guy. As he rammed his knee into the man's gut, the attacker's shirt flashed from gray to the dark brownish red of dried blood—the color our artistic friend no doubt wanted to leave in his wake.

I was about to jump in to join the fray when a third attacker leapt out of nowhere—straight at Lily. I didn't know if he meant to hurt her or simply take her hostage, but fury blazed through me in an instant.

"Leave her the fuck alone," I barked, throwing myself in front of her and swinging my fist.

Energy tingled through my limbs. My punch landed on the guy's nose with an electric jolt I felt in my bones. He backed up a step, clutching it and dribbling blood down his chin. I readied myself for him to make another lunge at her, but he glanced at Lily and then... backed away a little farther.

Odd.

The gears in my head started whirring, but a second later Nox tackled the guy to the ground. The other two attackers were already sprawled on the floor, one with a fatal slash across his throat and the other with his neck twisted at an unfortunate angle—well, unfortunate for him, anyway. He stared at his colleague over his shoulder with a dead-eyed expression that seemed regretful that he'd made this grave misjudgment.

"Hold on!" I shouted before Nox could bash the other guy's teeth through to the back of his skull, and dashed over. "We need one alive," I added under my breath, my senses twitching with the awareness of our audience—the frightened faces poking from doors up and down the hall. "We need to ask some questions."

"Right," the boss said gruffly, and motioned Jett and Ruin over as he hauled the guy to his feet.

I stepped closer. "Let me try something?"

Nox gave me a quizzical look, but he nodded— because he trusted me. He and the other guys might tease me about being a know-it-all, but they respected my knowledge, unlike a hell of a lot of the people I'd encountered in my life.

That was why I stuck with them, wasn't it? Because I gave them something they wouldn't have otherwise… and they did the same for me. I'd just lost sight of what that acceptance and respect meant in my exhilaration at being alive at all.

I smiled my thanks and didn't waste any time carrying out my test. The man jerked around like he thought he'd make a run for it, and I aimed another punch at his chest, tossing an order at him as I threw my fist. "Walk with us to the street, and don't make any other moves."

Another pulse of supernatural electricity quivered through my nerves. The man stiffened—and then turned toward the building's entrance. My smile grew into a grin.

When we started walking, the other guys staring at our captive, the man kept pace with us. His mouth had twisted at a horrified angle, and his shoulders twitched as if he was trying to move his arms, but he followed my command to a T.

Halfway down the hall, Ruin whooped and bounced on his feet. "You pulled his strings like he's a puppet!"

Nox glanced back at me, a pleased smirk playing with his lips. "I guess we found out what your ghostly superpower is."

I'd always been able to manipulate people's behavior

with my words—and now I could do it with my fists as well. I couldn't think of a more fitting complement to my skillset.

As we reached the doors, sirens sounded in the distance. Someone in our audience had called the police. Nox grunted and muttered, "Fucking cops. Let's move."

Jett frowned. "Are we going to stick this prick in Lily's car?"

"Better than on one of your motorcycles," Lily said from behind us. "Ruin and Kai can keep him under control."

Ruin pumped his fist. "Hell, yes, we can."

I gave the man another punch with the instruction, "Stay with us and follow us to the car." As we stepped out of the building, he turned as if to smack me, so I punched him again. "Follow us *and otherwise leave us alone.*"

With a strained grumble, he jerked forward again and walked stiffly with us to where Lily had parked the car.

She looked down at her paint-smeared clothes and skin and sighed. "There are ways to get it out of the upholstery," I said, and shoved the guy toward the back door with another shiver of supernatural energy. "Get in. Sit perfectly still."

He squeezed into the middle next to the giant teddy bear, giving it a nervous glance as if he thought it might turn out to be a living part of our gang too. I sat next to him in case I needed to pummel him into submission a little more. Ruin hopped in up front but stayed twisted in his seat, eyeing the enemy, while Lily started the engine.

"Where should we go?" she asked abruptly as she cruised down the street, ramping up the speed as the sirens wailed closer.

"Take a couple of quick turns so we're out of view of the cops," I said. Nox and Jett were roaring up behind us on their bikes, and I knew they'd follow. "And then…" We wouldn't want to take him back to her apartment. It wouldn't go over well with the rental company to splatter interrogation blood all over those hardwood floors after we'd just gone to so much effort cleaning up the joint. Although with my new talent, maybe there wouldn't need to be any blood involved.

No, still not a good place for holding criminal types. I motioned to the east after Lily had taken her second turn. "Let's head back to the new clubhouse. It's got a good basement. Basements are the best for putting the screws to someone."

Our captive let out a noise of protest where he was sitting rigidly next to us. "You fuckers," he spat out abruptly, as if he'd only just realized he could talk despite my orders about what he did with his body. "I don't know what crazy kind of—"

I socked him in the shoulder. "Shut up and just sit there."

Just like that, he did. Brilliant.

He might have been trying to spew intimidation at us, but he was obviously pretty shaken up. His eyes darted from side to side, the little bit of movement he was capable of after I'd given my commands, and his previously ruddy face had paled. With the dark V of his hairline adding to the effect, he looked like a vampire— a vampire who'd been taken hostage by a bunch of stake-twirling maniacs.

And really, the maniac part of that wasn't untrue.

Lily pulled up outside the clubhouse, and I rapped my knuckles against our reluctant guest's shoulder. "Get out and come into the restaurant with us."

I must have hit him too lightly. No jolt of electricity ran through me, and the guy shifted in his seat as if to take a grab at me.

With a shock of adrenaline, I smacked him again. "Get out and come into the restaurant with us. And that's *all* you're going to do until I say so." I whacked him across the head for good measure to drive that last point home.

The asshole's jaw worked, but he followed my directions this time. Nox and Jett converged on us in the clubhouse's dank basement, and Ruin gleefully brandished a length of rope he'd probably been dying for the chance to use. Since I didn't know whether my ghostly persuasive power might exhaust itself halfway through our little chat, I motioned for him to go ahead and tie the guy to a chair.

The guy's breath was coming in faint wheezes now. I studied him, stalking back and forth in front of him in a way I happened to know unnerved approximately ninety-three percent of all human beings.

"Got a mild case of asthma, do you?" I said. "Only comes out when you're really freaked out. Obviously you haven't had a very challenging job if you've been able to hide it all this time."

"You know fuck all about that," the man snapped, but there was a rasp in his voice. He wasn't shutting up anymore. I took note of the fact that it appeared my orders wore off as soon as I gave a new set. Probably the compulsion would fade given enough time too.

How kind of him to volunteer as a test subject for my trial run.

Since he was tightly bound to the chair now, I didn't have to worry about my previous command staying active. Most important things first—could I compel his vocal cords as well as his other body parts?

I cuffed him across the head. "Tell us who you work for."

"No," he snarled back. Okay, no luck there. I still had plenty of my usual methods to turn to. And I had another experiment to run.

"Wrong answer." I slapped him across the face. "Keep wiggling your fingers until I tell you to stop."

The guy immediately started jiggling his fingers in some very energetic jazz hands where they dangled by the sides of the chair. He couldn't move them any more than that with his arms tied from his shoulders to halfway down his forearms. I checked my phone so I could keep track of how long it took before he stopped and resumed my pacing.

The other guys hung back, watching eagerly but silently. They knew I'd get answers.

And if I needed any help with motivation, *I* knew they'd be only too happy to supply it. Really, it was the perfect symbiosis.

Our captive stared down at his hands, his face outright white now and strained as he must have tried to will his fingers to stop waggling. It didn't work. I strolled over and leaned close so my face was just a foot from his. "If you think that's creepy, wait until you see what else we can do."

His gaze jerked to me, and I grinned. Fear showed in every flicker of his eyes and the bead of perspiration that'd formed at the point of his hairline.

I'd never worked over a guy quite this terrified before. Even if I couldn't supernaturally persuade him into spilling his guts, my ghostly abilities were still giving me a leg up.

"There's a very simple way to get out of this horror show," I went on. "All we want to know is who hired you to go after our friend here and why." I motioned to Ruin.

"Well, you're not getting that," the guy said defiantly. "I don't fucking know."

Nox let out a growl, but I held up my hand to keep him still. I jabbed the man at the base of his throat. "You know who you work for, don't you? Who you take orders from?"

He glowered back at me, keeping his mouth shut. It'd have been a more impressive display if his hands hadn't still been wriggling away at his sides like butterflies on cocaine.

I kept grinning. "Let me put it this way. You've already seen that I can make you act any way I want. You could tell me, and we'll end this cleanly. Or before the end, I could order you to bite off your own dick. If your spine won't stretch that far, you could chew off those wriggling fingers one by one. Maybe we'll stop while you still have your thumbs and you can jam those all the way up your nose."

"Or his ass!" Ruin suggested helpfully.

"Or he could poke out his eyeballs," Jett said.

Nox chuckled. "Why choose? All three sounds good to me."

The bead of sweat had turned into a trickle that was streaming down the guy's face. I saw him make another attempt at controlling his hands... and fail. He'd now gone all the way from white to green. Maybe he'd be reborn as a chameleon.

"You want to do a little self-mutilation first to see how it goes?" I said conversationally when he stayed silent. "Well, I'm sure we'll have fun that way too." I lifted my hand to swing another punch.

"No!" the guy cried, with a pre-emptive wince. "Fine. I—I work for Ironguard Security. It was just a fucking job. We get our assignment; we follow through. That's it."

Lily tensed where she was standing at the edge of the room. My own thoughts had gone abruptly still.

Ironguard Security. We'd found their card in Nolan Gauntt's desk.

"What exactly was your assignment?" I asked.

He jerked his head toward Ruin. "The kid was supposed to be reporting to us on some girl he was monitoring. I don't know why. The orders came from someone high up. The kid stopped delivering, and we were supposed to end him."

"Who gave those orders?" Nox demanded.

"I don't know! I don't deal with the clients. I'm just one of the guys on the ground. I swear."

I cocked my head, raising my hand again. "I really hope you can tell me how your business is connected to the Gauntt family."

The man's eyes widened. "You mean Thrivewell. Sure —sure! I don't think it's supposed to be public knowledge, but I saw a form once—the company's owned by them. Ironguard is run by Thrivewell. Not really surprising, right, when they own half the businesses in the city." He let out a somewhat hysterical laugh.

A chill gripped me. I pulled out my phone, brought up the photo I'd taken of the business card with the numbers Nolan had scrawled on the back, and considered them. The second one was definitely a cell phone. I dialed it.

The phone we'd stolen from Ruin's previous attacker started to peal in his back pocket. Ruin snatched at it, but I ended the call, shaking my head. "Don't bother. That was just me."

The pieces were clicking together into a picture in my head I couldn't deny. Nolan Gauntt had been keeping tabs on Lily. So had Ansel Hunter. Nolan owned the security company Ansel had been reporting to. He'd written down the number of an Ironguard employee who'd gone missing while on Ansel's case. There wasn't a chance in hell this wasn't all part of the same scheme.

I could tell we weren't going to get anything more useful out of this dope. As much as I'd have liked to push the limits of my powers and see how far I could twist his sense of self-preservation, I preferred to stay a man of my word.

My other experiment had delivered results. The man's fingers were slowing in their frantic waggling. I checked my phone.

Fifteen minutes. Fifteen minutes for the effect to start to fade.

I motioned to Nox. "I'm done with him."

I turned my back while the shot rang out and found myself facing Lily. She was hugging herself, her face drawn, but she was looking to the other guys rather than me.

When we'd taken our turns helping her unwind, *I* was the one who'd offered her something that fit who she was. Hadn't that proven I understood her better than anyone?

But maybe I'd underestimated my friends' contributions there too. I'd given her what she already knew. They'd given her something of themselves. They'd shared part of who *they* were…

What did I have to offer up of myself that wasn't just information I'd gleaned from somewhere or someone else?

I glanced back at the man now slumped in his chair over a pool of blood, and certainty coiled inside me. I was what I was. And even if I couldn't present her with any great gifts that were all my own, I was damn well going to make sure every villain we crossed paths with coughed up everything in them that would help her.

twenty-six

Lily

I didn't know what the Skullbreakers did with the body, and I didn't have any interest in asking. Too many thoughts were whirling around in my brain for me to have much room to worry about it anyway. Even the rush of hot water when I showered off the paint on my hair and skin couldn't sweep the uneasy clamor away.

Ruin and Jett had brought me back to the new apartment while Nox and Kai handled the corpse situation. Technically my lease didn't start until tomorrow, but after the clean-up we'd done and the grudging approval I'd gotten from the rental company —and the fact that I already had the keys to the new doors—I'd unofficially moved in anyway. It'd given us a chance to get a little furniture set up for when I brought Marisol here tomorrow.

I'd wanted the place to look nicer than the old apartment without breaking the bank, especially considering I was out of my second job in a month's time, so everything was basic and modern but sturdy and clean. Mostly I'd given the guys the general specifications, and they'd picked things up here and there…

I hadn't asked much about how that'd happened either. I'd just insisted that no one get hurt in the process, and they hadn't given any indication that they'd broken that rule.

Among the few things I had picked up myself was a small, roll-top secretary desk that I'd already outfitted with pencils and pastels in the drawers and a stack of good drawing paper on the lower shelf. It sat by the window in the bedroom I'd figured would be Marisol's.

I wandered past it now, sweeping my fingertips over the curved top but barely feeling the old wood. The faint rumble of traffic carried through the window. I inhaled, tasting the "clean linen" air freshener I'd sprayed around the place to absorb any lingering odors from our cleaning.

It felt as though I'd traveled in a circuit of the entire apartment over a hundred times. The moment I stopped moving, my thoughts crowded even more heavily into my head, and I started feeling like I was drowning right there in the air.

I'd clearly been on Nolan Gauntt's radar from the

moment I'd returned to Lovell Rise. Had he ever *stopped* monitoring me? He'd had Ansel tracking me from the moment I'd returned, so he must have known I was being released from St. Elspeth's.

Was this all because he was worried that I'd spill the beans about what's gone on with my sister seven years ago? But then, why wouldn't he just have *me* offed instead of Ansel?

I had no answers to any of those questions, so they just kept gnawing at my brain.

Finally, Nox and Kai strode in. Ruin perked up where he'd been sitting on the boxy pull-out couch, shooting a hopeful glance my way. Jett turned around, but he never did perky. He'd been flicking his fingers against the wall to adjust the hue of the main room for the last hour, never seeming totally satisfied with what he ended up with. Right now, it was a muted olive green.

I moved to sit on the loveseat kitty-corner with the couch. As if sensing that we were about to have some kind of official debriefing, the rest of the guys assembled in the living area.

Nox took the spot next to me with his usual cocky air but slipping his hand around mine gently. He'd obviously wiped at the paint I'd trailed across his chest, but a smudge of blue remained. Jett dropped down next to Ruin, and Kai spun one of the chairs at the new dining table, which would be able to seat all six of us. If I ever decided to host a dinner party that involved both my sister and the former Skullbreakers, that was.

I should have been happy. I'd won this new home and I was getting Marisol away from Wade, but the interrogation made that victory feel like just one small bubble of okay in a vast sea of pretty-freaking-perilous. How easily would that bubble pop?

"The Gauntts hired this security company to hire Ansel to stalk me and then to kill him when he went AWOL on them," I said, laying out in as brief terms as I could what'd been obvious from the moment Ruin's attacker had mentioned Ironguard Security. "They've been keeping tabs on me since—hell, they must have had him ready to go before I even officially moved in. I guess they found out I'd gotten the old apartment, or heard from the hospital that I was being fully discharged…"

I paused, and a comment Nolan had made came back to me. I'd been so thrown by his blasé attitude about my powers that I hadn't totally wrapped my head around the rest before. "I think he paid off the hospital somehow to keep me under *their* supervision for as long as they did. He said something along those lines… but of course he denied it when I tried to get the real story out of him."

Nox growled, his fingers tightening around mine. "After everything else the bastard's done, I'm not surprised."

"Me neither. But that means…" I lowered my head and ran my free hand into my hair. "I thought all I had to do was find out what he'd done to Marisol seven years ago and make sure he didn't hurt her again. But he's been keeping me down this entire time. He's been trying to have Ruin *murdered*. Who knows what else he might have been doing that we haven't figured out yet?" The enormity of the situation and our enemy on the other side of it threatened to drown me again.

"He hasn't managed to murder me yet," Ruin said cheerfully.

"I know, but he's going to keep trying… and I don't know how to stop him. No wonder he wasn't scared by me hurling around some water when he's got so much regular power he could practically rule the world."

"No one's going to rule this city except for us when we're through," Nox announced.

Kai nodded. "We've learned things. We have a better idea what we're up against now, so we'll come up with better defenses—and offenses, when we're ready. We still have plenty of advantages. Our supernatural voodoo." He wiggled his fingers. "And the fact that we don't care if we break the law and he still has to consider it, even if he circumvents it sometimes."

"All our new friends on the streets, too," Ruin added.

"Friends," Jett scoffed, but he caught my gaze, his deep brown eyes steady. "We're not letting anyone screw you over again."

Their reassurances didn't comfort me the way they must have been hoping, but the worst of my nerves settled. I dragged a breath into my lungs. "Okay. I guess there's nothing to do but keep going forward anyway."

I didn't sleep well that night, though, and my

stomach stayed knotted with apprehension for the whole drive out to my old house to pick up Marisol. The guys had insisted on all coming along in case the Gauntts or the Skeleton Corps tried anything, and I'd insisted they stay on their bikes at a reasonable distance so I didn't have to explain about them to my sister just yet. Their forms cruised along behind me in the rearview mirror like they were haunting me, but I'd learned that being haunted wasn't so bad.

As I got closer and closer to the house, the knot balled even tighter. A hint of marshy scent crept into the car, and my chest started to contract too. Flashes of my nightmares flickered through my head, as if some part of me was afraid the lake would reach out and suck me back into it even if I didn't set foot anywhere near the shore.

I wasn't literally drowning, but I was in over my head, wasn't I? Taking Marisol under my protection when I wasn't even sure what I was protecting her from. When I was scared to even let her see the ways I *could* protect her.

How could I be her defender when I was so terrified myself?

The marsh and the shimmer of open water beyond the reeds came into view up ahead. My hands tightened around the steering wheel—and something cracked open inside me. A weird sense of certainty rose up through my chest. The mark on the underside of my arm prickled with a sudden itch, but I ignored it.

Nothing had unlocked my memories so far, but

maybe I simply hadn't opened up the doorway wide enough. I'd been afraid to know what'd happened, what I'd done, what I was up against… and I'd let myself become afraid of the source of the power I had.

The marsh didn't want to hurt me. It hadn't dragged me down on purpose. That'd been my six-year-old clumsiness, and when I'd fought through it and clambered my way out, the marsh had let a special piece of itself come with me.

What if it could help me unearth the piece of myself I'd lost?

The itch on my arms sharpened into a jab. That sensation only strengthened my resolve. I turned down the lane before the one that led to my old house, driving all the way out to the parking spot near the edge of the marsh.

The guys followed me. As I got out of the car, they parked their bikes around Fred 2.0. The damp breeze washed over me, and the cattails rattled together. My pulse stuttered with a sudden burst of panic, but I held strong against it.

"What's going on, Siren?" Nox asked, no judgment in his tone, only curiosity. His new nickname for me bolstered my confidence even more.

"A lot of things started here," I said. "And it was near here that everything went wrong. I want to see if the marsh can wash free the memories that I can't seem to get at on my own." I squared my shoulders and looked at the four of them. "No matter what happens or how it looks, I don't want you to come after me. You need to let me figure this out. I think—I think I'll be fine."

I couldn't say I was sure, but then, how many things could you be sure of in life other than taxes and a stomachache after a really greasy pizza?

A couple of frogs had hopped over to greet me. The familiar hum was spreading through my veins, even though I wasn't angry or particularly worked up right now. I was just determined.

I would own my power. I would own everything that'd happened in my life, no matter how horrifying. And that included embracing the moment when I'd nearly lost my life altogether.

I walked over to the water, kicked off my shoes, and stepped down into the mushy bottom. The chilly water lapped around my ankles. Pushing through the reeds and rushes, I waded deeper. The water wavered up to my calves, then my knees, then my thighs. My toes were going numb, but I didn't need them right now anyway.

I was a siren. I was a waterlily, an angelfish, a minnow. I was queen of the marsh, and the water moved to my will. I'd fallen down into it and risen again, and we knew each other now like old friends. Like mother and daughter, better than my birth mother had treated me lately.

My heart was thumping hard, but I kept walking until I was in up to my waist. The damp seeped up through my shirt. I shivered but held firm. Then I closed my eyes and threw myself forward into the water.

The cold liquid closed over me in an instant. Panic

blared through my limbs, but I held them rigid, refusing to struggle. Instead, I opened my mouth.

More water streamed down my throat and into my lungs, and weirdly, my body relaxed into it. As if I'd come home. The hum inside me rang out like a note strummed on a heavenly harp, its thrum resonating through my ears and into my mind, and I was abruptly aware of a pain in the mark on my arm and a wall in the back of my mind.

I willed the water's energy through my sinking body. Dug it into the mark to carve out that damned spot. Hurled it at the sense of a barrier within my thoughts.

The power sparked and sizzled, but I drew on more and more.

I was the marsh. The marsh was me. And nothing in me that wasn't part of it belonged.

Something in me that wasn't right at all strained and railed against the onslaught of watery magic. But I willed all the swell and stretch of the marsh into me, battering the strangeness again and again and—

The wall inside me shattered apart with a burst of refreshing cold, and images flooded into my mind.

I was thirteen years old, walking into the house after a wander down by the marsh seven years ago. Mom and Wade were sitting in the living room. Both of their expressions stiffened at the sight of me, but Wade's most of all.

"You're home early," Mom said faintly.

Wade jumped up. "Why don't you go out and play some more? There's nothing for you to do in here."

My senses prickled onto the alert. There was something they didn't want me to know. I glanced toward the stairs, and at the same moment the floor creaked and a gasp filtered through the floor from Marisol's room.

"Lily!" Wade barked, but I was already dashing for the stairs. I leapt up them two at a time, panic blazing through all my senses.

The door to the bedroom was closed. I hurtled to it and flung it open.

A man I hadn't known then but could now recognize as Nolan Gauntt was sitting on my little sister's bed next to Marisol. He was turned toward her, his knee touching hers, one hand stroking over her hair.

His other hand was tucked behind her back, but he withdrew it as I came in. Had he stuck it up her *shirt*?

My earlier panic crackled into rage. "Get the hell away from her!" I snapped, storming into the room. A weird hum tickled up between my ribs. I hadn't known what it meant back then. I'd been too busy wanting to rend him limb from limb to care.

Nolan stood up with a smile so calm it made me even more furious. He patted Marisol, who looked dazed, on the head and said something under his breath that I couldn't make out.

I lunged at him, throwing a punch, but he caught my arm. Holding it firmly, he set one hand on the underside, right by my armpit, and stared down at me with an eerie light dancing in his otherwise flat blue eyes.

"You won't remember this," he said. A thread of energy rippled through his voice and tingled into my flesh. "You won't remember."

"Of course I will," I retorted, and lashed out at him with my other hand.

He batted that one aside too, shoved me onto the bed next to Marisol, and stalked out of the room.

I sprang onto my feet and whirled toward Marisol. She was still sitting there so rigidly. The panic returned, clutching my gut.

"Are you okay, Mare? What did he do to you?"

"Nothing," she said in a distant voice. "It wasn't anything."

My teeth gritted. I dashed after the man who'd been messing with her.

He'd moved fast. By the time I raced to the bottom of the stairs, he was already by the front door. A car engine was revving to life outside. Both Mom and Wade were on their feet.

"I'm so sorry," Wade was saying. "I didn't mean for the interruption—"

"It's fine," Nolan interrupted briskly. "I've taken care of everything. You don't need to worry about her."

Then he swept out of the house.

I stared at Mom and Wade. They'd known. They'd fucking *known* he was up there with Marisol—they'd let him…

The hum that'd been seeping through me rose into a roar. I still hadn't known what it meant, but I did know I wanted to rain down all my fury on the two of them.

"Why did you let him come here?" I yelled, grabbing an empty mug off the coffee table and whipping it at Wade. "How could you do that to her?"

Wade winced as the mug hit his shoulder and held up his hands defensively. "Ellie, I think you'd better let me handle this," he said to Mom, who hesitated for only a split-second before dipping her head and ducking out of the room.

That made me even angrier. "You asshole! You shithead! He *hurt* Marisol, and you let him. I'm going to—"

"Now, Lily," Wade said. "You really have no idea—"

Those words triggered the biggest surge of anger yet. *I* had no idea? I'd been the one who'd gone up there and seen what the weirdo was doing to her.

An inarticulate sound of rage escaped my throat, the hum burst out of me—and a torrent of water exploded through the wall that bordered the kitchen.

The rest was mostly as I'd already pieced it together. Water I hadn't even fully understood I was controlling gushed out of the walls and pummeled Wade and the living room. Wade had shoved at me, and I'd given him a bloody nose and scratched up his cheek while I'd tried to fight him off. Then he'd fled to the kitchen and locked the door.

When the police had arrived, I'd run out of steam. I was standing soggy and screaming in the middle of the living room, with Wade's wounds and the destruction around me as evidence of my crazed meltdown. Someone had stuck a syringe in my arm...

And then I was back in the present day, heaving up out of the water with a groan and a sputter.

Swaying on my feet again, I doubled over and vomited marsh water back to whence it came. It poured out of me, somehow leaving me tingling clean on the inside rather than stinging raw.

"Lily?" Ruin's frantic voice carried from beyond the bullrushes. "Lily, can you hear me?"

I coughed again and found my voice, rough but steady. "I'm here. I'm coming back."

And now I was whole again.

As I strode through the water back to shore, my hand rose to rest on my other arm. I yanked aside the collar of my drenched shirt and peered at the underside.

The random birthmark was gone. It'd been right where Nolan had gripped my arm when he'd said I wouldn't remember, with that unearthly quaver in his voice.

That was how he'd been so sure I didn't remember.

I'd broken it. I'd broken the spell he'd put on me. My magic was stronger than his after all.

Nolan Gauntt had magic.

I hauled myself out of the marsh and went to join the guys, who'd come down to the shore to wait for me. Kai had pulled the spare blanket out of Fred's trunk, where I'd returned it once I had proper bedding in the apartment, and wrapped it around me with uncharacteristic tenderness. And the whole wrenching story spilled out of me.

"The Gauntts have their own voodoo," Nox said when I was done, his expression grim.

"Nolan does, anyway," I said. "But we can beat it. *I* just beat it. And now we know." Of course Nolan wouldn't have been that horrified by my water magic when he knew supernatural powers were possible because of his own. He had no idea how much farther I'd be able to take it.

Kai tipped his head. "Yes, and now that we know, we also know what we need to be watching for. We'll pick apart all his secrets until we figure out exactly how to take him down and make him pay."

For the first time, I completely believed that statement. A smile crossed my lips.

I knew all my own secrets now, and I hadn't done anything horrifying. I hadn't locked them away to protect myself from knowing the truth in the first place. It'd always been Nolan, trying to cover up his own crimes.

I rubbed the corner of the blanket over my hair and turned to look toward my old house. "I'd better go get Marisol." For the first time, that statement didn't come with any apprehension, despite the bizarre act I'd just carried out. My chin lifted higher. "And I think there's something I should show her."

When I pulled up outside the house, the guys staying far back on their bikes, my clothes and hair were still pretty damp. I didn't even have to knock on the door. Marisol had been expecting me. As I stepped out of the car, she came barging out of the house with a purse under one arm and dragging a carry-on sized suitcase by the other hand.

"You came!" she said, as if she hadn't been totally sure, and then took in my appearance. "What happened to you?"

"Nothing I couldn't handle," I said, running my fingers through my hair. "I wanted to make sure I can keep you safe. And I think I can. Definitely better than Wade and Mom have ever done. Do you want to see something crazy?"

Marisol arched her eyebrows, but a curious light flashed in her eyes. "Sure."

A flicker of anxiety still wavered through my chest, but I could ignore it. I drew on my love for my sister and my anger at everyone who'd threatened her, and swiped my hand over the front of my shirt in time with the hum resonating inside me.

A thin stream tugged off the fabric and wove through the air toward my palm as I moved my hand away. I urged it to dance in the air, swinging it higher and twisting it around, like it was a ribbon made out of water. Then I lowered my hand and let it splash to the ground.

Marisol's jaw had dropped. I watched her expression carefully, braced for any hint of fear.

A broad grin stretched across her face. "That's not crazy," she said. "That's fucking amazing! How did you do that?"

"Language," I chided, not that I was anyone to complain about swearing, and ushered her toward the car. "I'll explain everything while I drive."

twenty-seven

Lily

The day after Marisol moved in, Nox texted me while she and I were digging into a late breakfast. I'd made pancakes, which I was proud to say were not at all round but very fluffy, which was obviously what mattered the most. Maximum syrup absorption powers.

Is this a good time to come by and meet her? he asked. *Is she settled in?*

We'd already discussed that the guys should visit so I could introduce them to Marisol before too long. They were going to be a major part of her extended protection squad, so even though the situation was highly bizarre, she needed to at least be aware that they were on her side.

Give us an hour, I wrote back. *I want to prepare her a little more ahead of time.*

What's there to prepare for? We're undeniably amazing. Thankfully he added a winking emoji to show that he hadn't taken on Ruin's overly optimistic personality.

Ha ha. Be on your best behavior. No weapons, no blood.

And what do I get as a reward if I'm good, Siren?

We'll see. I added a tongue stuck-out emoji to emphasize the point and set my phone down. Although he'd probably get all sorts of not-totally-wrong ideas from that tongue.

Marisol had been watching me curiously. "Is everything okay?" she asked, giving her arm an idle scratch.

"Yeah!" I said quickly. "Just talking to some friends. Or, well, I guess more like boyfriends. In some cases."

Marisol's eyebrows jumped to her hairline. "Boyfriend*s*? There's obviously a lot you haven't filled me in on yet."

I let out an embarrassed laugh, wishing my brain had kept up better with my mouth so I hadn't blurted it out quite like that. "It's a long story. But what matters is there are some guys who care a lot about me, and they care about you too because they know how important you are to me. They helped me get to the point where I could look after you. They're going to stop by later today so you can meet them, but first there are a few things I should probably explain about them."

My sister popped another bite of pancake into her

mouth and chewed it thoughtfully. "Is this like your crazy water powers? Did they almost drown in the marsh and wake up as superheroes too?"

"I'm not a superhero," I had to protest. "And the guys, well—"

As I spoke, Marisol reached to scratch the underside of her arm again, and her posture went abruptly rigid. She stared at me, dropping her fork onto her plate with a clatter.

I hesitated. "Mare? What's—"

She leapt to her feet. "What are you trying to do to me?" she interrupted. Her eyes had widened. "You're trying to mess with my head, take me away from my family."

My heart started to thud painfully hard. "What are you talking about? *I'm* your family."

"No, you're not. Not after you left, and you've been doing all this crazy stuff—I can't trust you."

I scrambled up to reach for her, but the second I moved toward her, my sister jerked away, her hands flying up defensively. "Don't touch me! Don't come anywhere near me!"

What the hell was going on? It was like *she'd* been possessed—but from what the guys had told me, it couldn't happen in a blink to a person just sitting there eating pancakes.

I held up my own hands in a gesture of peace. "I won't come near you if you don't want me to. But you have to tell me what's going on, Mare. Everything was fine a minute ago. If something's bothering you—"

"Nothing was fine," Marisol shot back. "And I don't have to tell you anything. I'm getting out of here."

She dashed for the door without any further warning—in her short-sleeved pajamas and bare feet, without a single thing she'd brought with her. Like she couldn't bear to be in the same room as me for a second longer.

My gut lurched, but my need to protect her—even if from herself—was stronger than any remaining fear that I would hurt her somehow. I threw myself after her, snatching at her arm.

I caught the sleeve of her pajama top instead. She heaved herself away from me at the same moment, so hard the seam tore. Her arm flew up as she started to smack me away—

And I caught sight of a small, pinkish blotch like a birthmark on the underside of her arm, just a couple of inches from the pit. A blotch that was the same size and color as the one that'd marked my arm until I'd shook off the spell Nolan Gauntt had used to suppress my memory, in almost the exact same spot. Where she'd been scratching just now as if it was niggling at her.

Horror hit me in an icy wave.

Marisol hurtled away from me and flung the door open. "Leave me alone," she shrieked back at me. "Leave me alone!"

No way in hell. I charged after her, but she slammed the door in my face. In my panicked state, it took me too long fumbling with the doorknob and the two thousand automatic locking mechanisms Nox had insisted on. I raced after her, in my own pajamas and slippers, hearing her just a couple of flights below me on the stairs, then the solid thump of the new lobby door when it swung shut in her wake…

I shoved past that door and burst out onto the sidewalk, my head swiveling from side to side. "Marisol!" I cried out.

But she'd already vanished without a trace.

about the author

Eva Chase lives in Canada with her family. She loves stories both swoony and supernatural, and strong women and the men who appreciate them. Along with the Gang of Ghouls series, she is the author of the Bound to the Fae series, the Flirting with Monsters series, the Cursed Studies trilogy, the Royals of Villain Academy series, the Moriarty's Men series, the Looking Glass Curse trilogy, the Their Dark Valkyrie series, the Witch's Consorts series, the Dragon Shifter's Mates series, the Demons of Fame Romance series, the Legends Reborn trilogy, and the Alpha Project Psychic Romance series.

Connect with Eva online:
www.evachase.com
eva@evachase.com

Printed in Great Britain
by Amazon

25530766R00176